"I stand five foot ten in my stocking feet. I've got flaming red hair, and," Jamie added, her face flushed, "I'm Irish. Can you *imagine* how many stupid prejudices and dumb remarks I have to put up with?"

"People assume you've got a temper?" Daniel asked mildly, trying to hold back a smile.

"Damn right, they do!"

Daniel shook his head. "Well, Miss O'Rourke, I certainly have no fear of your temper. The reason I'm not going to hire you is simply because of your sex."

For a moment, Jamie couldn't believe he'd meant what she'd heard. When she finally replied, her voice had gone deadly cold.

"You're mistaken, Mr. Kelleher. First, you're going to interview me. Second, you're going to realize that I'm the most highly qualified physiotherapist in Calgary. And *then* you're going to hire me on the spot. And I don't care how rich or how powerful you are. We'll have no more talk about my sex...."

Dear Reader:

Meet twelve daring, passionate women!

You've seen many exciting changes in Harlequin books over the past few months, but one thing hasn't changed—our commitment to providing you with the most up-to-the-minute stories in romance fiction today.

In Superromance, we're delighted to introduce you to a bold new series, WOMEN WHO DARE. Through 1993, one book per month will feature a heroine who faces challenges head-on, a woman who will dare anything... for love.

And you will recognize some of your favorite authors as contributors to this new concept. In January, you won't want to miss Margot Dalton's *Daniel and the Lion,* in which physiotherapist Jamie O'Rourke saves the hero from himself. In February, Carol Duncan Perry drops modern-day stunt pilot Elizabeth Carmichael into perilous Prohibition-era Chicago in *The Wings of Time.* Dr. Caroline Charles shakes up the medical establishment in Janice Kaiser's March WOMEN WHO DARE title, *Cradle of Dreams,* and photojournalist Kelly Cooper stakes her life on her intuition when she finds herself held hostage in Sandra Canfield's *Snap Judgement.*

Whether emotional, adventurous, suspenseful or humorous, Superromance novels continue to reflect the ways that modern women live and love in today's society. I hope you'll enjoy all the wonderful stories our talented authors are planning for 1993!

Marsha Zinberg,
Senior Editor

P.S. We love to hear from our readers! Letters to the editor or to your favorite author can be sent to:

Harlequin Reader Service,
P.O. Box 1397
Buffalo, New York
14240 U.S.A.

Daniel and the Lion

MARGOT DALTON

Harlequin Books

TORONTO • NEW YORK • LONDON
AMSTERDAM • PARIS • SYDNEY • HAMBURG
STOCKHOLM • ATHENS • TOKYO • MILAN
MADRID • WARSAW • BUDAPEST • AUCKLAND

If you purchased this book without a cover you should be aware
that this book is stolen property. It was reported as "unsold and
destroyed" to the publisher, and neither the author nor the
publisher has received any payment for this "stripped book."

Published January 1993

ISBN 0-373-70533-6

DANIEL AND THE LION

Copyright © 1993 by Margot Dalton. All rights reserved.
Except for use in any review, the reproduction or utilization
of this work in whole or in part in any form by any electronic,
mechanical or other means, now known or hereafter invented,
including xerography, photocopying and recording, or in any
information storage or retrieval system, is forbidden without
the permission of the publisher, Harlequin Enterprises Limited,
225 Duncan Mill Road, Don Mills, Ontario, Canada M3B 3K9.

All the characters in this book have no existence outside the
imagination of the author and have no relation whatsoever to
anyone bearing the same name or names. They are not even
distantly inspired by any individual known or unknown to the
author, and all incidents are pure invention.

® are Trademarks registered in the United States Patent and
Trademark Office and in other countries.

Printed in U.S.A.

ABOUT THE AUTHOR

"My view of what a woman should be was shaped by my upbringing on the Canadian prairies just one generation removed from frontier times," says Margot Dalton. "It was the strength and tenderness, courage and compassion of the women that helped families survive and prosper even in the face of spring blizzards and summer droughts.

"When I wrote *Daniel and the Lion,* I looked to my upbringing and tried to embody everything I admire in a woman in my heroine, Jamie O'Rourke."

Margot and her husband now make their home in Vernon, British Columbia. They have three grown daughters and one teenage son still at home.

Books by Margot Dalton

HARLEQUIN SUPERROMANCE

Don't miss any of our special offers. Write to us at the following address for information on our newest releases.

Harlequin Reader Service
P.O. Box 1397, Buffalo, NY 14240
Canadian address: P.O. Box 603,
Fort Erie, Ont. L2A 5X3

CHAPTER ONE

AT ONE TIME Jamie's Volkswagen Beetle had probably been a rich dark green. Now it was the color of something found at the bottom of a swamp. Many, many people had owned this car, and each had tried to personalize it in some way with bumper stickers, happy faces, and racing stripes. All these were now tattered and peeling badly. A ragged dent in the door on the driver's side had the word *Ouch!* spray painted above it in glaring yellow. Jamie's own contribution was a crumpled right front fender, sustained in an argument between the Volkswagen, a patch of winter ice, and a lamppost...a battle that had been won, most decisively, by the lamppost.

Despite its occasional nasty temper, Jamie loved this car. It had a strong personality and a set of high and rigid standards. It would always get Jamie where she wanted to go, but only on its own terms and in its own time.

According to her brother Terry, Jamie's love for her cranky, beat-up car was another proof that she was crazy. But Terry had been saying this about her ever since she could remember, and it had never bothered her in the slightest. Jamie was, at all times, her own woman, confident, self-contained, and endlessly delighted by life.

Just now, though, she was feeling unusually tense and worried, and so was her car. She could tell because it was beginning to buck and hiccup, and was showing a dan-

gerous tendency to stall at intersections, a sure sign that
it was troubled.

Terry claimed the car always stalled because of a faulty
fuel pump. Jamie knew better.

The Volkswagen was fully aware of where it belonged.
And neither Jamie nor her car belonged in the neighborhood in which they now found themselves, driving slowly
up and down quiet tree-lined streets, searching for a house
number.

Jamie peered out the window at the elegant residences
flowing past her cracked windshield and wondered if she
would have even applied for this job, if she'd known it was
in this neighborhood.

The car, with startling suddenness, coughed and
bounced and lurched blindly toward the curb. Jamie
turned the key off to give the Beetle a moment to rest and
get over its sulk, while she gazed bleakly out the window,
biting her lip.

Knightsbridge Heights was the name given, infor-
mally, to this particular section of the sprawling, oil-rich
city of Calgary. The name wasn't found on any map, and
the addresses here were plain, innocuous street numbers,
so you didn't know until you got here just what you were
dealing with.

But what you were dealing with was something very
formidable indeed. The houses along these streets
weren't just large and expensive ... after all, there were
large and expensive houses all over the city. These particular houses represented a different kind of wealth—wealth
so vast that the people who lived here never even had to
think about money. They lived on top of deep, endless
deposits of riches. The money didn't come in monthly
paychecks or commission statements or dividends. It was

just *there*. And growing all the time, like some massive subterranean monster.

Jamie tapped the steering wheel absently and looked at the well-groomed grounds of the nearest houses. The houses themselves didn't even look large or opulent. Seen from the street, they appeared deceptively small, modestly fronted with brick or stone, hidden among towering trees. But Jamie had the uneasy feeling that once you stepped into one of those places, it would open out like the hole Alice stumbled into and swallow you up in echoing acres of luxury, filled with things so exquisite, so fabulous and so valuable that you could hardly put a name to them.

She squared her shoulders, drew a deep breath and turned the key in the ignition.

"Come on, troops," she muttered. "We've come this far. Might as well get it over with."

But the car was in no mood to respond. It snarled sullenly, rocked on its tires a couple of times, whined and subsided.

"Oh, damn!" Jamie said.

She stared for a moment at a long jagged rip on the dashboard, from which a mat of yellowed stuffing protruded.

Knowing her car's habits, she decided to leave it by the curb and walk the rest of the way. The car would start after an hour or so, and it might even be wiser not to have the thing in evidence, all things considered.

She opened the door and stepped out, gracefully unfolding her considerable height, then stretched briefly, sighing with pleasure at escaping the cramped confines of the tiny car. Opening her folder, she looked once more at the newspaper advertisement attached to her clipboard.

Wanted: physiotherapist to give daily massage treatment to paraplegic. Three hours' work daily, plus occasional extra treatments, full pay, live in.

There were further details about qualifications, application procedures and conditions, but the basics had been what most impressed Jamie's family.

They had been so excited when Doreen, Terry's wife, had spotted this ad. It looked perfect for Jamie. And when the unknown advertiser had called back a couple of weeks after she'd prepared and submitted her résumé, offering Jamie an interview, Doreen had been so flustered that she'd written the message on the back of little Sean's report card, and had to call the school to apologize.

But, Jamie thought gloomily, as she swung off up the quiet street with her lithe, graceful step, *how the hell was I to know that it was in Knightsbridge Heights? This place is downright scary!*

There was no sign anywhere of people. The late May afternoon was sunny, warm and languorous, rich with the scent of fruit trees in blossom and freshly mown grass, but nobody was out enjoying the day. There were no children's tricycles on the sidewalk, no old ladies with string shopping bags chatting at corner bus stops, no housewives visiting over side fences. The only evidence, in fact, of human habitation was a series of neat little signs at almost every residence, announcing that these premises were patrolled by guard dogs.

All at once, Jamie felt fervently grateful to Doreen for being such a cheerfully bossy and motherly person. Jamie had been planning to wear cotton khaki slacks and a casual plaid shirt to this interview, reasoning that nobody hired a private physiotherapist for her clothes. But

Doreen had called and persuaded her to wear a silk blouse, a dress skirt and heels. Now Jamie knew that her sister-in-law had been right.

Bless you, Doreen, she thought. *I owe you three nights of free baby-sitting, at least. I'd hate to be going into one of these places in my old khakis.*

Jamie now stood outside 1260 Herald Drive so the next place had to be 1270—the address she was looking for.

But it wasn't that simple. After 1260 came 1280, and there was no sign of 1270. Bewildered, Jamie checked the address again and then looked blankly up and down the street. 1270 Herald Drive didn't seem to exist. And then, suddenly, she saw it. Affixed to a high, beautifully constructed wall of fieldstone, there was a brass plate with the number 1270 on it. The wall ran up along an asphalt road, curving and disappearing into heavy foliage. Jamie had assumed this was a side street.

Staring up the broad, curving drive, flanked on both sides by that six-foot wall of stone, Jamie faltered. The urge to escape was almost overwhelming...to turn and run back to her car, down to her own cramped and colorful apartment, over to Doreen's cheerful, noisy kitchen full of sneakers and homework papers and broken toys and the good smell of things cooking.

As quickly as it had come, the urge passed. Jamie gathered her courage, briefly touched the little brass plate as if to draw strength from its golden surface and then started walking rapidly up the curving path between the high stone walls.

STEVEN WAS IN his favorite place when the lady came, hidden among the spreading branches of the mountain ash tree beside the drive. Although he climbed all the trees on the property that were accessible to a seven-year-old boy, the mountain ash was his favorite, because the branches swooped low to the ground, and the trunk forked not too high up, providing a comfortable resting place. And the foliage was so dense that he could hide in there unobserved, even by Hiro, who often passed by as he worked in the garden. Best of all, the clusters of bright red berries attracted flocks of birds. Sometimes, if he was very, very still, a little bird would alight near him to feast on the berries, almost close enough to touch.

One of the boys at school, Jeremy Fletcher, claimed to have a tree house, built for him by his father in a big tree in their backyard. The thought of that tree house aroused a longing in Steven deep enough to bring tears to his eyes. He had never seen the tree house, because he never went to other boys' homes. But he often imagined what it was like, even though the images brought him pain. He pictured the snug little shelter among rustling leaves, with walls and windows and roof, and a rope ladder, Jeremy boasted, that could be raised and lowered....

Steven lay back against the smooth bark of the forked trunk, dreaming about the tree house and what it would be like to have one here in his own tree to play in whenever he wanted.

But the thought made him too sad, and the arrival of the lady was a welcome diversion. Visitors hardly ever came up the drive of his home, and when they did, it was always an occasion of intense interest for Steven. He moved very carefully, so as not to rustle the leaves and give away his presence, and leaned down to study her.

She was a beautiful lady. She was slim and tall, much taller than Clara or Maria or even Hiro, the top of her head almost brushing the lower branches of the trees as she passed. And she walked with a bouncy, cheerful step, as if she liked being alive and was always going somewhere that made her happy. Her face looked happy, too, her wide mouth curving warmly to show that she smiled a lot.

As she passed close beneath his hiding place, he saw that her eyes were blue, blue, blue...like the hyacinths in Hiro's flower beds. Her hair was springy and curly in a wild mass all around her head, a vivid red-gold that caught the sun in a halo of fiery sparkles. She had golden skin, lightly dusted with freckles, and she wore a skirt the color of vanilla ice cream, and a blouse the color of coffee with lots of cream in it.

Steven frowned as she passed, trying to think what the lady reminded him of. Suddenly, it came to him—she looked like a lion. A warm, friendly lion, all red-gold and graceful, moving easily across the plains and into the jungle. All at once, he felt an overwhelming urge to be closer to her, to touch her and hear her voice.

Soundlessly, he slipped from the tree, retrieved his little football from the crevice in the branches where he'd left it earlier, and began to run beside the fence toward the gate, his small body invisible from the lady behind the high stone wall.

JAMIE ROUNDED A CURVE in the drive, and the house came into view, sprawling magnificently across the property. She hesitated, feeling more and more intimidated. The grounds themselves, she calculated, must cover four or five acres, in a section of the city where a standard fifty-foot lot cost more than Terry and Doreen's entire house.

The house was fronted with glass and stone, shadowed by trees and massed shrubbery, architecturally designed with unusual angles and planes and slanted windows. At her left, a huge garage ran down at right angles to the house, joining the stone fence to block access to the grounds beyond. Jamie counted five separate garage doors, all closed and silent. Did this guy really have *five* cars?

She stood in the golden sunlight on the drive, fighting off an eerie impression of being watched. She had felt it as soon as she started up the entry, and the sensation was even stronger now. She felt as if there were eyes everywhere, silently boring into her, measuring her and evaluating her. The trees had eyes, and the stones in the curving fence, the shrubbery and flower beds, and the graceful planes of the silent house. . . .

Sternly, she reminded herself that she had a right to be here, she had an appointment, she was expected. There was no reason to feel like a trespasser or a door-to-door salesman. She took one more deep breath and studied the front of the house, wondering which door to use. There was a massive oak front entrance, flanked with broad panels of stained glass, and a smaller one just off to her left near the garage.

Whoever has to answer the door is probably in the kitchen, she decided. *No point in being pretentious and going to the front door, just to prove I'm important. I'll use the side entry.*

Having decided this, she marched briskly toward the corner of the house. As she did so, she passed a heavy wrought iron gate on her right, and almost screamed aloud.

A human figure had materialized behind the gate with ghostly suddenness, almost as if it had appeared out of thin air. It stood regarding her in steady silence.

But after a breathless, panic-stricken moment, she realized that the person behind the gate was just a little boy, no bigger than her nephew Sean, and there was nothing sinister about him at all. In fact, his small body looked thin and vulnerable in tan shorts, a brown striped T-shirt, and sneakers with one of the laces dragging. He had dark, straight hair and huge brown eyes that looked both frightened and wistful.

"Hello there," Jamie said softly, touched by the shy, eager look on the boy's face. "What's your name?"

"I'm Steven." He watched her through the black iron bars, and then stood on tiptoe, straining to unlatch the gate and swing it open. "Do you want to come inside?"

"Well..." Jamie hesitated. "I'm supposed to go into the house now. I have an appointment with—" She searched her memory briefly "—with Daniel Kelleher."

"That's my father."

"I see." Jamie looked down at him. "You shouldn't invite strangers into the yard, you know, Steven. It's not really a good idea."

"Why not?" He climbed up to swing on the gate, hanging on to the iron railing with one hand and cradling his little football in the other.

"Well, because... you should be careful with strangers. People aren't always nice, you know."

"But you are," the little boy said matter-of-factly. "You're really nice. I can tell. I bet you'd be fun to play with."

Jamie smiled at him. "Well, Steven, you're right about that. I certainly do love to play. Almost any game you can think of."

His eyes brightened. "Football? Do you play football?"

"Like a pro," Jamie said cheerfully.

"All *right!*" he shouted, and ran off across the yard, turning to sail the little ball toward her with surprising accuracy.

Jamie, still standing by the partly opened gate, grabbed the ball neatly and tossed it back to him, taking care to throw it low and easy. The little boy caught it, and his face blazed with joy. He sprinted, turned and threw the ball a little to the right, so Jamie had to run down onto the grass just inside the stone fence and leap to snag the pass out of the air.

Awkward in her high heels, she slipped and fell, landing safely on her hip on the soft grass and sliding a little way down the slope of the lawn, clutching the ball triumphantly in her hands. Steven came pounding across to her, his face pale and terrified.

"I'm sorry, lady," he said anxiously. "Are you all right? I didn't mean to—"

"I'm fine." Jamie grinned, still sitting on the freshly mown grass, and reached up to punch his arm lightly. "But we're going to have to work on your positioning a little, quarterback. If I weren't such a fabulous pass receiver, we just might have lost that one."

Steven threw his head back, laughing with relief, and Jamie was touched by the transformation. Instead of a shy and lonely waif, he looked, for the moment, like any other happy little boy.

"Can we play some more?" he asked, holding her hand as she got to her feet, brushed some stray grass clippings from her skirt and tucked her blouse in firmly once again.

Jamie smiled down at him, and ruffled his hair. "Not just now, Steven. I have to talk to your father. Maybe later."

He walked beside her toward the house, still holding her hand. Jamie felt immeasurably better, even though she still had the sensation of being watched, and now she was certain that she wasn't imagining it. A shadow flitted around the corner of the house by the garage, another stirred in the shrubbery off to her right, and a curtain dropped into place at a window in the house.

But the moment of boisterous play had completely restored her equilibrium. She was herself again, buoyant and happy, full of confidence, and this place wasn't going to intimidate her any longer.

She was spared any further decisions about doors, because Steven dragged her firmly to the side entry, opened it and went in calling, "Maria! Come quick!"

Jamie barely had time to absorb the details of the massive, gleaming, modern kitchen, before a small, slender young woman appeared from a recess at the back and stood twisting her apron nervously in her hands.

"This is Maria," Steven said cheerfully, "and this is the lady. We played football," he added for Maria's benefit, and crossed the room to open the fridge door and study its contents.

Jamie smiled at the other woman. Maria looked about Jamie's own age, probably late twenties. With her slim figure and coal black hair and eyes, she was quite attractive but her face had a shy, terrified look and was extremely pale, as if she never saw the light of day. She stood very still, gazing timidly up at Jamie, apparently overwhelmed by her sheer size and her robust golden presence. Jamie returned her look in grave silence, conscious of the smaller woman's painful shyness.

"I'm Jamie O'Rourke," she said gently. "I have an appointment with Mr. Kelleher at two o'clock."

Maria's eyes widened in startled alarm, and she stared at Jamie.

"Oh, no," she murmured. "There must be...there must be some mistake."

"Why?" Jamie asked in surprise. "I do have the right day, don't I? Yes, I know I do. My sister-in-law wrote down the appointment. Saturday afternoon, two o'clock, 1270 Herald Drive. And here I am.''

"But...but he doesn't..." Maria began, and then subsided helplessly. "If you have an appointment, I guess it's all right," she concluded in bewilderment. "But I was sure he didn't—"

"Maria," Steven interrupted, still squatting by the fridge, "can I have a bowl of pudding?"

The young woman turned to him. "All right," she said. "But just a little one, Steven. You mustn't spoil your dinner."

"What's for dinner?" he asked.

"I don't know. Clara won't tell me. She said it's a surprise."

The little boy's eyes brightened. "When she says that, it's usually oysters and asparagus. Yummy!"

Maria smiled at him, and her face momentarily lost its tense and frightened expression.

Jamie stood uncertainly, battling a mounting impression of unreality. She felt more and more like Alice, stumbling into an unreal world, a silent, withdrawn place where the walls and trees had eyes; and everyone seemed shy and lonely, and little boys actually *liked* dining on oysters.

She struggled to recall Terry's house, with Doreen, plump and cheerful, serving bowls of macaroni and cheese to a table circled by noisy children, any of whom would have greeted a plate of oysters and asparagus with a resounding and graphic "Yuck!"

That was the *real* world, she reminded herself, and this place was strange, indeed. Even stranger, she somehow sensed, than it appeared on the surface.

Maria turned back to her. "Mr. Kelleher is in his private rooms, upstairs," she said softly. "You can use the elevator. I'll show you."

Jamie followed the other woman out of the kitchen and into a huge, marble-flagged foyer, her sense of unreality growing. Vistas spread out beyond archways and opened doors, echoing expanses of luxury and beauty, with exquisite paintings hanging on the walls and priceless statues standing in lighted alcoves. And everywhere, there were plants, masses and forests of greenery fronting the huge windows, brightening the corners, and massed in an atrium that was just visible beyond the living room, opening, it appeared, onto a private, semi-enclosed swimming pool.

As they moved through the house, doors slid open in front of them with ghostly silence, responding, apparently, to invisible pads beneath the flooring like the doors in supermarkets. Jamie was astounded by this, trying to recall if she had ever heard of such a thing in a private home.

But then, she recalled, this house belonged to a paraplegic who obviously had enough money to customize it to his needs. For someone confined to a wheelchair, the automatic door openers were an extremely sensible idea.

She smiled warmly down at Maria as they waited by the brass doors of the elevator in the foyer, and the other woman, startled, gave her a quick shy smile in return. Just at that moment, Jamie heard an eerie whirring sound coming from somewhere quite nearby, and saw a gray, shadowy human form vanish in the distance around a potted palm.

Badly startled and a little frightened, she clutched her leather folder tight in her hands, stepped into the elevator behind Maria and waited as it rose smoothly and silently to the next level.

Maria led her down a hallway floored in polished oak, and paused in front of a heavy wooden door. This one, Jamie noticed, did not open as they approached it. The door, she thought, must be locked, or possibly operated by some inner control panel.

This guess, it turned out, was correct.

An intercom, cleverly set into the door molding so it was almost invisible, crackled by Jamie's ear, and she jumped a little.

"What is it?" a voice asked, strong and masculine in the tiny speaker.

Maria leaned toward the concealed intercom. "Someone to see you, sir."

"All right," the voice said. "Send him in."

The door slid sideways with that same sinister, invisible ease, opening into a large, square room flooded with sunlight. Jamie blinked a little after the dimness of the hallway, and, as she did so, Maria waved her hand in the direction of the room with an awkward, jerky motion and then fled rapidly down the hallway. Puzzled, Jamie watched the smaller woman's slender departing back for a moment and then stepped inside.

Her first impression was one of warmth and comfort, and an appeal far greater, in her opinion, than the opulence of the lower floor. This room was designed for someone to live in, with massive, well-worn leather furniture, walls of books and bright, vivid splashes of color in wall hangings and throw rugs. A huge rosewood desk equipped with a bank of sophisticated computer equipment was set near the wide mullioned windows.

A man sat beside the desk in the sunlight, near a giant fern, and as soon as Jamie's eyes focused and she saw him clearly, she was unable to see anything else. The man's face was dark and commanding, with an arrogant, handsome, male appeal that left her almost breathless. His eyes were black and intense, and his hair, too, was dark, very thick and straight, with a light frosting of gray at the temples, though Jamie judged him to be, at the most, perhaps in his early thirties. His nose was strong and highbridged, his mouth wide and finely sculpted, with a full, sensual lower lip above a rugged square chin.

The man sat regarding her steadily, unsmiling, his brown strong hands resting casually on the arms of his wheelchair. He wore a short-sleeved white polo shirt, open at the neck, which made his deep tan even more pronounced, and accentuated the muscular bulk of his torso. He was, Jamie could see, incredibly strong in his arms and upper body, with muscles that rippled and bulged beneath the thin fabric of his shirt. He wore navy blue jogging pants and neat gray sneakers tied onto the feet that rested useless and immobile on the footrest of the wheelchair.

The black eyes flicked coldly over Jamie, taking her all in, the curly reddish crown of hair, the rich ample bosom beneath the mocha-colored silk blouse, the trim waist and firm thighs and long shapely legs. She felt embarrassed, almost exposed. There was something searching and merciless in that unwavering dark gaze.

"Well?" he said finally.

"I beg your pardon?" Jamie said.

"Could you state your business, please? I assume you have some reason for being here, or my housekeeper wouldn't have let you in. And I'd like you to get on with it, because I have an appointment at two o'clock."

"That's me," Jamie said, abrupt in her awkwardness. "I'm it. Your appointment, I mean."

He stared at her, and she tried to meet his gaze, struggling to overcome the sensation of unreality that had haunted her since she first set foot in this place. Jamie was a confident person, accustomed to being in control of her life. But there was something about this place . . . and this man's piercing black eyes. . . .

He stared at her a moment longer and then leaned over to lift a folder from the desk and leaf through it before glancing sharply up at her again.

"*You're* Morgan James O'Rourke?" he asked in disbelief.

"Yes, Mr. Kelleher. I am."

There was a moment's silence while he absorbed this information, and Jamie waited.

"What happened?" he asked finally, with a sardonic little twist of his mouth. "Did they get the babies mixed-up at the hospital and not notice for a while that they didn't have a boy, or what?"

Jamie flushed at his tone and lifted her chin to look steadily at him.

"Morgan is a fairly common girl's name, amongst the Irish, Mr. Kelleher."

"Okay, I'll grant you that. But *James?* Is that a common girl's name in your family, too?"

He was making fun of her, and Jamie hated the feeling. She controlled herself firmly, not letting any emotions show, and answered in as calm a voice as she could muster, "James was my mother's maiden name. In earlier times, it was a general custom, in the county in Ireland where my parents grew up, to give one or more daughters their mother's maiden name. That way, when a girl married and took her husband's name, she still retained some of her own heritage as well."

"I see," he said, nodding, a brief humorless grin flitting across that powerful sculpted mouth. "A sort of feudal feminism, you might say."

Jamie decided that she really didn't like this man very much at all.

But she wanted the job he was offering, wanted it badly, and so she stood still in front of him and said nothing. She was uncomfortable standing there in the middle of the room and terribly afraid that at any moment her knees were going to start shaking. She would have loved to sink into one of the deep, soft leather chairs placed invitingly nearby, but he made no move to offer her a seat, and so she lifted her chin again and looked at him, waiting for his next words.

"I see that most of your official documents indicate that you customarily use the name Jamie. Why not Morgan, since that's your first name?"

None of your damned business, Jamie thought furiously.

Then she reminded herself just how much she wanted this particular job, drew a slow, ragged breath, and answered him.

"Because," she said evenly, "when I was a little girl, I was fat and carrot-haired and bouncy, and Morgan just didn't seem to suit me. I was more like my mother's family...a real little James, everybody said. So they all started calling me Jamie."

He grinned suddenly, and white teeth flashed in his tanned face. Jamie was startled at the transformation. For a second, he looked boyish and appealing.

But, as soon as it appeared, the smile vanished, leaving his face so dark that Jamie wondered if perhaps she had imagined that sudden flash of light and warmth.

"Well, I'm sure that all this Irish family history is really fascinating," he said, with a sarcastic edge to his voice that made Jamie flush with angry embarrassment, "but I'm afraid that we're just wasting each other's time. I have no intention of hiring you for this job, and I'm sorry to have troubled you."

Jamie stared at him, her eyes wide, her mouth poised to frame an indignant protest.

"But..." she began helplessly, "but you haven't even—"

"I want a man for this position," he interrupted, his voice firm and dismissive. "You'll forgive me, I trust, for assuming that Morgan James O'Rourke was a male. It's an understandable error, after all."

Jamie felt as if the world were slipping away from her, and she wanted to clutch at something, but she was, she realized, too upset to trust her own voice. She stared at him, unmoving.

"Goodbye, Miss O'Rourke," he said with a touch of impatience. "I'm sure that you can see yourself out."

Jamie stared at him a moment longer, thoughts whirling and colliding within her mind in a sort of crazy confusion.

He turned aside deliberately, wheeling himself skillfully around into position at the desk, the muscles in his big arms bulging as he manipulated the chair.

Jamie walked slowly toward the door, which slid silently open at her approach. In the doorway she paused and turned back to look at him once more, and then stared in surprise.

He was watching her and grinning broadly. This time, there was no doubt about the smile... it lit up his whole face, drove deep creases into his tanned cheeks, made his dark eyes dance. But, Jamie realized, there was nothing friendly about this smile. It was genuinely amused, but faintly, privately derisive, as if, for some reason, he was laughing at her.

She turned away angrily, stepped through the door and heard it slide shut behind her. After a moment's hesitation, she began to trudge down the hallway toward the brass panels of the elevator, wondering what she was going to tell Terry and Doreen and her father.

Suddenly she remembered Daniel Kelleher's parting grin and had a quick, dreadful thought. She arched her back, peered over her shoulder, and felt a hot flush of pained embarrassment that spread in a slow tide of red from her neck to the roots of her hair.

On the seat of her trim, dressy, cream-colored gabardine skirt, there was a long green grass stain, spreading vividly over one firm, rounded hip. She remembered catching the little boy's football, slipping on her high heels, sliding down the slope of freshly cut grass....

Then she recalled that amused, sparkling grin, and felt the growth of a deep, welling fury that, strangely enough, both warmed and steadied her.

The *bastard!* she thought. *The goddamn, smug, arrogant, vicious bastard! This is just too much....*

Without further thought, she turned on her heel, blue eyes blazing, red hair electric with anger and strode back down the hall to the wide oak door of his room.

CHAPTER TWO

JAMIE POUNDED on the door and eventually heard his voice booming through the little intercom again.

"'What is it now, Maria?" he asked.

Jamie leaned toward the speaker, exercising considerable self-control to keep her voice calm and level.

"It's not Maria. It's me…Jamie O'Rourke. I'd like to speak with you again for a moment."

After a brief hesitation, the door slid open and Jamie stepped inside the room. Daniel Kelleher glanced up at her, switched off his computer monitor and waited politely for her to speak.

Jamie drew a deep breath, allowing some time for the hammering of her heart to subside a little. Just the look of the man, the arrogant set to his mouth, the inquiring, sardonic arch of his eyebrows, was enough to make her furious.

"I wanted," she said finally, "to do two things. To tell you something and ask you something."

"Is this going to take long? I really do have to get back to work."

Jamie bit her lip. "No, Mr. Kelleher. It won't take long," she said softly. "First, I want to tell you that the grass stain on my skirt, which you apparently found so intensely amusing, was the result of a little impromptu football game I was playing with your son when I arrived here today. He strikes me as a very lonely little boy, Mr.

Kelleher. Maybe someone should see that he has a few playmates, so he doesn't have to accost strangers for company."

This shot, Jamie observed with satisfaction, appeared to have hit home. Daniel Kelleher paled slightly, and his dark eyes flashed dangerously.

"And," Jamie went on before he could reply, "I wanted to ask you if you had any applicants for this position—any at all—who were better qualified than I am. And I'd appreciate an honest answer, Mr. Kelleher."

Her voice had steadied by now, though her blue eyes were still vivid with anger. She stared at him, her gaze level and challenging, and the man in the wheelchair returned her look, Jamie realized in surprise, with something approaching respect.

"No," he said calmly, after a moment's thought. "No, I didn't. You have..."

He paused, leafing quickly through the file on his desk. Jamie recognized one of the papers as her own résumé, heavily marked with unfamiliar notes and underlining in black ink. The man glanced up at her again.

"You have a degree in physiotherapy and five years of experience in a clinical setting, and that makes you by far the best qualified applicant. Most of the others, in fact," he added with a touch of bitterness, "appeared to be attracted primarily by the idea of a job where they could earn room, board and full pay for three hours of work a day."

"That's what I thought," Jamie said. "Now, if I'm the best-qualified applicant, am I not at least entitled to an interview?"

"I told you," he said patiently, in the elaborately gentle tone one uses when addressing a very young and possibly backward child, "that I want a man for this position."

"I don't even think that's legal, you know, Mr. Kelleher. There are laws about that sort of thing, these days."

"And what are you going to do? Report me to the Human Rights Commission, because I refuse to hire a physiotherapist who comes to an interview with grass stains all over her bottom?"

Jamie bit her lip and looked at him steadily. "You really are a bit of a bastard, aren't you, sir?"

Unexpectedly, he grinned. "Yes," he agreed calmly. "I really am."

"Well, I'm not going to report you." Deliberately, uninvited, Jamie walked across the room and seated herself gracefully in the leather chair nearest his desk, leaning forward to look at him intently. "I'm just going to demand, Mr. Kelleher, that you give me this job. Or, at the very least, give me a fair interview."

He met her gaze, unmoving, and the quiet, luxurious, sun-washed room seemed almost to vibrate with the intensity of two powerful personalities locked in grim combat.

"As you know," Jamie went on, "I've had five years of clinical experience. The sex of my patients has long ceased to be an issue, Mr. Kelleher. It's immaterial to me whether the body I'm working on is male or female. To any professional person, it really doesn't make the slightest difference."

"I assure you, Miss O'Rourke," he said dryly, "that it doesn't make much difference to me, either. So many people have poked and prodded at my body over the course of the last two years that my physiotherapist could be a trained gorilla, as long as he gave a proper massage. I require a man for the position for other reasons."

"What other reasons?" Jamie asked bluntly.

Her anger was quickly ebbing away. Jamie could never stay angry for very long, no matter how severely provoked. But she was still grateful for that initial surge of fury, because it had made her brave, wiping away her intimidation at all this wealth and luxury and freeing her to speak her mind.

"Reasons of discretion," he said mildly, apparently unoffended by her brusqueness.

"Discretion?" Jamie asked. "In what way?"

He leaned back against the padded leather back of his chair, balancing a pencil carefully between his strong brown hands and looking at her in steady silence. Jamie gazed back at him, waiting.

"I am, as it happens, a rather well-known person," he said without emotion. "Not under my own name, but under another name which is familiar to the public. I have taken great care, for many years, to keep the two identities separate, because I value my privacy. Do you understand?"

"Not entirely," Jamie said. "I mean, I can certainly understand you valuing your privacy. I don't understand what it has to do with your choice of a private physiotherapist."

"Come on, Miss O'Rourke. Think about it. This is a live-in position. The person I hire will, I hope, keep the job for a long time and will become an integral part of the household. He will inevitably become privy to information that I don't wish to make public knowledge. So I need somebody for this job who can be trusted to be discreet. *Now* do you understand?"

Jamie felt the hot, searing spread of a new rage, even more sweeping and compelling than her earlier anger. She was furious all the way to the tips of her well-shod feet, her whole body trembling in the grip of an emotion that she could just barely control.

"That's just . . . It's just so bloody *stupid!*" she burst out.

Too agitated to remain seated, she leaped to her feet and stood in front of him, hands on hips, glaring furiously down at him as he sat behind his desk.

"'Bloody stupid,' Miss O'Rourke?" he asked, in a tone of amused surprise that enraged her further. "To what, exactly, are you referring?"

"To the ridiculous, asinine stereotype that says men are somehow more discreet than women!"

Jamie hesitated, her full, shapely bosom heaving, and drew her breath in slowly, fighting to calm herself, while he watched her curiously.

"I've had lots and lots of friends in my life, Mr. Kelleher. Both male and female. And it's been my general impression that there are women who can be trusted with secrets more than men. I think there are men who tend to be terrible gossips, especially amongst themselves. And there are women who will go out of their way to respect a friend's confidence. It's a personal, individual thing. And, in my job, I learn all sorts of things, about all kinds of people, and I never tell anybody. I think I'm probably more capable of discretion, Mr. Kelleher, than any man you've ever met."

She paused. Her first hot surge of anger began to ebb away, leaving her feeling empty and a little foolish.

"I just loathe stereotypes," she murmured, somewhat lamely, her face hot. "I hate the way people classify each other by superficial things like that."

"Do you, now? And what, Miss O'Rourke," he asked bitterly, gesturing toward the chair that he sat in, "would *you* really know about being stereotyped?"

Jamie met his eyes steadily. "I'll grant you, probably not as much as you. I've been working in therapy for years, and I know, all too well, what the disabled suffer at the hands of ignorant, insensitive people." She hesitated, and then continued. "But I *do* experience my own small share of it, too, Mr. Kelleher."

"You? In what way?"

"Look at me," she commanded, still standing in front of his desk. "Look at me, Mr. Kelleher. I'm five feet eleven inches in my stocking feet. I have bright red hair. I'm Irish. And if that's not enough, I give massages for a living. Just *ask* me how many stupid, stereotyped remarks I have to listen to!"

He chuckled with sudden genuine amusement, the first entirely human reaction he had shown during the whole interview, and Jamie relented slightly, her mouth tugging upward in a little answering flicker of a smile.

"Yes," he said finally. "Yes, I can see how you might have to deal with your share of clichés, at that." He grinned at her. "Please sit down, Miss O'Rourke. Not to cast any unkind aspersions on your height, God forbid, but you *are* a little intimidating, towering way up there above me."

Jamie sank back into the chair and gripped her folder, still trembling slightly as she looked at him.

"Tell me," he began in a casual tone, "why you want this particular job enough to fight for it so convincingly."

"Because it's perfect for me, at this point in my life," Jamie replied promptly. "I've always enjoyed clinical work, but it's so time-consuming and emotionally draining to carry a full caseload that there's not much room for anything else."

"I see. And you've reached the stage where you want something else in your life?"

"Yes, I have. I'm working on developing my own exercise program for cardiac patients and pregnant women. It's a combination of low-impact aerobics and water exercise, and it's very complex to get just the right balance of muscle work and stress control. It's going to take years to get it refined."

He nodded thoughtfully. "And what will you do with this program when you've developed it? Make a video, and get rich and famous?"

Jamie smiled. "I'm hardly the type to be rich and famous, Mr. Kelleher. But I do like to help people. I think I'd be satisfied to see it printed and distributed to hospitals around the country where they could make some use of it. Right now," she went on, "I teach experimental classes four nights a week, three at the clinic and one at the community center, and in my free time I'm doing research and developing new routines. But I quit my job to concentrate on my program. I haven't been working for a couple of months, and I'm running out of savings."

He nodded thoughtfully, and in the new easy tone of their conversation, Jamie was able to appreciate the way the sun glinted on the planes of his strong handsome face, and gilded the springing dark hairs on his muscular tanned forearms.

He was such a commanding, powerful presence, she thought, that he filled the whole room with the sheer strength of his personality, and the brilliant intelligence in those blazing dark eyes. They were eyes that seemed almost able to see right through you, look into your soul and read your most private dreams.

She shivered a little, and forced her errant thoughts back under control, trying to catch what he was saying.

" . . . for you, wouldn't it?" he asked.

"I beg your pardon?" Jamie asked. "My mind was wandering," she confessed, blushing a little. "This whole . . . this interview has been a little . . . a little upsetting."

He grinned, but made no comment. "I was saying," he repeated, "that considering your personal interests, this job would, indeed, be ideal for you. It would pay you the salary you're accustomed to, but still leave you large blocks of free time in which to do your own work."

"Yes," Jamie agreed eagerly. "That's what we thought."

"We?" he asked, his voice suddenly wary.

"My family," Jamie said. "My brother Terry, and his wife Doreen. She's the one who took the message from you about the interview."

She looked up at him with a questioning glance, and he nodded quietly, watching her.

"And my father, who's a widower, lives with them, too. They have a house over on the north side, and they have five children."

"Quite a houseful," Daniel Kelleher observed dryly.

"Yes," Jamie agreed, with a fond reminiscent smile. "It certainly is. But I love them all."

"If I offer you this job," he said, "you would have to understand that, although it's a live-in position, and you would have a private suite of rooms here in the house, you could never invite anybody here. Nobody at all, family or friends."

Jamie stared at him, and said nothing.

"You would have the weekends off," he continued. "From Friday at four o'clock until Monday morning. If you wished to pursue a social life, you would have to do it then, away from these premises. Do you understand?"

Jamie nodded. "Yes," she said. "I understand."

"Your résumé states that you're not married. Do you have a boyfriend?" Kelleher asked abruptly.

"Yes," Jamie said, startled. "Yes, I do."

"Well, I don't want him here, either. Ever. When you have a date, you will have to make arrangements to meet him, or have him pick you up elsewhere. Not in my home. Is that understood, as well?"

"Yes," Jamie said once more. "What I *don't* understand, Mr. Kelleher, is whether you're actually offering me the job or just outlining conditions or what."

"Good question." He looked at her, and their eyes met and held, his gaze dark and piercing, hers as blue as the square of summer sky beyond the windows.

He grinned suddenly, with another flash of white teeth against his tanned face.

"I guess I'm offering you the job, since I have the distinct feeling that it's inevitable, somehow. You're really rather overwhelming, Miss O'Rourke."

"So are you," Jamie said truthfully.

"Good. Let's maintain that degree of mutual respect, for a healthy working relationship. We will continue to address one another as Miss O'Rourke and Mr. Kelleher," he went on, his voice suddenly crisp and dictatorial, "and we will not become cosy and confiding friends. We will remain therapist and patient, nothing more. You will not, at any time, discuss the occupants of this house with people outside the house or impart any information you might learn about me to anyone else. I will not tell you any of my psychic traumas, and you will kindly refrain from confiding in me the details of your love life."

"Count on it," Jamie said dryly. She looked over at him. "What level of treatment are you proposing?" she asked in a more businesslike tone. "Are you currently in any kind of therapy program?"

"I've been driving over to the hospital three afternoons a week, for hydrotherapy and massage, but I hate it. It's always so crowded and I feel that the treatment is hardly worth the time it takes."

Jamie nodded. "All the facilities in the city are overcrowded. It's a problem everywhere."

"And," he continued, "I've had some outpatient assistance here at home, with therapists coming to the house a couple of days a week, but they seem notoriously unreliable, and I like to run my life on a tight schedule. I don't appreciate sitting around and waiting for somebody who's going to turn up an hour late, if at all."

Jamie glanced over at the grim set to that powerful mouth, and thought that it would take a considerable nerve to keep this man waiting.

"They're busy, too," she said softly. "The outpatient therapists, I mean. They all have impossibly heavy caseloads. There just isn't enough money for proper staffing and programs."

"I know," he said wearily. "I feel genuinely sorry for the poor unfortunates who are in my position and have to depend on the generosity of the government to get the help they need. But I can afford to hire my own care, and that's what I've decided to do. The only reason I haven't done it sooner was that I was reluctant, for various reasons, some of which I've already mentioned, to add another person to my household."

"I gather," Jamie said, "that your injury is fairly recent?"

"In medical terms, yes, I suppose it is," he said, gazing bleakly out the window at the blue square of summer sky. "But it feels like an eternity to me," he added quietly.

Jamie was silent, waiting.

"It was just over two years ago, in the early spring," he said. "I was playing hockey, in an unimportant little amateur neighborhood league. Nothing impressive or anything, but I've always...I always used to like rough sports, as an outlet, I guess, for the mental energy that my work demands."

He glanced over at Jamie with a quick, raking glitter of brilliant dark eyes, and she nodded.

"I was checked into the boards, extremely hard, at an awkward angle, and had to be carried from the rink on a stretcher. I knew right away that something was wrong with my lower body, although I wasn't aware of the full extent of the injury, of course, until they told me later at the hospital."

Jamie gazed at him, wide-eyed, gripping her leather folder so hard that her knuckles were white. No matter how many times she heard stories like this, she could never quite get over the agony of it...the pain of sharing that dreadful moment when a person realizes, fully and horribly, that his life will never, ever be the same again.

And, she thought, wretched with sympathy, it must have been even worse for him...an athletic man in the prime of his life.

But she was a trained professional, and she knew enough to keep her emotions hidden. The last thing men like Daniel Kelleher wanted, the thing, in fact, that they most detested, was pity.

Instead, she drew herself together and asked a few brisk technical questions about the nature and location of the spinal trauma, and the degree of impairment.

"I'm one of the lucky ones," he told her without emotion. "At least, that's what the doctor tells me. The damage was low enough on my spine that I still have some sensation in my lower torso. I am, for instance, fully in control of my bodily functions."

"You *are* lucky, then," Jamie told him. "That's the exception, rather than the rule, for paraplegics."

"I know," he said, "but you'll forgive me if I find it damned hard to feel lucky."

"Yes," Jamie said softly, "I'll forgive you. You said the trauma to your spine was situated low down. Do you have any range of movement at all below it?"

"None. Absolutely none. I'll never walk again, and I've adapted to that. I do have some fleeting sensations in my legs...a little pain and cramping sometimes, which the doctor feels is probably more of a phantom limb type of phenomenon than actual feeling. But it does seem to be eased by massage."

Jamie nodded. "So, basically, you require the standard treatment...massage to maintain circulation and skin tone in your legs, and to ease pain in your spine."

"Right. And not just in my spine." He looked at her, a little abashed. "I like to make the most of the part of my body that's left to me, and I sometimes overdo the weight training and swimming, and suffer afterwards as a result."

"Well," Jamie said severely, "I'll expect, as your therapist, to have something to say about *that,* Mr. Kelleher. Now, you want three hours of massage and exercise daily, isn't that right? Did you want this all in one session or spaced through the day or what?"

"Oh, my God. Spaced throughout the day," he said emphatically. "I could never endure the boredom of three consecutive hours of therapy. That's why I want a live-in therapist, entirely for my own convenience. An hour in the morning after my swim, an hour at lunch, and another at four o'clock. And, occasionally, there will be the need for extra massage, when I'm in pain at night and can't sleep."

"Does that happen often?"

"Often enough," he said grimly, "and I have no intention of becoming addicted to painkilling drugs."

Jamie nodded, calculating rapidly in her mind. The schedule as he outlined it was perfect for her, allowing her time to work on her own programs and leaving her evenings free for teaching.

He was watching her face. "Does this all sound satisfactory to you, Miss O'Rourke?"

"Oh, yes, excellent. Even better than I'd hoped."

"Good. There is, as I mentioned earlier, a small suite of rooms provided for you, and you will take your meals with the rest of the household. You may also feel free to avail yourself of all the facilities here...the pool, and the sauna and sun-room, the media room and the library."

"The library?" Jamie interrupted. "You have a *library?* Besides this, I mean?" she went on, indicating the book-lined walls on two sides of her.

He smiled. "Oh, yes, Miss O'Rourke. Much more than this. The library downstairs contains some four thousand volumes, in a wide variety of fiction and nonfiction titles."

A small, involuntary sigh of bliss escaped Jamie, and he looked at her curiously.

"Are you a reader, Miss O'Rourke?"

"Yes, Mr. Kelleher, I'm a reader. I love books almost more than anything in the world. I always have."

His dark eyes kindled with sudden interest, and he seemed on the verge of questioning her further, but

checked himself and turned away, his face falling once
more into its customary cold and guarded expression.

"I hope you will enjoy your life here," he said in a cool,
formal tone. "Maria will show you where your rooms are.
Are you able to start on Monday morning?"

"Yes," Jamie said.

"Very well, then," he said, turning to switch his computer monitor on again, his voice curt and dismissive.
"Thank you, Miss O'Rourke."

Jamie got up to leave, painfully conscious, as she
turned to the door, of the vivid grass stain on her skirt.

"Miss O'Rourke?"

"Yes?" Jamie paused in the doorway, and turned to
look at him.

"You will park in the garage bay nearest the street.
Each door is controlled by its own remote opener, with a
numbered combination. Maria will give you the one for
your door."

"Thank you, sir."

Jamie had a sudden, overwhelmingly vivid mental image of her battered little car lurching up to that massive
luxurious garage, and waiting imperiously for the door to
open. In spite of herself, she smiled, a wide, sparkling grin
that crinkled her nose, dimpled her cheeks and showed her
even white teeth.

"Is something amusing, Miss O'Rourke?"

"I was just thinking about . . . Mr. Kelleher, my car is a
little . . . disreputable looking. It's a really old Volkswag-
en Beetle, covered with dents and happy faces, you know,
and I was just trying to imagine . . ."

Her voice trailed off, and the man behind the desk
shook his head sadly.

"Miss O'Rourke," he said, "I fear that you are going
to be a great trial to me."

Jamie couldn't tell if his words were serious or not. But, as she nodded and stepped from the room, she suspected he hadn't been joking.

JAMIE WANDERED through the marble-flagged hallway on the lower floor, a little dazed by everything that had happened. She still couldn't quite believe that she had the job, and that she would actually be living in this beautiful place.

She hesitated by one of the lighted alcoves containing a marble statue of a winged horse, so fluid and exquisite that it seemed poised and ready to soar from its pedestal. Awed by the graceful beauty of the figure, Jamie reached out a trembling hand to touch one of the fragile wings.

At that moment, she heard the eerie whirring sound again. Turning abruptly, her heart thudding, she glimpsed a gray shadow as it disappeared around a corner.

God, she thought, pressing her hand against her chest. *This place is going to take some getting used to. What is that? A ghost, or what?*

At the same moment, one of the windows darkened slightly, and Jamie whirled to see the vague outline of a face staring in at her. Then it vanished as abruptly as it had appeared.

In sudden panic, she hurried from the foyer and bolted for the relative safety of the kitchen. She found Maria there alone, energetically scrubbing the floor, which already looked spick-and-span to Jamie.

"Hello, Maria," she said.

The other woman jumped and turned, still on her knees by the stove, gazing up at Jamie in alarm.

"Sorry," Jamie said. "Did I startle you?"

"It's all right." Maria got to her feet, wiping her grimy hands awkwardly in her apron and giving Jamie a shy, inquiring look.

"Well, I got the job," Jamie told her cheerfully. "I start on Monday, but I guess I'll be moving in tomorrow evening. Mr. Kelleher said that you might have time to show me where my—"

She paused, surprised by the sudden expression of happiness that illuminated Maria's youthful features.

"He hired you?" Maria asked in disbelief. "Really? You're coming to live here?"

"Really," Jamie said.

"Oh, Miss O'Rourke, that's wonderful! That will be so nice! We were afraid that he—"

Maria paused, beaming up at her for a moment longer, while Jamie hesitated, puzzled by the other woman's reaction. "Call me Jamie," she said finally. "I'm sure we're going to be good friends, Maria."

"All right. Come, Jamie," Maria said, still smiling with pleasure. "Come, I'll show you your rooms. They're quite nice, and they open onto the patio."

Maria took a key from a rack in the corner and went briskly ahead of Jamie, out of the kitchen and down a wide corridor toward the rear of the house.

The rooms in this wing appeared to be living quarters. Glancing through open doorways, she saw television sets, cosy armchairs drawn up to fireplaces, and bright rugs on the floors.

"We live down here," Maria said, "and this is where guests stay, too, although we hardly ever have any visitors anymore."

"Who's 'we'?" Jamie asked. "How many people work here?"

"Not many. Just three. Four," Maria corrected herself with a smile, "counting you." She took the key from her apron pocket and unlocked a door, stepping inside and handing the key to Jamie.

Jamie followed her and drew her breath in sharply. The room in which she found herself was about fifteen feet square. It was thickly carpeted and tastefully furnished. On one wall, a small oak-framed fireplace held a gas firelog. A white sheepskin rug was spread in front of the hearth. Two doors in the main sitting room opened onto a bedroom and a bathroom. The suite was warm, rich and surprisingly luxurious.

But the most wonderful thing was the view. The far wall of the sitting room was almost entirely glass, and it overlooked the whole city, giving the room the feeling of being suspended in midair. Jamie realized that the house was built right on the edge of the cliffs on the outskirts of Calgary. The view from this window was a sweeping panorama of the city and the surrounding prairie, all the way to the horizon, fifty miles distant in some places. Yet it was completely private, so high up that it was isolated from anyone's view.

"Oh," Jamie breathed. "Oh, my." She wandered over to the window, fingering the sheer fabric of the draperies, and gazed out in pure bliss.

"I'm sorry," Maria said behind her, watching her anxiously. "It's the only suite left with a sitting room, but we could get that wall covered with heavier drapes, if you don't—"

"Oh, no!" Jamie exclaimed. "I love it! It's gorgeous. I've always loved light and space."

Maria looked at her in disbelief. "Well, I hate it," she said flatly. "I'd be scared all the time if I had to live by that window. I don't think I could stand it."

Jamie looked around, surprised by the smaller woman's terrified expression, and then went over to peer into the bedroom. It was also comfortably furnished, with a set of French doors opening onto a shady patio beside the deck of the pool.

"I can't believe it," Jamie said finally. "I feel like I'm dreaming, and somebody should pinch me. Go ahead, Maria," she added cheerfully. "Pinch me."

Maria chuckled. The tenseness smoothed from her face, and all at once, she looked a good deal younger and prettier.

"Who else lives here?" Jamie asked again, pausing to inspect the beautiful, modern bathroom, equipped with bathtub and tiled shower stall.

"My rooms are right across the hall," Maria said, "and Clara...that's the cook, you'll meet her soon...she lives just up there." Maria pointed in the direction they had come. "And Hiro, he's the gardener and handyman, he has his own rooms behind the garage. Steven's room is upstairs, of course."

"He seems . . . he seems like a really lonely little boy," Jamie said hesitantly.

Maria looked troubled. "I know. His father tries to...to do things for him, but he doesn't go out much, and I can't . . ." She paused, biting her lip, and went on. "Besides, Mr. Kelleher can't stand to have any interruptions when he's working. And," Maria added grimly, "you never know when he might be working. All hours of the day and night, sometimes."

"What does he do?" Jamie asked.

Maria looked at her directly. "He writes books," she said.

Jamie stared back, amazed. "He's a *writer?*" she repeated.

"Yes. You look surprised."

"Well . . ." Jamie hesitated, and then waved a hand at the luxury all around her. "I didn't think writers earned this kind of money, you know?"

Maria smiled. "I don't know about that. Mr. Kelleher inherited this house from his parents. His father was a really big man in the oil industry. But I think he makes lots of money from his books, too."

Jamie looked at her, intrigued, remembering his comment that his name was well-known to the public. "I wonder if I've read any of his books," she said.

"I'm sure you have," Maria said dryly. "If you read much at all."

"Really? What's his pen name, Maria?"

The other woman closed her mouth firmly, as if regretting her careless flow of words, and shook her head.

Jamie looked at her, and suddenly the name clicked in her mind, along with a vivid mental image of the row of books that stood alone on a shelf behind Daniel Kelleher's desk, books with bold, unforgettable covers.

"Dan Kelly," she whispered. "I saw the whole set of books there in his office. Is he *Dan Kelly?*"

Maria turned away, trembling, and plucked nervously at the tasseled corner of a cushion on the sofa. "I didn't say anything," she murmured in panic. "I didn't say that."

Jamie stared at her in stunned silence. "It's true, isn't it?" she breathed. "He's really Dan Kelly."

Maria still refused to look up, and Jamie gazed at her, wide-eyed. "Oh, my God," she murmured, shaking her head in disbelief. "Dan Kelly. I never dreamed that he lived here in Canada. I thought he lived . . . on a private island or something."

Maria turned quickly, her face white, her eyes pleading. "Look, Jamie," she said rapidly, in a low, uneven voice. "You mustn't ever, *ever* say anything about this, to anybody. Please. I would lose my job, right away. And then," she concluded simply, "I think I'd die. I don't know what I'd do, if I didn't live here."

"Don't worry, Maria. He's already impressed me with the need to be discreet. Look at me, Maria," she commanded.

The smaller woman raised her face, still pale with fear, and met Jamie's eyes.

"Maria," Jamie said, looking directly at her, "I swear to you by everything that's holy to me that I'll never tell anybody who he is without his permission. Never, as long as I live. Now, stop worrying, okay?"

Maria stared up at her for a moment, and then gave Jamie a misty smile and reached out to give her arm a quick, grateful squeeze. "You're good, Jamie," she murmured. "You're a good person. I knew the minute I first saw you, and so did Steven."

Jamie patted the little woman's hand absently, still trying to absorb who her new boss really was. Then, horrified, she remembered their interview and the fact that she had actually called him a bastard.

Dan Kelly, the author, was a legend. He wrote huge, complex spy-and-espionage novels, about one every two years. They topped best-seller lists around the world, sold millions of copies, and were always made into movies that grossed millions more at the box office. He was, in fact, one of Jamie's favorite authors. She never missed his latest book, even if she had to stand in line at the bookstore and pay an exorbitant price to buy it in hardcover.

"Maria," Jamie whispered in horror, "I got mad at him during the interview, and called him a bastard! Oh, my God, Maria, I actually called *Dan Kelly* a bastard!"

Maria chuckled, looking much more at ease, even a little mischievous. "Well," she said comfortably, "sometimes he is, you know. You should hear what Clara calls him in the kitchen, some days. But," she added loyally, "he's a really good boss. He's stern, and sometimes he gets mad if things aren't done right, but he's always fair and generous."

"How long have you been here, Maria?"

"Twelve years. I came before his mother died when I was just seventeen. That was in the old days, when there were parties and company all the time. It was a different house in those days, let me tell you. Ten people on staff, and always something happening." Maria smiled in fond reminiscence. "But then the old lady died of cancer, and Mr. Kelleher got married. They led a different kind of life after that, traveling so much and shutting the house up for half the year. And then there was his accident, and she left."

"Who left?" Jamie asked. "His wife, you mean?"

Maria nodded. "About a year and a half ago, not long after he came home from the hospital. She said . . ." Maria hesitated, and then continued. "Clara heard her on the phone, telling one of her friends that it gave her the creeps, seeing him sitting in that wheelchair all the time. She couldn't stand it, and she left him." Maria turned to Jamie, her face ashen. "Did you ever hear of anything so terrible? To leave a man, just because he's been hurt?"

"Yes, Maria," Jamie said quietly. "I've heard of it."

In fact, though it horrified Maria, this type of behavior was all too typical. Books and movies, she thought, were full of the stories of gallant families who rallied around the injured person and gave him the kind of love and support necessary to rebuild a shattered life. In reality, many people were like Daniel Kelleher's wife. They just couldn't cope with the disaster and abandoned their disabled spouses or children or parents to the care of others.

"Are they divorced," Jamie asked, "or just separated?"

"Oh, they're divorced," Maria said grimly. "Believe me, they're divorced. She wanted her share of the money, all tied up and legal."

Jamie nodded. "I get the picture. What was she like, Maria?"

Maria pondered a moment. "Empty," she said finally. "A sad, empty person. Beautiful, you know, but nothing else. It's amazing, isn't it, that smart men can be such fools sometimes?"

Jamie grinned at this observation. "You're right," she said cheerfully. "It really is amazing." She hesitated, and then drew herself together. "Well, I'd better get moving, Maria. I have to go home and start packing, and I'm supposed to have supper at my brother's house...."

She slipped the room key into her handbag and walked briskly toward the door.

"I'll give you the garage opener," Maria said behind her, trotting to keep up with Jamie's longer stride, "and a key to the kitchen door. When did you say you're moving in?"

"Tomorrow evening, I guess. I start Monday morning."

"Will you be here for dinner? I should tell Clara."

Jamie shook her head, suddenly shy. "No...no, I don't think so. Monday will be soon enough to start meeting everybody else. Although, since I know you and Steven, I guess I've already met half the household, haven't I?''

She smiled at Maria, who returned the smile with another burst of warmth. "We were so afraid," she confessed. "Clara and I, we thought he was going to hire some awful man, who'd be living right down here with us." Maria shuddered. "You should have seen some of the ones he interviewed!"

Jamie grinned. "Well, he didn't. He hired a six-foot redhead with grass stains on her skirt, and you're just going to have to live with it!"

Maria laughed. "Bring that skirt to me tomorrow when you come," she said comfortably. "Lemon juice and vinegar will take that stain out like magic."

Jamie walked with her through the house, waved goodbye and started off down the curving path.

She looked at her watch, and realized in amazement that only an hour had gone by since she'd walked up this drive. She felt dizzy, as if she had traveled to a faraway country, met amazing people and had had a lifetime of adventures.

And yet, out here in the real world, the same sun was shining, her old car was still sitting by the curb, Doreen was across the city getting the meat loaf ready to go in the oven, and only an hour had passed.

CHAPTER THREE

THE VOLKSWAGEN seemed to have recovered completely from its earlier sulk...seemed, in fact, almost to be sharing in Jamie's triumph as it sailed smoothly across town with hardly a burp or a hiccup. But, Jamie had to admit to herself, this could also have been because the journey was all downhill from Knightsbridge Heights.

Gradually, as she drove through the busy Saturday afternoon traffic, her sense of unreality faded, to be replaced by warm, rich exultation. The job was wonderful, the working conditions ideal, the problem of living accommodations all taken care of, no hassle driving to and from work. And if Daniel Kelleher was a moody, irritating man, well, he was still just another grouchy patient. And she'd dealt with hundreds of *those* over the years.

She pulled up behind her shabby apartment block, took her high heels off in the lobby, and ran lightly up the stairs to the fourth floor, letting herself into her apartment with her key. Inside, she tossed her handbag and folder onto a cluttered hall table, looked around and frowned.

The small two-bedroom apartment was already stiflingly hot, long before the true heat of summer was ready to descend. And it was depressingly untidy, even dirty. Two of the girls had thrown an impromptu party the previous evening, and then had obviously gotten up and gone shopping without bothering to clean up. Sticky glasses, spilled drinks, scattered potato chips and overflowing ashtrays littered the apartment. The air smelled stale and used, and Jamie's plants were drooping, withered from the heat.

She thought of the private apartment in Daniel Kelleher's home, so quiet and gracious, with its breathtaking view and the cool shady patio beyond the French doors. Jamie sighed with pleasure.

She had lived in this cramped apartment with three other girls ever since she graduated from college and started work. She was the only one remaining of the original occupants. An endless procession of former roommates had all gotten married or moved on to better jobs and better living quarters. But Jamie tended to cling to familiar things, and she had stayed on, welcoming a succession of bright-faced hospital colleagues who seemed, every year, to get a little younger and a little sillier.

Just now, she was living with two nurses and a lab technician. And at times their boyfriends seemed to be living there, too. At any time, she ran the risk of finding a man in the bathroom or lounging in the kitchen in his undershorts. She was growing sick of it. She would leave this place, she realized, without a single pang of regret.

When she began gathering her things she was surprised at how little she would actually take with her. By tacit agreement, all the cooking utensils and equipment belonged to the apartment, and if somebody bought something for the kitchen, they left it behind when they moved on. Jamie's only real belongings were her plants, books, clothes, a small stereo and a couple of good prints that she'd bought over the years to hang in her half of the bedroom.

She went into this room, which she shared with one of the nurses, and shuddered. The contrast here was striking enough to be funny, provided you didn't have to *live* with it. Jamie's half of the room was impeccably neat; bed smoothly made, night table organized, clothes hung away out of sight.

Carol's half was such a wild, heaping jumble of disorder that Carol herself could be in there somewhere sleeping, and it would be impossible to tell. The bedclothes were mussed and pulled aside to reveal the mattress in places. Piles of clothes were everywhere, interspersed with dirty underwear, empty shopping bags, spilled make-up, hair dryers, hot rollers, curling irons and other appliances.

Jamie shook her head, thinking about how Carol looked when she was ready for work, all neat and crisp and fresh, and wondered, as she always did, how such beauty could possibly emerge from this squalor. She moved across the room to her own side, taking folded jeans and a T-shirt from a drawer, and hanging her silk blouse away in the closet. She rolled up the stained skirt and put it in her small wicker hamper, thinking with a smile that tomorrow she would ask Maria to help her clean it. Maria, who knew all about grass stains.

Suddenly, as she changed into her casual clothes, Jamie felt a surge of joy so intense that her body could scarcely contain her happiness. She wondered how she had endured it all these years, living in this cluttered little place with its ceaseless procession of noisy, messy young women. In the early years, life here had been fun sometimes. But now it was almost unbearable. She was ready to move on, more than ready.

Cool and comfortable in faded jeans, sandals and a Garfield T-shirt that her nieces and nephews had given her for Christmas, she watered her plants, then paused to take one final look around the apartment. All at once, with a vivid smile of pure, shining joy, she grabbed her handbag, spread her arms wide, and pirouetted gracefully across the living room. Then she let herself back out into the hallway and ran down the steps and into the parking lot.

AS SHE APPROACHED her brother Terry's house, activity seemed, as always, to have spilled from the door to flow across the trampled front lawn. There appeared to be some kind of impromptu pet show in progress, probably organized by her ten-year-old niece, Teresa, who was good at that sort of thing.

Neighborhood children stood about, dragging cats and puppies on leashes and turtles on strings. There was even, Jamie observed, a long-suffering goldfish swimming valiantly about in its bowl in the hot afternoon sunshine. Furious arguments and accusations raged around Teresa, but she remained serene. Her mop of red curls shining in the sunlight, Teresa moved among the hopefuls awarding crayon-colored ribbons with lofty disregard for the protests of the pet owners.

"He's *dirty*," she said calmly to one little boy, who clutched his mongrel puppy to his chest and glared at her through his tears. "How can you get a prize for your dog when you didn't even bath him before the pet show?"

As Jamie parked and approached across the lawn, smiling, controversy began to rage in earnest, centering on accusations of conflict of interest.

"She *can't* give a prize to Howard! That's *her own cat!* That's not even *fair!*"

"Howard is the nicest cat here," Teresa replied, unruffled. "Why should your mangy old cat get a prize, just because I'm the judge? Sean, pin it to his collar," she instructed her younger brother, who was following reverently behind her, carrying the ribbons in a shiny brass toffee tin.

"Aunt Jamie! Aunt Jamie!" Beaming with pleasure, five-year-old Kevin hugged her knees and jumped up and down. "Look! Howard won a ribbon! He won first prize!"

The big calico tomcat wore a large red bow on his collar and a leash that was being firmly held by Kevin. Howard glared up at Jamie with slitted eyes and looked dangerous.

"It's not *fair!*" The cries of favoritism began to swell again, gaining momentum. "Miss O'Rourke, it's her *own cat!* Tell her that she can't—"

Sensing mutiny and possible revolution in the air, Jamie escaped quickly into the relative quiet of the house. Miriam, aged three, was in the front room watching the baseball game on television with Jamie's father. Little Dougie, nine months old, lay placidly in his playpen, kicking his bare legs and sucking, wide-eyed, at a bottle propped on a pillow by his cheek.

"Hi, Da," Jamie said, crossing the room to kiss her father's cheek and giving little Miriam a loving cuddle. "Hi, Miriam. How are the Blue Jays doing?"

Kevin O'Rourke snorted angrily, his heavy eyebrows, still black and expressive, lifting in disgust.

Miriam, sitting beside him on the couch, looked up at Jamie with wide blue eyes. "Two men bumped into each other. One of them fell down and dropped the ball," she reported solemnly. "Gramp was *mad.*"

Kevin chuckled and lifted the quiet little girl onto his lap, kissing her dark hair. "Gramp was mad, indeed," he muttered, his brogue more pronounced than usual, as it always got when he was upset by the Blue Jays. "Playing like a bunch of old ladies, the lads are. Shameful."

Jamie grinned. "They need you as field manager, Da. You'd shape 'em up."

"I don't know," he said mournfully. "This season, they might even be beyond *my* abilities. 'Tis a sad sight, indeed." He looked up at her with a grin. "Well, Jamie girl, aren't you the smug-looking one, now? Did you get the job, then?"

"Shh. I want to surprise Terry and Doreen." She smiled fondly back at her father. "But I can never keep a secret from you, can I, Da?"

Gazing down at him, she had the same sense of terrified love that she'd felt ever since his heart attack, over a year ago. She knew that he was recovering well, but he still looked alarmingly frail, not at all like the man Jamie remembered from her childhood.

After his wife's death, Kevin O'Rourke had raised his young family alone—Jamie and Terry and their two older brothers, now both married and working back East. He had always been a gigantic figure to his children, one of the black Irish. Full of laughter and music and fun, he'd worked longer and played harder and sang louder than anybody else. Now he seemed fragile and pale, his powerful body stooped and shrunken.

He had a good home here, with Terry and generous, kind Doreen, who was as loving with him as if he had been her own father, and who genuinely appreciated the help he gave with her noisy brood of children. But Jamie worried about him all the time. It was mainly because of her father's condition that she'd first become interested in therapy for cardiac patients.

He pressed her arm and gave her an impatient little pat. "Don't be standing there looking at me as if I'm already in my coffin, girl," he said. "There's lots of life in the old man yet. Dougie, my lad, does that nappy need changing, then?'' He put Miriam gently back on the couch, got up stiffly and approached the playpen.

Dougie, seeing his grandfather coming, dropped the bottle and began to crow, waving his arms and legs furiously. Kevin grinned, and turned to his daughter.

''They're in the kitchen,'' he told her. ''Terry's eating early. He has to be on shift at five.''

Jamie nodded. ''Thanks, Da. See you later.''

She left him dealing competently with the diaper, and went down the hall toward the kitchen, giving a moment's sympathy to her poor brother, a city policeman who frequently worked shifts on weekends and had to manage somehow to sleep during the day in the midst of all this uproar.

Terry was already in uniform, eating his meat loaf and baked potatoes, while Doreen sat opposite him, keeping him company with a mug of coffee. Doreen would eat her meal later with Jamie and Kevin and the children.

Jamie entered the kitchen quietly, patted her brother's wide shoulder, gave Doreen a little hug and crossed the room to pour herself a mug of coffee from the pot on the counter.

''So, Jamie,'' her brother said, spearing another slice of meat loaf and grinning at her, his broad, freckled face cheerful. ''How's that car running?''

''Terrible,'' Jamie said as she sat down opposite him. ''It stalled twice on the way over here, and the second time I was in the center lane on the cloverleaf. It was really scary.''

''I keep telling you,'' he said patiently, ''that you need a fuel pump. You shouldn't wait any longer. But,'' he added, ''it's going to cost you a bundle, because you'll have to have it done at the shop. We're going on double shifts, right through the Stampede, and I won't have time to put it in for you."

"Well, Terry, that's no problem," Jamie said calmly. "Because, you see," she added with elaborate casualness, "I just got this terrific job, and now that I'm an employed person again, I can afford to have my car serviced."

Doreen, who had been watching Jamie's face in tense, tactful silence, suddenly beamed and hurried around the table to hug her sister-in-law. Jamie laughed, protesting at the stream of eager questions that followed.

"It's a nice house," she said, "up at the west end. I'll have my own little apartment there, and it's just like they said in the ad. I'll get full pay for three hours of work a day, plus some on-call periods. The rest of the time is my own."

Already, instinctively, she avoided direct questions about the house and particularly about Daniel Kelleher, giving only vague answers, mindful of her promises to be discreet. But Terry and Doreen appeared satisfied, and were genuinely delighted at her good fortune.

"How's the pet show coming out there?" Terry finally asked with a smile, changing the subject as he accepted a dish of ice cream from his wife.

"It's getting pretty ugly," Jamie reported. "I think they're going to riot and lynch the judge in another few minutes."

"Good," he said with satisfaction. "Then maybe we can have some peace around here for a little while."

He finished his coffee, took his visored cap from a peg near the door, kissed Doreen, patted his sister's shoulder, shrugged into his patrol jacket, and went jauntily out the door and down the walk to his car. Jamie watched the other woman's face in this unguarded moment, and suddenly saw her, not as a plump mother, but as a young girl in love. And like the wife of any policemen watching her man leave for work, praying that he would come safely home again.

Jamie reached across, patted Doreen's work-worn hand and smiled at her. But their quiet moment was disrupted by the arrival of the children, tumbling into the kitchen in a solid wall of noise.

Teresa, it appeared, was not at all bothered by the bitter reaction to her pet show. In fact, she was already deeply involved in planning tomorrow's activity, a circus, to be presented in the backyard, with kitchen chairs set up for the audience and admission tickets to be made and sold. She and Sean and little Kevin were to play the principal parts, with poor, long-suffering Howard doubling as man-eating tiger and dancing bear.

"Can you come, Aunt Jamie? You can be the Giant Lady."

"Thanks a lot," Jamie said dryly, "but I think I'll be busy tomorrow, Tessie. I'm moving."

"Where? Where are you moving?" little Kevin asked in alarm. Tears began to form in his wide blue eyes.

"Just across town, you dummy," Teresa told her small brother. "Mom already *told* us."

But Jamie's father reached over to give his grandson a comforting hug. "Auntie Jamie's not going far away," he murmured. "She's moving into a fine big house right here in the city, and she'll make lots of money and have lots of free time to visit with us. You'll likely see her even more than you did before."

Reassured, the little boy brushed at his tears and looked hopefully at Jamie. "Can I come and see the big house?"

Jamie thought about the huge, sweeping, lovely grounds, and the pool, and poor little Steven, with his pinched and lonely face. "Maybe," she told her small nephew. "Maybe someday I'll take you over there, just for a visit."

Having other children to play with would be good for Steven, she thought. That poor little boy, all alone in such a huge place.

Then Daniel Kelleher's dark features came into her mind, looking outraged. But she resolutely ignored him. The man couldn't control everybody all the time, she thought. Other people had some rights, too.

After their meal, Kevin herded the children downstairs for their Saturday treat, an hour of cartoon videos, while Jamie and Doreen tidied the kitchen and did the dishes, talking quietly. Then Jamie immersed herself in the up-roar of bath-and-bedtime, scrubbing wriggling bodies, drying curly mops of hair, tucking in, and telling stories and listening to whispered secrets.

Finally, when the house was at last silent and peaceful, Jamie sat with her father and sister-in-law in the front room, enjoying the quiet and a cup of coffee.

"Care for a hand of bridge, Jamie?" Doreen asked. "We could get Mrs. Elliott from across the way to make a fourth." She grinned significantly. "Terry and I think that Mrs. Elliott fancies our Gramp," she confided.

Kevin snorted in outraged disgust, and Jamie chuckled.

"Sorry, Doreen," she said. "I'd love to, but I have a date with Chad. I'm supposed to meet him at the gym at closing time. We're going bowling with Mark and Cindy."

Doreen nodded. "That sounds nice. How is Chad, any-how?" she asked, her voice casual.

"Oh . . . fine. Busy, like always," Jamie said.

"I suppose he was pretty thrilled about your new job," Doreen said.

"Actually, I . . . I haven't told him yet."

"You haven't told him yet! Jamie, I can't believe it."

"Well," Jamie said reasonably, "I haven't seen him today. I told you, I'm just meeting him now."

"Yes," Doreen said, "but I would have thought you'd stop by the gym on your way here, to tell him you got the job."

"You know," Jamie said, "I honestly never even thought about it. I was driving over here, and I just didn't think of stopping at the gym."

She got up to stroll into the kitchen and rinse out her mug. As she left the room, Kevin and Doreen exchanged a troubled glance, but Jamie was not aware of their concern.

CHAD'S GYM was a lively operation, increasing in popularity and profits every day. You had to give him credit, Jamie thought, parking in front and hurrying into the lobby. Chad had bought this tumbledown building with a huge bank loan, installed all the equipment himself and worked hard to get a clientele established. Now he had a faithful group of regulars, and although he worked long hours, he was happy with the progress of his business.

The place was closing as Jamie entered. The outer lobby was filled with lithe and lively young people, all carrying equipment bags and wearing expensive casual clothing, noisily making arrangements for the remainder of the evening. Jamie smiled and greeted a few of them who knew her, then slipped through the entry door and into the gym.

Chad was alone in the big room, wearing white shorts and a thin red singlet, working out on a rowing machine. He grinned to acknowledge her presence and went on rowing while Jamie watched. Chad was Jamie's own physical counterpart, strong, handsome and golden blond. And a good four inches taller than her. Heads turned when they walked into a room together, because they were so well matched.

Jamie had known Chad since their high school days when he had been one of Terry's friends, but she had only started dating him a few months ago. Now, as he worked the rowing machine, his muscles bulging in his powerful upper body, his long legs pumping and flexing, she found herself comparing him to Daniel Kelleher.

As far as upper body strength, she thought, Chad had nothing on Daniel Kelleher. If anything, Daniel was a little more muscular and powerful. And, though he lacked Chad's blond, movie star good looks, he had a definite charismatic appeal of his own.

But then she looked at Chad's legs, his heavy, steel-hard thighs knotting and flexing as he rode the machine in a smooth even tempo, and she knew that there, all similarity ended. She thought of Daniel's wasted lower limbs and his sneakered feet resting neat and unmoving on the footrest of his wheelchair. For some reason, the memory made her feel irritated with Chad. She wished that he would get off the damned machine and greet her properly.

"Look," she said, more sharply than she'd intended, "you'd better hurry up. You're going to want a shower, and Mark and Cindy said they'd meet us by nine-thirty."

"Okay, okay." He flashed a grin at her, his teeth white against his golden tan, his blond head gleaming under the overhead lights. "Just forty more strokes. Then I'm all yours."

Jamie wandered across the room to toy with the settings on the weight-lifting equipment while Chad finished his workout. When he came to stand beside her, he was panting.

Jamie looked up at him. She had always liked being with a man taller than she was. In fact, it had been one of Chad's chief attractions. But now, for some reason, his sweaty, looming presence seemed oppressive to her.

Realizing that she was being unfair, she turned to him with a bright smile.

"I got the job, Chad. I start on Monday."

He grinned and hugged her. "Hey, babe, that's great! Is the whole setup as good as you thought it'd be?"

"Even better. Three hours of work a day, with full pay, and I have a nice set of rooms there, all to myself."

"Well," he said with a slow significant grin, "that *is* good. I know that you've never been comfortable at your place or at my apartment, when there's always people wandering in and out. Now that we've got a place all to ourselves, maybe we can finally—"

"Chad," Jamie interrupted in horror, "it's not going to be like that! You can't come there. Not ever."

"I can't? Why not?"

"Well, because he...the man who owns the house, my boss, he..." Jamie floundered awkwardly. "He's kind of a private person. One of the conditions of the job is that I don't invite anybody over there. I'm supposed to meet my friends away from his house."

"I see," he said, his voice suddenly cold. He released her and leaned back against the weight-lifting equipment, extending his long muscular legs. "That's the cripple, is it? The guy in the wheelchair? He's the big boss?"

"Yes," Jamie said briefly, irritated with Chad again.

"And how old is this guy? Real old? Seventy or so?"

"No," Jamie said. "Not real old."

"Yeah?" he stared at her. "*How* old, Jamie?" he asked softly.

Jamie stiffened. Chad's jealousy had caused problems between them in the past, but she had never expected this sort of difficulty to arise in relation to her job.

"I don't know," she said evasively, and then decided with some impatience that she shouldn't be forced to lie, just to keep the peace. "Early thirties, I'd guess. A couple of years older than you, maybe."

His handsome face darkened. "Well, well. Sounds cozy. No wonder he doesn't want me around, when he's going to have you all to himself, massaging him all day long."

"Chad, for God's sake. The man's a paraplegic. He's paralyzed, Chad. He lives in a wheelchair. Can't you be reasonable, just for once?"

"Hell, Jamie, a guy in a wheelchair, that's just your style. Somebody you can *really* feel sorry for. Right?"

Jamie refused to answer.

"Like that damned artist...what was his name...Eric? The guy who was going to be world famous. But he needed you just to keep him propped up or he was going to kill himself. Remember that guy, Jamie? Remember the misery he put you through? Or how about the other one...the guy with the two little kids, who couldn't manage without you. *That* one just about did you in, didn't it, Jamie-girl?"

"Damn it, Chad..."

"Face it, babe. You collect losers. You're looking for a man to take care of. I should've figured it was only a matter of time before you got involved with a patient. You like feeling sorry for people. And they always bring you to grief, all those losers you get tied up with, because all they want is to use you."

Jamie was silent, staring at the opposite wall. She knew that his harsh words contained a core of truth. At times,

Chad was capable of this kind of insight, particularly where his own interests were concerned. She turned to give him a level glance.

"And are you really any different, Chad? Don't you just want to use me, too? You'd like to use my body, to satisfy you sexually, and you really enjoy using my size and my looks as a kind of ornament for your gym, right? You like having me around just because we look so great together, and people are always impressed by us. Isn't that a way of using me, Chad?"

He flushed angrily. "Baby, I don't need to use *anyone*. I'm on my way up. I'll make it with you or without you. But if you're smart, you'll stick with me, and we'll make it together."

They stared at each other, two beautiful golden faces locked in angry confrontation.

He was the first to waver and turn aside. "Look, Jamie, I don't want to fight. Let's just forget the whole thing, okay? I just get edgy, sometimes, because I want you so damned much it hurts, and you won't even—"

She opened her mouth to respond, and he went on hastily.

"Forget it, I said. Don't say anything. I'll go have a quick shower, and we'll go bowling and have a great time. Okay?"

"Okay," Jamie said mechanically. She smiled at him absently, responded briefly to his kiss and watched as he strode off toward the change rooms.

Alone in the gym, she sat quietly on the padded weight bench, hugging her knees and staring thoughtfully at the opposite wall. But Jamie wasn't really thinking about Chad or their conflict or the evening to come.

She was looking forward, with dreamy anticipation, to the next day when she would load all her possessions in her car and drive across the city to the big house in Knightsbridge Heights.

CHAPTER FOUR

STEVEN LAY ON THE FLOOR of his room in a pair of brown polo pajamas, his rumpled dark hair standing on end, his eyes solemn as he played with his model train.

Steven had no interest in the modern toys that most children of his age favored . . . monster figures and scary haunted castles, and blood-soaked violent battle scenes. He found them terrifying and much preferred his trains and books and teddy bears.

He even had a small family of dolls—a father and mother, a little boy and a baby, complete with clothes and furniture, who lived in a big decorated box in one corner of his room. He spent hours dressing and undressing the dolls, talking to them, and taking them out for walks and treats.

Fortunately for Steven, his father was an intelligent, educated man who understood the small boy's need for family. He encouraged Steven's affection for his little people, and even entered into the game sometimes, having long solemn conversations with the father doll about the stock market and baseball, and pretending to make a great mess of feeding the baby, while Steven giggled in delight.

Those times, to Steven, were the best of all . . . the times when his father would come into his room and play or wheel his chair out into the yard and enter into whatever solitary game Steven was involved with. But the happy times didn't happen often, because his father was so busy.

His mother, by now, was just a faint shadow in Steven's mind. He had never seen her much, even when she lived at home, because she was always going out, talking on the phone, doing her hair or fussing with her clothes.

When he got too close or touched things or bothered her, she would raise her voice and slap him. Soon Steven had learned to avoid her.

But his mother had gone away, and she never even came back to visit ... probably, Steven thought sadly, because he was such a bad boy, and she couldn't stand to live with him. Now there were just the five of them: Steven and his father, and Clara and Maria and Hiro. Steven loved them all passionately, but sometimes he felt so lonely.

All at once, he remembered the golden lion-lady, who was coming today to live with them. He remembered her warm face, her shining hair and the way she smiled at him. His heart lifted with happiness. He rolled over on his back, pumped his legs in the air in a sudden paroxysm of excitement, and then drummed his small bare heels on the thick pile of his carpet, smiling dreamily at the ceiling.

Daniel appeared in the doorway, his strong brown hands resting lightly on the arms of his wheelchair, his dark hair wet from his morning swim, wearing nothing but his sweat pants and a soft white beach towel draped over his muscular shoulders.

"What's all this?" he asked, looking thoughtfully at the windmilling body of his son.

Steven sat up, his hair more rumpled than ever, his eyes bright, and smiled. "Hi, Daddy."

"Aren't you going to be late for school?"

"It's *Sunday,* Daddy," Steven said patiently. He was used to this. His father didn't have to go to an office like other boys' fathers, and his days were always the same, so he sometimes lost track of what part of the week it was, especially if he was busy working on something.

"Right," Daniel said. "So it is."

"And the lady comes today," Steven said.

"Miss O'Rourke?"

"Yes," Steven said, and drummed his heels again.

"You like that lady, don't you?" Daniel asked.

"She's nice. She played football with me, and she hugged me."

Daniel felt a brief wrench, looking at the little boy's radiant face, and changed the subject. "So, what are you planning for today?"

"I want to go to the zoo and see the pandas. You said maybe I could go this weekend," Steven said. "The pandas are visiting from China. They'll only be here for a little while."

"Certainly," Daniel said absently. "Which of them is going to take you?"

"You'd have to take me," Steven said. "It's Clara's day off, and she's gone out into the country. And Hiro left already to go to a woodworking show at the arena."

Daniel regarded his son in dismay. "Me? But, Steven, I don't know if I . . ."

Steven's face crumpled with disappointment.

"How about Maria?" Daniel asked hastily. "She's here, isn't she? I saw her watering plants in the foyer, when I finished my swim."

Steven looked pityingly at his father. "*Maria* can't take me to the zoo."

"Why not? Does she have plans for the day, too?"

"Maria doesn't go anywhere," Steven said matter-of-factly. "She doesn't *ever* go anywhere."

Daniel wheeled his chair inside, shutting the door behind him, and paused beside his son, bending to scoop the thin little body onto his lap. Steven cuddled blissfully, burying his face against the warm softness of the big white towel.

"What do you mean, Maria doesn't go anywhere?" Daniel asked. "Of course she goes places. She must have to go shopping, and visit her family, and . . . and keep appointments, and that sort of thing."

Steven shook his head emphatically. "She never goes anywhere. She never even goes into the yard. She's scared to go outside."

Daniel looked down at his son, startled and troubled. "I've noticed that she stays home a lot," he murmured, half to himself, "but I didn't realize . . . Steven, are you telling me that she never, *ever* goes out of the house? Not at all?"

"Never, ever," Steven repeated solemnly. He wriggled out of his father's lap, then wandered across the room to squat by his dollhouse.

Daniel watched him in troubled silence.

"Can I?" Steven asked, lifting the baby from its crib and examining it closely.

"Can you what?"

"Go to the *zoo*," Steven said, his voice still patient.

"Well . . ." Daniel hesitated. "Let's play with the train instead, shall we? Remember, we were going to start building the new station? Today would be a good day for that, wouldn't it?"

"Okay," Steven said without expression, taking out the little boy doll and beginning to remove his pajamas. "Maybe," he added, "the lady will take me, when she comes. I bet the lady would love the pandas. And," he added, concentrating on his doll, "I bet *she's* not scared to go places, like you and Maria are."

Daniel's head jerked up quickly, and he cast his son a deeply troubled look. But Steven was still kneeling by the dollhouse, intent on his task, his head lowered and his thin shoulders jutting through the soft fabric of his pajamas. Daniel hesitated a moment longer, began to speak, changed his mind, and wheeled himself silently from the room.

"You have to get dressed now," Steven murmured to the little boy doll. "You have to put your clothes on, because you're going to the zoo with your mommy and daddy. And the baby's going, too, in her stroller, and you'll have so much fun. You're going to see the pandas, and buy candy floss and an apple on a stick, and look at the monkeys...."

His voice continued, in a soft singsong, lost in the ghostly Sunday morning silence of the vast, luxurious house.

JAMIE DROVE SLOWLY up the curving, rock-lined drive, uncomfortably aware of the spectacle she presented. Her old Volkswagen was sagging with her possessions, which, as usual, had turned out to be far more space-consuming than she had anticipated. The front trunk lid was tied precariously over a set of bulky suitcases, and the backseat overflowed with her stereo equipment, her books and framed prints and winter boots. Leafy plants teetered and wobbled in all the windows, adding to the general vagabond appearance.

She pulled up and parked in front of the garage door that had been assigned to her, looking around in the mellow spring twilight. The house and grounds were just as spacious and lovely as she had remembered, and even more intimidating. The house looked cool and unwelcoming, and she had that same eerie impression of many eyes watching her from behind darkened windows.

Jamie shook her head and set her jaw, determined not be overwhelmed by all this opulence. People, she reasoned, were just people, after all, no matter how they lived.

But her sense of depression and unease persisted. She knew part of it was due to her own mood. All her earlier exultation at getting the job seemed to have faded, to be replaced by a sense of oppressive foreboding.

Most of her uncharacteristic gloom, she suspected, was because of the previous evening with Chad. They had tried to patch things up and enjoy themselves, but Chad just couldn't leave their earlier discussion alone. He had picked on her and needled her until, finally, they had a miserable, full-blown fight before he took her home, and they'd parted in cold anger. Jamie hated fighting, hated the sour, flat feeling that you woke up with after saying and hearing all those unkind words.

Maybe, she thought miserably, examining the row of polished garage doors, it was time to say goodbye to Chad.

She tapped her fingers idly on the steering wheel, postponing the moment of getting out and approaching the house by thinking about Chad. She wondered now what had attracted her to him in the first place. Probably just the fact that he was so strong and confident, so absolutely not one of the dependant types who had caused her such misery in the past. And yet, despite his arrogance and conceit, he was painfully jealous, and needed all kinds of praise and admiration.

Jamie sighed, wondering if *every* man wasn't a lame duck of one sort or another.

Just as she framed this gloomy thought, the kitchen door flew open, and a small figure catapulted into the entry drive and came running toward her, legs pounding, arms pumping.

Jamie waved and got out of the car, feeling, all at once, a great deal better.

"Hello, Steven," she said, smiling down at the little boy. "How are you tonight?"

"Hello, Miss... Miss..." Steven hesitated, struggling with the name and feeling shy, although he had spent the past several hours watching tensely for her arrival.

"Jamie," she said. "You can call me Jamie. It's easier."

"There's a boy at school called Jamie," Steven offered, standing on tiptoe to peer, fascinated, at the mountain of things in the back in the back of the Volkswagen.

"Is he nice?" Jamie asked.

"He's okay," Steven said casually. "He can make his ears wiggle, all by themselves."

"I can't," Jamie said.

Steven turned to smile at her. "Me, neither," he said. "I tried lots of times, but I can't."

"Well," Jamie said cheerfully, "we all have our own special abilities, I guess. Now, do you think you can help me to unload all this stuff?"

Steven beamed with pleasure and then looked concerned. "There's lots of things here," he said. "I'd better get Hiro to help us, too. I'll be right back."

Before Jamie could protest, he vanished somewhere into the recesses of the treed area behind the garage, and returned almost at once, followed by a thin Japanese man in clean, neatly patched jeans and a navy blue sweatshirt.

"This is Hiro," Steven said proudly, gripping the young man's thin brown hand with the air of someone introducing a very important person, "and this is Jamie. She's going to live here."

"Hello, Jamie. Welcome to our house," Hiro said in a gentle, lightly accented voice. Jamie smiled warmly at him. He was about six inches shorter than she was, and probably several years younger, but with a calm intelligence in his dark eyes that made him seem older than his years. His movements were spare and graceful, and when he opened the car door and began lifting things neatly onto the paved drive, Jamie was amazed by his wiry strength.

"Hiro's taking me to the zoo to see the pandas next Sunday," Steven offered, obviously feeling the need to be a gracious host and make conversation. "Today he went to a woodworking show and he saw a jewelry box all full of secret compartments, and you had to press in just the right place to get the little secret drawers to open."

Jamie pondered this information, fascinated both by the image of the magical box, and by the close and confiding relationship that Steven seemed to have built with all these shy, withdrawn people who worked for his father.

Hiro lifted the stereo receiver gently from the back seat and placed it on the pavement next to the turntable. His hands, Jamie noticed, were beautiful, with long, graceful, callused fingers, and bones that were strong and finely articulated.

"Do you like woodwork, Hiro?" she asked, handing a wrapped ivy plant to Steven, who held it proudly against the front of his T-shirt.

"Yes," Hiro said briefly. "Very much."

Jamie smiled. "You'll have to show me some of your own work," she said. "I'll bet it's beautiful. My father would say that you have the hands of an artist."

Hiro glanced up at her, startled.

"Hiro doesn't *do* woodwork," Steven said. "He just looks at it."

"Oh," Jamie said in confusion. "I see."

"Hiro doesn't have any tools," Steven continued. "He's going to make all kinds of beautiful things, when he gets some tools. He's going to build a..."

The young man reddened, and bent swiftly to whisper in Steven's ear. Then he handed the little boy one of the framed pictures to carry along with his plant. "Here, Steven," he said. "Take these to the side door. Maria will let you in."

Steven started across the open expanse, balancing his two objects with extreme care. Hiro cast an apologetic look at Jamie, bent to pick up the stereo equipment and followed Steven toward the house. Jamie came behind, lugging two of the suitcases, more than ever bemused by the mysterious occupants of this household.

DANIEL KELLEHER SAT high up in his office, hidden behind the drapes, watching his new physiotherapist arrive and unload her car. He looked with masculine appreciation at her tall lithe figure in jeans and sweatshirt. She seemed much more comfortable now than she had the previous day in her high heels and the dressy gabardine skirt with the grass stain....

Daniel grinned suddenly and then sobered. He knew that he had been brusque with her, and he genuinely regretted his behavior. His response had been triggered partly by her overwhelming physical beauty, the lush firmness of her body and her appearance of health and vitality. A woman like Jamie O'Rourke aroused powerful desires in any man, desires that, for a man like Daniel, often seemed just a painful mockery.

But that alone wouldn't have been enough to make him react so rudely. Normally, Daniel was a firmly disciplined man, hiding his angers, fears and frustrations deep beneath a facade of brittle, polite detachment. He knew, all too well, that he had been reacting to her red hair, her roses-and-cream complexion, her mention of Ireland....

For Daniel, the thought of Ireland still aroused painful, almost unbearable memories.

Immediately after his accident, after he was home from the hospital with a wrecked body and a ruined marriage, Daniel had tried to ease the pain and numb the reality of his condition by throwing himself into a new book, one he had long been contemplating, on the smuggling of weapons by the IRA. And, refusing to acknowledge his disability, he had hired an assistant and traveled to Belfast to do his research.

Daniel shuddered, gazing out the window with an intent, brooding expression, his dark arrogant face drawn with pain as he remembered.

It had been just this time of year. Ireland had been almost unbearably lovely, rich, fertile and green....

At first, traveling in his wheelchair had seemed awkward and strange, but not impossible. He'd had even begun to believe that perhaps it was true what they said about disabilities. Maybe disabled people *could* travel and accomplish things, maybe his vital, useful years didn't have to be over after all....

A few days into his stay, Daniel ventured out onto the streets of Belfast, alone in his wheelchair, sniffing the damp mossy fragrances and delighting in the beauty of the ageless stone buildings washed with sunset colors of rose pink and gold.

Deliberately, Daniel had sent his assistant out to the shops to pick up some writing supplies, and he was all on his own for the first time, savoring his independence. He wheeled his way along the narrow cobbled street, feeling his pain begin to ease away.

Suddenly, without warning, the horror struck.

A little tobacconist's shop down the street rocked with the harsh booming violence of an explosion. A flood of broken glass and a rain of fire spewed into the street. There were screams, the acrid smell of smoke and burning. People ran past him in panic, jostling and stumbling over his wheelchair.

Daniel was rocked, then toppled out of his chair. Unable to help, unable to flee, he lay on the cobblestones, praying he wouldn't be trampled.

At that moment, on the cool gray streets of that poor battered city, Daniel Kelleher finally realized what it was to be disabled. He huddled there, shivering with terror until his assistant came rushing back, found him and wheeled him to the safety of his hotel room.

The next day they took the first flight out, and Daniel fled to the safety and isolation of his home.

Now, years later, he could never hear mention of Ireland or see a fresh-complexioned woman with a cloud of red hair, without reliving the horror of that scene. The smell of cordite and the agonized screams of the dying were still with him. And he was deeply ashamed—ashamed of the terror he'd felt, ashamed that he'd been unable to help himself and, most of all, ashamed that he'd been unable to help the people injured by the bomb. He was useless . . . a cripple.

Daniel shifted awkwardly in his chair, staring down at the driveway where Steven was trying to drag a suitcase almost as large as he was. Jamie bent over him, laughing, and took the heavy piece of luggage from him.

Frowning and gripping the arms of his chair, Daniel turned away, his dark face somber, still thinking about that night in Ireland.

In the years following the painful incident, almost all his connections with his past life had fallen away one by one. Daniel could no longer risk the dangers of traveling, nor could he endure renewed encounters with his writing colleagues around the world. The shock and pity on their faces, the false heartiness of their words, were so terribly painful to him that he had severed all ties with former acquaintances. Gradually he had become trapped within the confines of his own city, conducting all business with his publishers and his agent by telephone, venturing out only to do brief errands, and then hurrying back to the safety of his home.

Slowly, his face a cold mask of suffering, Daniel wheeled himself away from the window, crossed the room to his desk and switched on the computer monitor, hoping that a long night of work would hold the dark demons of memory at bay.

IN A SURPRISINGLY short time, all of Jamie's belongings were packed neatly away in the closets of her suite, plants were arranged in various windows, and her pictures were leaning against the walls, awaiting a final decision as to where they should be hung.

Jamie luxuriated in a deep hot bath in her elegant, tiled bathroom, overwhelmed by the knowledge that this place was all her own, and nobody was waiting outside the door, clamoring for her to hurry so they could get in.

She stepped from the tub, dried herself briskly on one of the huge yellow towels and wrapped up in her dark green terry cloth robe. She emerged into the living room, turned on the gas firelog and looked around with a blissful sigh.

She was surprised when a timid knock sounded on the door.

"Come in," Jamie called.

The door opened and Maria entered, carrying a tray and followed by a brisk woman of about fifty with clipped gray hair and wire-rimmed glasses, wearing a clean pink cotton housedress.

"This is Clara," Maria said. "She just got back, and she's the only one you haven't seen yet."

"Pleased to meet you," Clara said brusquely, extending a firm hand and giving Jamie a level, appraising look.

With the possible exception of Daniel himself, Jamie thought, Clara seemed on first impression to be the only member of the household who was entirely confident and self-contained.

Jamie smiled at the older woman, but Clara remained expressionless, seating herself on the edge of the most uncomfortable chair in the room and staring intently at the vast spangled array of city lights in the blackness beyond the huge window.

"We thought you might like a cup of hot chocolate," Maria said, her cheeks pink with shyness and excitement. "We usually have a cup after the news on TV, before we go to bed."

Jamie smiled warmly at her and took the proffered cup. "That sounds lovely, Maria. Thank you."

While the two younger women sipped their chocolate and chatted, Clara drank steadily from her own small pot of unsweetened tea and continued to gaze fixedly out the window.

"Fabulous," she exclaimed with sudden abruptness. "I'd like to shoot in here one night."

"I . . . I beg your pardon?" Jamie said, bewildered.

"The view from your window." Clara waved her hand impatiently at the starry vista of velvet sky and dancing lights. "I had no idea it was so magnificent this time of year. I believe it's the layering, with the willow framing the scene in the foreground, and the sweep of land to the northwest. . . ."

"You're talking about photography," Jamie ventured.

"Well, of course," Clara answered, as if amazed that anyone would talk about anything else. "Would you mind?"

Jamie looked at her, still puzzled. "Oh," she said finally. "You mean, if you were to take some pictures in here?"

Clara drew in the slow, patient breath of an artist forced to deal on a regular basis with lesser mortals. "Yes. That's what I mean."

"I don't mind at all," Jamie replied. "I'd love to see the pictures. I'd even like to buy one, to have for myself. It's a wonderful view."

Clara stiffened. "I don't show my work," she declared coldly, "to *anybody*."

"Oh," Jamie murmured.

"Hiro says he'll come in tomorrow," Maria interjected hastily, "and hook up your stereo. He understands all about things like that."

"He seems very nice," Jamie acknowledged.

"He has gorgeous skin tones," Clara said abruptly. "I like shooting him in shaded sunlight. Marvelous depth."

Clara, Jamie thought, could take some getting used to. Suddenly, she recalled the strange whirring sound in the foyer as she arrived for her interview, and the eerie flitting shadow.

"Do you take a lot of pictures here, Clara?" she asked. "Around the house and grounds, I mean?"

"Some," Clara admitted judiciously.

"Oh," Jamie said again, wondering if there was some polite way to request that in the future Clara refrain from snapping candid shots of her. She looked at the woman's stern face and decided that there probably wasn't.

Instead, she returned to the topic of Hiro.

"Why," she asked, voicing a question that had been on her mind since she arrived, "does Hiro just *look* at woodworking? Why doesn't he get some tools and make things himself?"

Clara and Maria exchanged a glance, and then Maria turned to Jamie.

"Hiro only emigrated a few years ago, you see," Maria said. "When he was just learning English, Clara and I used to help him with his business and banking and so on, so we know that he sends all but fifty dollars of his salary, every month, to his family in Japan. That's all he leaves for himself to live on, for everything he needs. Fifty dollars."

Jamie stared at the other women, appalled. "Fifty dollars! But that's...."

"Not enough to buy woodworking tools," Maria concluded. "And I think that's probably what Hiro wants more than anything."

"How long will he keep sending the money away?"

Maria shrugged. "I don't know. Hiro never talks about himself. But I suppose he'll keep on until they've saved enough to emigrate, too...his parents and brothers and sisters.''

Jamie was silent, stunned by such self-sacrificing generosity. "I guess he doesn't have a car, either, then?" she said finally.

Clara snorted and poured herself more tea.

"Poor Hiro can't even afford a bicycle," Maria said.

"Then who drives all the other vehicles in the garage?" Jamie asked.

"Well, the small car is Clara's, and the little truck belongs to the house," Maria said. "Mr. Kelleher keeps it for everybody to use, running errands and so on. The Porsche and the Lincoln are both his. They're equipped with hand controls and special seats for him."

"And you don't have a car, Maria?" Jamie asked.

"I don't drive," Maria said flatly, her pale cheeks reddening.

"Would you like to learn?" Jamie asked gently. "I'd be happy to—"

"*No!*" Maria burst out in sudden panic, and then smiled awkwardly. "It's nice of you to offer, Jamie, but I don't think I..." She hesitated, plucking nervously at the rough tweedy fabric of her chair arm while Clara gazed out the big window with an unreadable expression.

Jamie watched them both for a moment in puzzled silence and then, seeing Maria's obvious discomfort, changed the subject.

"I haven't seen Mr. Kelleher since I arrived, Maria. I assume he still wants me to start tomorrow morning?"

Maria nodded. "He left a schedule for you. It's in the kitchen, but I can bring it down if you want. He just says he wants a massage for an hour at nine o'clock, after his swim, another at noon, and again at three."

"And where does he usually take his massage?"

"In the sun-room off the pool," Maria said. "I can show you in the morning."

"Thanks, Maria. I think," Jamie added impulsively, "that I'm really going to like this job."

Clara chuckled without humor. "You won't last a week," she said flatly.

But when Jamie looked at her, startled and appalled, the older woman's expression wasn't mean, just matter-of-fact.

"He can be so rude and difficult," Clara explained, startling Jamie further. "He takes a lot of getting used to and most people just can't take it. They don't have the patience."

"Why?" Jamie asked. "Why is he like that?"

"He's still learning to deal with pain," Clara said. "Not physical pain . . . the man's tough enough physically, God knows. But his spirit has been badly damaged, and now he lives like a prisoner here in his own house. It makes him bitter."

Maria was listening quietly, and something in her eyes gave Jamie the sudden impression that Maria, too, knew what it was to live with spiritual pain. She turned back to Clara.

"Well, I might just surprise you, Clara. I'm trained to deal with physical pain, but I've seen my share of the other kind, too. I'm not going to burst into tears just because somebody says a harsh word to me."

Clara regarded her steadily for a moment. "Good," she said brusquely. "Glad to hear it. Around here, you have to be tough if you want to survive."

Jamie thought about the occupants of this house, of Maria, timid and withdrawn, of lonely little Steven, and of Hiro, so shy and puzzling. She wondered if she had ever met a group of people less qualified to be described as "tough."

"I'll survive," she said aloud, getting up and walking with the other two women to the door. "Wait and see."

CHAPTER FIVE

THE MASSAGE TABLE was set up in a spacious atrium just off the pool deck. The glass walls overlooked the city and, like Jamie's room, the atrium seemed to be suspended above miles of open space. Leafy plants lined the walls, and windows opened to the outdoors on three sides, admitting a warm morning breeze that carried the sounds and scents of summertime.

Daniel had equipped the room with an eye to comfort and professionalism. The wide leather-covered massage table was a modern clinical model, electrically equipped to tilt, raise and lower. He had also installed a fine stereo system, and soothing semiclassical music mingled with the muted outdoor sounds of birds, insects, and Hiro's lawn mower.

Concealing her nervousness, Jamie began the first massage with calm mechanical expertise. She kneaded Daniel Kelleher's long motionless legs, bending and flexing and applying pressure to them, and then moved to the upper body, working at pulse points to stimulate circulation. All the while he lay on his back in his white swim trunks with his eyes closed against the cool filtered sunlight.

Jamie stole a look at the powerful sculpted features of his face, the strong nose and wide unsmiling mouth and straight dark hair. His expression seemed bold and arrogant even in repose, even when he was supine and help-less under her hands.

And yet, the man gave no impression of helplessness. The well-developed muscles of his chest and arms bulged and rippled, flexing powerfully against her skillful hands. Despite his obvious strength, his sun-browned skin was surprisingly fine and silky, with a warm, firm texture that seemed rich and intimate under her hands.

She gazed down at his closed eyes, the shock of dark hair falling across his forehead and the rich sensuous fullness of his lower lip, and found herself wondering what he was thinking.

Is he thinking about me? Does he feel it, too, this strange, electric kind of warmth between my hands and his body? Or is it just my imagination?

Suddenly realizing how unprofessional her wayward thoughts were becoming, Jamie was shocked at herself. She'd given thousands of massages and her thoughts had never strayed like this before.

"Could you roll over now, please, Mr. Kelleher?" she asked tonelessly. She watched without expression while he obediently braced his muscular arms, heaved his body over with athletic quickness and lay on his stomach on the leather table, cradling his head in his arms.

Jamie smoothed cream onto his tanned back and con-tinued with her massage, kneading and smoothing the heavy bands of muscle, pounding gently on the long ridges that ran up beside his spine and across his collar-bone. He stretched and gave a little involuntary sigh of pleasure, causing Jamie to smile privately. But she kept massaging in steady silence.

The work was hard, and far more physically taxing than a casual onlooker might suspect. Motivated by an urgent desire to do the best possible job and make a really favorable first impression, Jamie pushed herself to perform at the peak of her skill. Soon, beads of perspiration began to gather along her brow and trickle down her face. She brushed at them furtively, resolving to wear a headband and some cooler clothes the next time she worked out here.

Her movements became mechanical and rhythmic and her mind wandered. She tried to discipline her thoughts, to drag them away from an obsessive concentration on the beautiful tanned body and the brilliant creative mind of the man before her on the wide leather table....

"So," Daniel said suddenly, startling her. "Who won?"

"Won what?" Jamie asked in bewilderment.

"The Great Breakfast Challenge," he said, turning his head on his folded arms so his voice was less muffled.

Still puzzled, Jamie gazed down at his tanned cheek and the curve of his mouth, and realized that he was smiling.

"I'm still... I'm not sure what you mean," she said.

"This morning, on my way down for my swim, I chanced by the kitchen door and heard a great deal of laughter. I gathered that some kind of competition was under way."

Jamie flushed scarlet and returned to her work, her hands trembling. "It was just... it was silly," she murmured. "We... Steven found this little car in the cereal box, one of those kind that you wind up with an elastic band, you know, and Hiro got it working, and then we started setting up..."

Jamie fell abruptly silent, painfully conscious of the warm skin beneath her hands, and Daniel's strong smiling mouth.

"Come on, Miss O'Rourke," he said, with laughter in his voice. "I have the right to know what's going on in my own house, you know. *What* were you setting up?"

"Rows of Cheerios," Jamie confessed, still blushing furiously. "Then we took turns shooting the little car through them, from a fixed distance, you know, and the one who passed cleanly between the rows and knocked off the fewest Cheerios in a single sweep was the winner."

"I see," Daniel said, his voice carefully sober.

Jamie peeped down at him, but he had buried his face in his arms again so she couldn't see his expression.

"So," he repeated patiently, "who won?"

"Clara," Jamie admitted. "The woman's got a deadly accurate aim. It must be from all that photography."

Daniel roared with laughter, and Jamie jumped a little, watching his powerful shoulders flex and heave in spasms of mirth.

Awkwardly at first, and then with rising merriment, she joined in.

"Lord," Daniel said finally, wiping his streaming eyes, "it feels good to laugh like that. It's been a long time, Miss O'Rourke," he added, lifting his head to glance up at her, "since I've heard laughter in this house at breakfast time. I want to thank you for bringing it."

Jamie watched him a moment, still flushed with embarrassment but absurdly pleased by his words. Then with a small businesslike gesture she moved his head back into position, thrilling unexpectedly to the feel of his crisp dark hair against her palm, and returned to her work.

Finally, she brushed an arm over her hot face and checked her watch, observing with relief that there was only five minutes to go. She devoted the last few minutes to a brisk, bracing rubdown, to stimulate cell activity and circulation. Then she applied a mild astringent and toweled off his gleaming upper body.

"Okay," she said finally, panting a little. "All done. Have you fallen asleep?"

For a moment he didn't stir, lying very still with his dark head still cradled on his arms. Jamie thought perhaps he had, in fact, dropped off after the rigors of his swim and the soothing comfort of the massage. She frowned, wondering anxiously if she should wake him or just tiptoe away and leave him.

But, finally, he rolled his head on his folded arms, lifted it, and heaved himself onto his back, opening his eyes to gaze up at Jamie.

"Wonderful," he murmured. "That was wonderful. Superb. Miss O'Rourke, you're a real professional."

Jamie smiled with pleasure and wiped her streaming face again. "Thank you," she said.

He looked at her with concern. "You're warm," he said. "I'm sorry. The room is air-conditioned, but I didn't have it turned on. It was thoughtless of me not to."

"That's all right," Jamie said. "Really. I'm fine. But next time, I'll wear some lighter clothes, I think. Shorts, or something, if you don't mind."

He smiled. "If you keep giving treatments like that, I don't care in the slightest what you wear. Scuba gear, a ball gown, whatever you like."

Jamie had a sudden mental image of herself in a long sequined gown with a diving mask and flippers, rubbing cream into his back. She chuckled involuntarily, and he arched an inquiring eyebrow.

"Nothing," she said hastily. "Just a...just a silly thought."

He grinned at her, his dark eyes dancing, and she giggled again. Still smiling, Daniel sat up, reached out a long arm, drew his wheelchair close and set the control to lock the brake, then swung his useless legs skillfully down into the chair.

He rolled himself over to a wall near the stereo and flipped a switch, setting a small rush of chilled air whirring into the room.

"Just stay here a minute and cool off," he said over his shoulder, starting toward the door. "I'll go to the kitchen and get you some iced tea."

"Oh, really, " Jamie protested. "Please, you don't have to...."

But he was already gone, wheeling himself rapidly off across the tiled deck of the pool while the latticed door swung shut behind him, blocking him from view.

Jamie gave herself up to the enjoyment of the cool, refreshing flood of air. She crossed the room to shut the windows and, sighing with relief, sank gratefully into one of the comfortable metal chairs that were grouped along one wall under a high bower of plants, and then looked briefly troubled.

She hadn't really known what to expect from her enigmatic employer. But she certainly hadn't counted on him being nice. And certainly hadn't expected to feel both warmed and confused by his company.

Daniel reappeared suddenly, bearing a tray across his knees with a frosted pitcher of iced tea, two clear glass mugs, a crystal dish of lemon slices, and a plate of warm, fragrant cookies.

"Maria was baking," he said cheerfully.

Jamie watched in startled silence while he grabbed a towel, tossed it around his wide shoulders, and then arranged the contents of the tray on the small metal table between them. He poured out the iced tea, added lemon, and handed her the plate of fresh cookies.

Jamie accepted one and bit into it hungrily.

"Oh," she said in bliss. "They're gingersnaps. And they're delicious! I haven't eaten a warm gingersnap since..."

She interrupted herself to demolish the rest of the cookie, and take an appreciative gulp of iced tea.

"Did you say Maria was baking?" she asked finally. "I thought Clara was the cook."

"She is. Clara looks after menu planning, meal preparation, marketing, household accounts, all that sort of thing. For Maria, baking is more of a diversion."

Daniel watched Jamie for a moment in thoughtful silence.

"What do you know," he asked suddenly, "about emotional disorders, Miss O'Rourke?"

"I beg your pardon?"

"I mean," Daniel said, selecting a cookie and examining it carefully, "you're clearly a professional physiotherapist of great skill. You know all about pains and traumas in the physical body. Do you know anything about the nature and treatment of emotional traumas?"

"A certain amount," Jamie said cautiously. "After all, the emotional and physical problems frequently go hand in hand."

He nodded thoughtfully, sipping his iced tea. "I was thinking," he said finally, "about agoraphobia. Do you know anything about it?"

Jamie glanced at him, her eyes widening in surprise.

Could he possibly be talking about himself? Clara had referred to him the night before as a "prisoner" in his own home.

Concealing her reaction, she answered him as calmly and professionally as she could.

"Agoraphobia," she said, "comes from a Greek word meaning, literally, 'fear of the marketplace.' It describes an emotional condition in which the patient is actually afraid to leave his or her own home.''

He raised an inquiring eyebrow. ''Have you ever encountered it yourself, in anyone?''

Jamie nodded. ''It sounds unusual, but it's far more common than people suspect. We sometimes came across it when we were working on the visiting therapist rotation at the hospital. People who are suffering more severe disabilities can begin to stay at home so much that they sometimes find they're unable to venture back out into the world at all.''

She paused, flushing in embarrassment, wondering if she was, in fact, describing the condition of the man sitting opposite her. But he just listened intently with a thoughtful frown on his face.

''And in the severest forms,'' he asked, ''what's it like? How bad does it get?''

''I remember one woman,'' Jamie told him, ''who hadn't set foot outside her house in three years. Not even out into the front yard to pick up the newspaper. She was even terrified to stand by a window or an open door. She ordered everything she needed through the mail, had the doctor make house calls. She actually had her husband pull one of her teeth when it was aching to avoid going out to the dentist.''

Daniel listened, appalled. ''My God,'' he murmured.

Jamie nodded. ''It was so sad. And she was such a nice person, too. Didn't want to cause anybody any trouble, had no idea why she was like this. She was just certain that if she ever stepped outside of the house, some horrible danger would overtake her and she'd die.''

''What finally happened to her?''

''Nothing. As far as I know, she's still in her house, still afraid.''

Jamie peeped over at him, fascinated by the way the slanted rays of light fell through the banks of foliage by the window, dappling Daniel's dark face with patterns of light and shadow, playing across his cheeks and lips.

She caught herself and looked hastily away, feeling warmth rise to her face again.

This whole experience, she thought, was becoming more and more surprising and troubling. The pleasure of their impromptu snack beneath the potted plants and the ease and comfort of their conversation were so different from anything she had expected. And feelings were rising and swelling within her, strange, haunting emotions and yearnings that she knew she didn't dare to examine.

She wondered again if his interest in agoraphobia was just a writer's curiosity or something more personal. She was nerving herself to ask when he spoke again.

"I believe," he said, "that Maria may be agoraphobic."

Jamie looked over at him, wide-eyed with surprise. "Maria?" she said finally. "Why? What makes you think so?"

"Well, I'm not very observant about these things, I know." He paused, and gave Jamie a sardonic smile, as if he were laughing at himself and his own isolation. "But I've never seen her actually leave the house, although I occasionally see the others coming and going...."

Jamie was silent, waiting for him to continue.

"More important," he went on, "Steven told me yesterday that Maria *never* goes out. He said she's scared to, and that she doesn't even go into the yard."

Jamie felt a shiver of apprehension. "If Steven says that," she began slowly, "I think I'd tend to believe it. He's...he's very close to all of them," she added.

"I know. They're his family," Daniel said, with a sudden expression of brooding sadness that chilled Jamie.

But as soon as the look appeared it was gone, and he glanced up at her with a calm, pleasant smile.

"Do you think you could look into the situation with Maria, and get some idea of what her condition actually is?"

Jamie looked at him, startled, her knees suddenly weak. But before she could reply, he was gone.

A FEW HOURS LATER, Jamie floated on her back in the big pool, eyes closed, relishing the silence and peace of the morning. It was going to take time to absorb the fact that this was her life from now on, this comfort and luxury and security, with so many free hours to entertain herself and pursue her own interests.

Lazily, she rippled her fingers in the water beside her and smiled, enjoying the warm play of sunlight on her face through the skylights overhead. Finally she opened her eyes, gathered her wandering thoughts and forced herself to get back to work, planning and designing aerobic exercises for her programs.

She was clinging to the side of the pool, bracing her feet against the concrete wall and arching her back out, holding and counting, when Maria appeared on the deck and smiled down at her.

"Jamie, there's a phone call for you."

Jamie shook the wet hair from her eyes and looked up, startled and alarmed, wondering who could be calling. She had given the number to her family, of course, but had stressed that it was only to be used in case of an emergency.

Her first thought was her father, who always seemed so frail these days. Thoroughly worried, she climbed lithely from the pool and wrapped herself in one of the huge white pool towels. Then she bound another towel around her head, stepped into her yellow thongs, and followed Maria to the kitchen.

Clara was there as well, stirring something in a steaming copper saucepan that smelled deliciously of chicken and seasonings. She glanced at Jamie without expression, jerked her head toward the telephone and returned to her stirring.

"Hello?" Jamie said breathlessly into the receiver.

"Hi, babe! How's the first day of work?"

"Chad!" Jamie said, feeling a flood of relief, and then a quick stab of annoyance. "Why are you calling me here, Chad?" she asked in a lower tone. "I told you this number was only for emergencies."

"Sure," he said, his voice lazy and teasing. "And this is an emergency. I'm in desperate need of somebody to take to lunch."

Jamie drew in a long breath and struggled to keep her temper. "Chad, I already *told* you that my lunch hours aren't free. I have a therapy session scheduled at noon. I'm going to hang up now, and I don't want you to call here again."

"Hold on! How about tonight? Are we still on?"

Jamie paused. She realized she didn't want to see Chad tonight. "Okay," she said at last. "Pick me up at eight-thirty after my class at the hospital. There's something I need to talk to you about, anyhow."

"Great," he said with satisfaction. "I'll be there. So long, Jamie."

Jamie hung up slowly, and stood staring out the window.

No, Chad, she thought. *Not "so long." This time I'm afraid it's goodbye.*

She shook herself and turned, forcing a bright smile.

"Just a friend of mine who didn't realize he wasn't supposed to call here," she said to Maria and Clara. "It won't happen again."

Clara ignored her, stirring her soup in grim silence, and Maria smiled timidly.

Jamie smiled back. "Maria," she said on impulse, "could you come to my room with me for a minute? I want to ask you something."

Maria immediately set aside the sweater she was knitting for Steven and got to her feet to follow Jamie from the kitchen.

In her own sitting room, Jamie rubbed herself briskly with the towel and turned to Maria, indicating one of the chairs near the fireplace. "Sit down, Maria, while I just slip out of this wet suit."

Jamie vanished into her room and emerged almost at once in a brief blue cotton sunsuit, rubbing at her mop of damp curls.

"Would you like to sit out there?" Jamie asked casually, indicating a comfortable grouping of chairs on the cool, shaded patio. "Then my hair could be drying while we talked."

Maria turned even paler than usual, and shook her head. "I'd...I'd rather not, Jamie," she murmured. "The sun is so warm."

Jamie glanced briefly at the shady depths of the patio, but said nothing. Instead, she sank into a chair opposite Maria, crossed her long tanned legs, and smiled gently.

"Maria, how'd you like a little outing this afternoon? I have to go downtown to pick up a few things, and I thought you might like to ride along. We could do some shopping," Jamie went on, warming to her subject, "and have coffee somewhere, and visit, just the two of us. What do you think?"

Maria stared at the other woman, her eyes wide with terror, searching for words.

"I...I can't, Jamie," she said finally. "I have to...I'm stripping all the beds this afternoon and airing out the bedding. It'll take hours. I have to—"

"Okay," Jamie said hastily, moved by the small woman's obvious distress. "That's okay, Maria. It was just a thought. What's Clara making?" she added casually. "I can even smell it here in my room. It's heavenly."

"Her grandmother's chicken soup," Maria said with a shaky smile. "It *is* heavenly. And she's making hot biscuits for lunch to go with it. Mr. Kelleher loves them."

"Does he always eat alone?"

Maria nodded. "Usually. Except in the evening when Steven eats with him in the dining room. The rest of the time, he usually just has his meals on a tray up in his room while he works."

"And this therapy session at noon... He'll want that before he has his lunch? He'll eat when we're finished?"

Maria nodded again.

"Well, I'd better get ready, then," Jamie said. "It's amazing," she added with a grin, "how fast the time flies when you're just doing nothing but enjoying yourself."

Maria returned the smile awkwardly, got to her feet and moved toward the door. "I'm sorry about this afternoon, Jamie," she murmured. "It really sounds like fun, but I'm just...just too busy."

"That's fine, Maria. We'll do it some other time."

"Yes," Maria said in relief. "Some other time."

She escaped up the hallway, fleeing back to the safety of the kitchen, while Jamie stood by her fireplace gazing out at the patio in thoughtful silence.

THE SUMMER MOON was almost full, a glittering disk of silver in a sky of velvet black. Stars shimmered against the wide expanse of prairie sky, millions of them, while bright fingers of northern lights rayed across the darkness like nighttime rainbows.

Jamie parked in the big garage, walked out onto the drive, and hesitated, gazing up at the sky. The vastness was somehow soothing, putting her own misery and unhappiness into perspective. But she still felt lonely and upset, and longed for someone to talk with.

Her final evening with Chad had been dreadful, even worse than she had feared.

She trudged across the huge drive to the side door, let herself in quietly with her key and crept down the hallway toward her room. The big sprawling house was locked in that strange, deep silence of midnight, so still that the occupants seemed not to exist, and the house took on a mysterious life of its own.

Jamie fancied that the big place really *did* seem to be alive. She could almost hear it murmuring and breathing softly in its sleep.

Suddenly she paused in the carpeted hallway, held her breath, and listened intently.

That time, it wasn't imagination. She had really heard a sound, a soft rustling or stirring noise, impossible to identify, coming from somewhere beyond the foyer.

Jamie hesitated, working her way through a rapid sequence of emotions.

Being Jamie, her initial reaction was one of private amusement. She grinned to herself, picturing Clara roaming around sleepwalking, camera in hand. But her smile faded instantly as she thought about little Steven and Maria and Daniel, helpless without his chair, and the possibility of prowlers in this luxurious house.

Without further thought, Jamie turned soundlessly in her padded sneakers and crept back along the hallway toward the foyer, straining to listen, hearing more furtive sounds. She slipped through the foyer and the atrium, and into the dim expanse surrounding the pool, keeping to the shady plant-lined areas along the walls.

The pool lay silent and still in the filtered moonlight, like a huge cloth of beaten silver, glimmering faintly. Jamie looked out at it, frowning in concentration and holding her breath. She had a strong, terrifying sense of someone nearby, of someone watching her.

Battling her fear and wondering how she had gotten herself into this position in the first place, she edged her way along the banks of plants, trying not to make a flicker of movement.

"One more step," a voice said calmly, "and we're both in big trouble."

Jamie gasped and jumped, clapping her hand to her mouth to choke off her scream.

Then, abruptly, she relaxed in a flood of relief.

Daniel sat quietly in his wheelchair beside a giant fern, directly in her path. As he had sensibly pointed out, one more step and she would have been upon him, tripping herself and possibly upsetting his chair.

"Oh," Jamie said, still stupid with relief. "It's you. I thought..."

"Sorry to frighten you," he said mildly. "I heard you unlocking the door while I was in the pool and thought I'd just slip out without letting you know I was here, and hide myself back in the foliage to avoid startling you. Obviously," he added with a wry smile, "I failed miserably."

"You sure did," Jamie said bluntly, beginning to recover her equilibrium. "You scared me half to death. Probably took several years off my life."

"Well," he said, still smiling, "when you've determined what several years of your life are worth, Miss O'Rourke, let me know and I'll try to reimburse you."

Jamie looked at him, finding that her eyes were growing more accustomed to the moonlight and she could discern his face and form quite clearly. His fine arrogant features were etched with silver in the moonlight, and his muscular chest, with its dark curly mat of hair, gleamed dully, while his lower body was concealed beneath a towel that he had thrown over himself.

"Why didn't you stay in the pool?" she asked. "I hope you didn't feel you had to get out just on my account."

"Actually, I did," he said, with another flash of white teeth in the darkness. "You see, when I come down to swim at this time of night, I don't usually bother with swim trunks. And I didn't want to give you any nasty shocks so early in your employment."

"Oh," Jamie said helplessly.

To her absolute amazement, she felt a warm flush mount her cheeks and was grateful for the darkness. Astounded, she tried to sort out her own reaction. She had meant it earlier when she had told Daniel that after five years as a physiotherapist she found that the sex of a patient, or his nudity, meant nothing to her. And yet the thought of Daniel Kelleher, close enough to touch in the moonlight, with just a towel thrown across his naked loins, was somehow intensely disturbing.

She wondered what was happening to her and forced her thoughts into some kind of order, retreating gratefully to safer ground.

"Did you... Weren't you able to sleep?" she asked hesitantly. "Are you in pain?"

He shook his head. "Swimming doesn't usually help when I'm in pain. But it does ease the mental turmoil sometimes, when my mind is working overtime and I can't get to sleep.''

''I should try it, then,'' Jamie said gloomily, staring out at the silent, shimmering expanse of water.

Daniel looked thoughtfully up at her delicate profile and reached out a long arm to pull up a nearby deck chair.

''Please sit down, Miss O'Rourke,'' he said courteously.

Jamie hesitated and then sank into the proffered chair. She continued to gaze across the quiet silvered surface of the pool in brooding silence.

''This is rather late for a prenatal aerobics class, isn't it?'' Daniel said casually.

Jamie glanced at him, briefly puzzled, and shook her head. ''The class ended hours ago. I had . . . I had a date afterwards.''

He stole another look at her tense, unhappy profile. ''Not a success, I take it?'' he said with surprising gentleness.

''Hardly,'' Jamie said grimly. She turned to look directly at her employer. ''We broke it off. It's over.''

''I see.'' Daniel hesitated. ''Your idea or his?''

''Mine,'' Jamie said, and was too preoccupied with her own feelings to notice the sudden tensing and relaxing of Daniel's lean brown hands on the arms of his chair. ''It's been coming on for a long time,'' she went on, ''but when it really happens, it still just feels so . . .''

She paused and turned to him, trying to smile.

''Sorry,'' she said abruptly. ''One of your specific requirements when you hired me was that I refrain from confiding in you the details of my love life. So here, on my second night in the house, what am I doing? Confiding in you. Forgive me.''

"This is different," Daniel pointed out mildly. "I asked."

"Yes, I guess you did. It's nice of you to express an interest," Jamie said, looking absently back out at the pool. "I was feeling so miserable when I got home, and now, just from telling someone, it's already a lot better."

"You say that so naturally," he commented.

"What's that?"

"You said, 'when I got home,'" Daniel repeated. "It sounded so natural to you. Do you really feel at home here?"

"Yes," Jamie said slowly. "I think I really do. In fact, partway through the evening tonight, even in the midst of all that misery, I found myself thinking about this place." She waved her hand at the quiet pool, the atrium, the sunroom with its sweeping view of the sky and the city lights. "And I just kept thinking how nice it would be to go home," she concluded simply.

"I'm glad," Daniel said.

The two of them sat quietly for a moment, not looking at one another. But Jamie was intensely aware of him, of his arrogant silvered profile, of his high flat cheekbones and sensual sculpted lips.

She shivered again in the moonlight, and he looked at her in quick concern.

"Are you cold, Miss O'Rourke?"

"No, no. I'm fine. I was just..." Jamie hesitated, and then turned to him. "I've been thinking about what you told me about Maria," she said, "and I think you're probably right. I think there's a real danger she's agoraphobic."

Daniel frowned. "I was afraid that's what you'd say. Is there any way to help her?"

"I don't know. Certainly not without prompting."

Daniel cast her a quick glance. "You sound hesitant."

"I guess I am, a little." Jamie bit her lip and turned to him, her eyes troubled. "It's just that this kind of thing seems to happen to me all the time, you know? I get involved in people's problems and get all wrapped up in their lives, and sometimes, later, I think it would have been better for them and for me if I'd just minded my own business. You know what I mean?"

Daniel nodded. "You're quite a sympathetic person, Miss O'Rourke. I can see how you'd be a target for people with problems."

Jamie nodded gloomily.

"If you don't care to involve yourself in Maria's condition," he went on, "you certainly don't have to."

"But I *do* want to!" Jamie burst out. "That's just the problem! I always *want* to get involved, even though I know I'm going to regret it later."

Daniel smiled. "It's late, and you're tired. Let's sleep on it, shall we? I'll do some reading about the condition and give it some thought, and you can do the same. And in a day or two we'll compare notes and see if we can decide what to do for poor Maria, if anything. How's that?"

Jamie smiled at him gratefully and got out of the chair, her tall body lithe and slender in the moonlight. "That sounds just fine, Mr. Kelleher. Good night," she added softly. "See you in the morning."

As she moved quietly past his chair, he reached up to grasp her arm. Jamie paused, startled, and looked down at his face, her heart hammering wildly just at the feel of his firm callused hand on her bare skin.

"I think," he said, " that this is an unusual circumstance, and you are a most unusual person. I'd like, with your permission, to suspend one of my own rules."

"What's that?" she asked, still distressed by ᵤer own turbulent emotions.

"I'd like to call you Jamie. And I think you'd better call me Daniel. If we're going to be counseling partners," he added cheerfully, "we might as well be a little less formal, don't you think?"

Jamie stared at him, her eyes shadowed and enormous in the moonlight. "I don't know if I could...."

"Try it," he said briskly, releasing her arm. "Call me Daniel."

"But it seems so..." Jamie whispered, looking down at him. "All right...Daniel," she said softly.

"There, you see? Nothing to it. Now, Jamie I think we'd better say good night, because I'm going in for another swim, and we don't want to embarrass each other so early in our friendship, do we?"

He gave her a quick, teasing grin. Jamie nodded, gulped and beat a hasty retreat along the edge of the pool and through the atrium.

Once more, she was astounded at herself, amazed at the way she could be so passionately aroused and disturbed by the simple mental image of his naked body slipping into the pool, and his powerful shoulders knifing through the water in the moonlight.

At least, she thought, escaping gratefully down the hallway to her own room, this whole unsettling interview had accomplished one thing.

It had succeeded in driving all thoughts of Chad completely out of her mind.

CHAPTER SIX

JAMIE WHEELED the massage table across the sun-room to the sliding glass doors, pausing to allow them to slide open with ghostly efficiency. Happily, she passed through the doors and out onto the shaded warmth of the patio, followed closely by Daniel in his chair.

"Is this all right?" she asked, stopping the table near the low stone wall that flanked the edge of the patio and overlooked that same dizzying view of the city and the foothills.

"Maybe a little more under the trees," Daniel suggested. "You know how warm you always get."

"Right," Jamie said, pushing the table farther into the shade. "This is good. It's nice and cool, and the view is still lovely. Look, Daniel, it's so clear you can see the mountains today! Aren't they beautiful?"

"Beautiful," he said absently. But he was not looking at the view to the west. He was watching Jamie's face, and her long shapely body.

Unaware of his thoughtful scrutiny, Jamie worked carefully to position the table in the shade with room for her to work, lowered it, and set the brakes.

"Okay," she said finally. "All set."

She watched as Daniel, wearing nothing but a pair of gray gym shorts, heaved himself out of the chair and onto the broad leather surface of the massage table. His face was intent and grim with effort as he twisted expertly in midair, using his powerful upper body muscles to swing his useless lower limbs into a sitting position, then reached down to straighten and arrange his long, motionless legs.

Jamie watched silently, knowing better than to help him. She wondered involuntarily what Daniel Kelleher must have looked like before his accident, when those legs were as powerful and active as his upper body.

He would have been well over six feet tall, lithe and athletic, with a quick, catlike grace and an overwhelming physical presence.

She shivered suddenly in the heat and rubbed her bare arms.

"Okay," she said briskly, reaching into a lower cabinet for her tube of cream. "Let's go. Left leg first."

He closed his eyes, hands beneath his head, face raised to the dappled shade while Jamie worked over his legs. She stole a glance at him, almost unbearably stirred by the sculpted planes of his face, the dark thick hair falling across his tanned forehead, the fullness of his lower lip.

Jamie worked on mechanically, distressed by her own thoughts and reactions. She wanted so passionately to lean forward and kiss that powerful, sensual mouth.

She forced herself to look away, trying to analyze and control her own reactions. After the first couple of days, they had fallen into the pattern of having the noon hour massage out here on the patio, and it was in this setting that Jamie suffered the most from her strange, nearly uncontrollable urges.

Maybe, she thought, it had something to do with the laziness and peacefulness of the setting—the fragrant scented breezes, the muted hum of insects. There was something intoxicating, almost hypnotic, about the beauty of the early summer days and the place where she worked.

But that still didn't explain her intense attraction to this man, her urgent stirrings of desire. She thought of Chad, and his beautiful, powerful male body, and realized that never, in all the time they had spent together, had she felt for him the kind of sexual yearnings that she felt for the man beneath her hands.

She knew that the problem lay with her. It was some strange twist of her personality, something that she couldn't explain and was even reluctant to think about. None of this was Daniel's fault. He had never done anything to encourage such feelings in her. After their initial skirmishes he had accepted her fully and proven to be unfailingly courteous, friendly and considerate, with just the right mixture of cheerfulness and reserve for a good patient-therapist relationship. Jamie knew that she was responsible for these errant, disturbing reactions, and she would just have to try, somehow, to deal with them.

"Are all the doors closed?" Daniel asked, opening his eyes and giving her an exaggerated conspiratorial wink. "Can we talk?"

Jamie glanced around at the sliding glass doors opening from the patio into her room, the sun-room and the living area.

"All closed," she said, in a light, cheerful voice that belied her inner turmoil. "Unless the patio's bugged, you can talk freely."

He chuckled. "Can't you just see a little audio room, like in the cop shows on TV, with Clara and Hiro huddled around receiving sets with headphones on, monitoring the household's private conversations?"

Jamie, who could see this very clearly and found it a most engaging picture, laughed with him, and then sobered. "I spent the evening in the downtown library yesterday," she said. "How about you?"

"I called some people I know," he said a little evasively, "and got some more information."

"Anything new?"

He shook his head, wincing a little as she pressed hard
on a nerve high in his hip.

"Does that hurt?" Jamie asked quickly.

"Just a little."

She nodded thoughtfully, and went on with her work.

"So, what we know," he continued, "is that agoraphobia is a fairly straightforward condition. People suffering from it have a morbid fear of leaving the house,
believing that some harm will befall them if they do.
Caused by..."

He cast Jamie a questioning glance, waiting for her response as if he were a college professor quizzing a bright
student.

She smiled. "Caused by general timidity," she said
obediently, "perhaps compounded by some traumatic
event in the past which has in all likelihood been forgotten, but the damage remains."

He nodded approvingly. "Therapy?"

"Roll over," she said.

He laughed, and heaved himself deftly onto his stomach. "What a simple cure," he observed cheerfully.
"That'll be four thousand dollars, please."

Jamie laughed. "If only it *were* so simple. Poor Maria." She began to stroke and stimulate the sensitive areas at the backs of his knees, looking up at his wide brown
shoulders, admiring the way his thick dark hair grew low
on the nape of his tanned neck.

"Therapy?" he prompted again, his voice muffled in
his folded arms.

Jamie grinned once more, enjoying this game they
played, and then collected her thoughts. "First, patient

acknowledges problem and confesses need for help. Second, a friend or therapist offers assistance. Third, standard behavior modification procedures are implemented. Patient faces the feared situation a step at a time, starting with less threatening situations and then moving on to scarier things in gradual steps. Is that uncomfortable?"

"I can feel it all the way up into my back."

"Here?" Jamie asked, pressing the flat heavy band of muscle beside his spine.

"Yes. Right there."

She paused with her hands on her hips and glared down at him. "Well, it *shouldn't*. Have you been using those heavier weights again?"

He rolled his head on his arms and peeped up at her. "Maybe a little," he confessed.

She continued to frown at him. His face was solemn and contrite, but his eyes were bright with laughter.

"I'm warning you, Daniel, I'll quit. I *won't* go on trying to keep your body in condition, if you insist on deliberately damaging—"

"Jamie, Jamie . . . don't be mad. I promise I'll be more restrained from now on."

She hesitated, still suspicious. "You *promise?*"

"I promise."

"All right," she said grudgingly, and returned to her work, being more gentle with the long muscles that he had strained in his private workout.

"So," he said finally, resuming their previous conversation, "where do we go from here?"

"I don't know," Jamie said. "We could hire a professional therapist, but that's awfully expensive, and unless it's someone Maria trusts and decides to confide in, it wouldn't do any good anyhow." She hesitated. "I think I should give it a try, first. She seems to like me."

Daniel grinned, and glanced up at her again. "Come on, Jamie. Is there anybody who doesn't like you?"

Jamie thought of Chad on their last evening together, of his handsome flushed face and his furious, outraged expression, and felt a little chill. But she kept her voice light and casual. "Oh, I can think of a couple."

"So," Daniel said, ignoring this, "what you have to do is get her to admit to a problem, right? How will you do it?"

"I'm still working on that," Jamie said. "I'll think of something."

He nodded, and she looked at his dark head resting against the powerful muscular arms.

"These people you called," she asked casually, "the ones who gave you all this information. Are they your regular research staff?"

He rolled over abruptly and stared up at her, his dark eyes intent and piercing. "You know," he said slowly.

Jamie nodded, biting her lip. "I'm tired of pretending that I don't. We might as well be honest about—"

"Who told you?"

"Nobody. I just guessed. I knew that you were a writer, and you're obviously prosperous and successful, and the coincidence of the names was just too much to—"

"How did you happen to make the connection?"

"Oh, come on," Jamie said, looking down at him in disbelief. "Who wouldn't? I mean, Dan Kelly is one of my very favorite writers, has been for years. How could I not make the connection?"

He relaxed on the leather surface of the table, and Jamie stole a glance at him, relieved to see that he didn't appear to be angry.

"One of your favorite writers, eh?" he asked thoughtfully, gazing at the dappled shadows above his head.

"Absolutely. I've loved every one of his..." Jamie gave an awkward little laugh. "Every one of *your* books," she corrected herself.

He stared up at her in silence, his face unreadable.

"But," she went on, considering, "I think my very favorite was *Astrakhan*. I thought that was such a wonderful story. I just loved it."

Unexpectedly, he smiled, the rare, shining, boyish smile that never failed to move her. "Me, too," he said. "I mean, I loved writing it. I lived in a little mountain village in Nepal for six months while I was researching it, and became like one of the people. They have the most incredible storytellers, and their pageants and feast days are just unbelievable."

Jamie lifted and flexed his legs automatically, her eyes glowing.

"What a wonderful adventure," she said softly. "No wonder the book seemed so real." She hesitated. "Did you always do that sort of on-location research?"

He nodded. "It's not the same, getting your facts secondhand. Unless you actually live the life, it's difficult to make it all seem real. I've traveled all over the world, spent time in some of the strangest, most godforsaken places you could imagine...."

He fell abruptly silent, staring up at the leafy curtains of greenery above his head.

"But you don't anymore," Jamie said quietly. "Now you have other people who do your research."

"Yes," he said, his voice curt and dismissive. "Now I have a research staff."

Jamie looked over at him, a little intimidated by his cold, withdrawn expression that was so different from his earlier warmth and friendliness.

"Why?" she asked cautiously. "Why did you quit doing your own traveling and research?"

"Oh, come on, Jamie," he said impatiently. "Don't pretend to be stupid. It doesn't become you."

She looked down at him thoughtfully, ignoring his brusque tone. "I'm not pretending," she said. "If there's something so obvious here, I seem to be missing it."

He glared up at her, startling her with the angry flame in his brilliant dark eyes. "I don't know how you can miss it," he said coldly. "After all, it's right under your hands, isn't it?"

"Daniel, disabled people travel, you know. They do all kinds of things. There are facilities for—"

"Oh, certainly," he interrupted bitterly. "All kinds of facilities for disabled people. And then you become one of the people using the special facilities, somebody that everybody else has to help and wait for and pity. No thanks, Jamie. I find it much easier just to stay at home."

Like Maria? Jamie thought. *Is that what you're saying, Daniel... that it's easier to hide from the world than to risk all the dangers out there?*

"Well," she said aloud, trying to sound casual and cheerful, "to each his own, I guess. But if *I* were like you, with a career that allowed me to travel as part of my work, and enough money to do it in style..." She grinned, panting as she gave his legs a final brisk rubdown with the towel. "Well," she concluded finally, "you wouldn't find *me* paying someone else to do my traveling. I can tell you that."

Daniel gazed up at her as she wheeled the chair back over near the table and set the brake for him. His angry expression was already fading into the bleak distant sadness that so often showed on his face when he was alone.

He sat up and grasped the chrome supports on the table, swung himself carefully down into his chair, and then looked at Jamie again.

"That's easy for you to say, Jamie," he said finally. "You're almost six feet tall, and you're as strong and graceful as a lion. You can go anywhere and do anything. If you were in this chair, looking up at the world, maybe your viewpoint would change."

Without another word, he turned and wheeled himself away, off across the patio and into the sun-room, vanishing at once through the atrium and into the lonely reaches of his upper apartment.

Jamie watched him go, thinking about his words, wondering if she really would view things differently in his position.

It was so hard to know, she thought miserably. Nobody *ever* knew, really, how they would react to a disaster until they were actually confronted with it.

Still silent, she tidied the sun-room, took a last wistful look at the glowing sunny world beyond the windows, and went off toward the kitchen for her lunch.

IT WAS A FRIDAY AFTERNOON, about a week after that troubling conversation with Daniel. The day was gray and swirling with leaden clouds, and a strong prairie wind sobbed and howled around the tall windows, sending occasional gusts of rain rattling against the glass. Jamie sat cross-legged on the deep carpet in her sitting room, surrounded by tangled skeins of brightly colored yarn. Her gas fireplace was on, filling the room with a cheery glow, and she sighed with pleasure at the cozy, snug feeling of warmth and hominess.

Beside her, Maria lounged happily in one of the padded armchairs, munching popcorn and watching an afternoon talk show on Jamie's small television set. She wore casual white cotton slacks and a red pullover that accentuated the delicate beauty of her pale skin, her dark hair and eyes. Jamie glanced up at her with admiration, thinking how pretty Maria looked when she was relaxed and comfortable.

"Okay," Jamie said aloud. "I've got all those little stitches made. Now what?"

She held up her crochet hook, adorned with a trailing length of bright yellow wool, and Maria leaned forward to study it.

"Now," Maria said, "you join it into a circle, remember? And then you chain up to set the base for your next row. Right here," she said, pointing.

Jamie nodded, and absently took a handful of popcorn from Maria's bowl before continuing with her work.

"Oh, I see how it's going to work!" she said suddenly. "This row sets the corners, right?"

Maria nodded. "That's all a granny square is, just endless repetitions of that corner row, with extra units set in for the sides."

"And now that I can do this," Jamie said happily, "I can make cushions, afghans, bedspreads...."

Maria smiled and shook her head. "You have so much energy, Jamie. Who else would think, as soon as they learn to crochet, of making a *bedspread?*"

Jamie chuckled, and then sobered. "What are you doing tomorrow, Maria?" she asked, concentrating intently on her crochet hook.

"Why?" Maria asked.

"Well, it's Saturday. I thought you might be planning something."

Maria shook her head. "Just...just the usual, I guess," she said evasively. "How about you?"

"I'm going over to my brother's house. You remember, I told you about Terry and Doreen?"

"And all the little ones?" Maria asked wistfully.

Jamie nodded. "Five of them. Terry and Doreen are taking the three older kids to the circus tomorrow afternoon, and my father's going to be at a bridge tournament, so I'm baby-sitting the two littlest ones. That's Miriam and Dougie. She's three, and he's nine months. They're so sweet."

Maria's thin gentle face took on a dreamy, faraway expression of yearning that was painful to observe. "I'd love to see them," she said softly. "I wish..."

"Why don't you come with me?" Jamie asked, as if on impulse. "It'll only be for the afternoon and probably for supper, and we'll be home early in the evening. Come on, Maria. You'd love the babies. They're just darling."

Maria looked down at her friend, her face twisting in anguish. "Oh, Jamie," she whispered.

Swiftly, Jamie set her work aside and crossed the room to kneel beside her, slipping an arm around the other woman's thin shoulders. Maria sagged forward in the chair, covering her face with her hands, her body heaving, and Jamie held her, waiting for the first storm of emotion to pass.

"Maria," she whispered finally. "Maria, look at me."

Maria looked up in mute appeal, her cheeks streaked with tears.

"Maria," Jamie said gently, "you never go outside, do you? You're afraid to go out of the house at all."

Maria gulped and nodded, hiding her face again. "It's...it's awful," she whispered in a muffled voice. "I'm...some kind of crazy person, Jamie. I just can't..."

"Listen to me," Jamie said with quiet firmness. "Are you listening?"

Maria nodded, keeping her face turned away.

"First, you're not a crazy person," Jamie said. "Not at all. And you're not alone, either. As a matter of fact, a lot of people suffer from the same thing you do. It even has a name, Maria. It's called agoraphobia."

Maria turned to her in stunned amazement, dark eyes wide and staring. "What? What did you say?"

"I said," Jamie repeated patiently, "that a lot of people are afraid to go out of the house. It's a clinical condition called agoraphobia."

"You mean..." Maria whispered in wonder "...you mean I'm not the only one like this? Other people feel the same way?"

"Lots of them," Jamie said briskly. "And they can be helped, too. Many, many people have been cured of agoraphobia."

Maria shook her head, still trying to absorb what she was hearing. "I never knew. I always thought it was just me, that I was crazy." She turned to Jamie in sudden excitement. "You said people have been cured? They can get over it and go outside again?"

Jamie nodded. "Absolutely."

"But... but how?" Maria said haltingly. "Jamie, I've tried. I've tried so many times. You just don't know. It's been years since I could... Jamie, I've tried to force myself, but as soon as I get out the door, even just a few inches, I get dizzy, and I can't breathe right, and I start to feel like I'm going to faint or suffocate...."

She paused, trembling violently, and Jamie hugged her again. "It's like anything else, Maria," she said softly. "It's awfully hard to do alone. Sometimes you need a little help to take the first steps."

"I don't have anybody to help me," Maria said simply. "My mother died just after I came to work here, and my sisters live so far away. This place is all I have." Maria looked up at her in childlike appeal. "Jamie, do you think . . . Could *you* help me?"

Jamie smiled. "Yes, Maria," she said. "I'll help you. I'll help you every step of the way."

"What's going on here?"

Both women turned, startled by the harsh, familiar voice. Clara stood in the doorway with several cameras hanging around her neck and a case of filters in her hand.

Maria glanced over at her timidly, her face pink with embarrassment, but Jamie crawled back to her place on the rug and gave the older woman a cherubic smile.

"Maria's teaching me to crochet," she said, holding aloft her tiny square of yellow. "And," she added cheerfully, "as soon as I've got this mastered, I'm going to crochet you a whole set of matching camera cases and a big equipment bag."

Clara continued to regard Jamie with a severe expression.

"I think," Jamie went on innocently, concentrating on her work, "that I'll make them fluorescent green and orange, so people can see you coming, Clara. No more of those sneaky candid shots."

Unexpectedly, Clara snorted with laughter, Maria giggled, and Jamie grinned impudently. "What do you think of that?" she asked.

"I think you're a very rude girl," Clara said, her mouth still twitching. "I also think it's a nasty cold afternoon, and we all seem to be taking the day off, so we should have some coffee and hot apple turnovers. They're just ready to come out of the oven. Come on, you two."

Jamie set her work aside with alacrity, and she and Maria got up to follow Clara's brisk figure eagerly down the hall.

Maria already looked different, Jamie thought, younger and happier, and she walked with a light, eager step. A cloud passed briefly over Jamie's face, and she frowned, wishing that she was really as confident as she had pretended to be about her ability to help.

"AND THERE WAS an elephant," Sean said excitedly to his grandfather, "and he stood up on this stool, with his front feet waving in the air."

"Did he now?" Kevin O'Rourke asked, deftly spooning mashed banana into little Dougie's mouth.

"I felt sorry for the elephant," Teresa muttered to Jamie, who was beside her.

Jamie looked down at her niece's fiery red curls and unhappy freckled face. "Why, Tessie?"

"They made him look silly," Teresa said darkly. "They put this dumb little skirt on him and a stupid frill on his head. I bet he just hated it."

Jamie said nothing, but felt a surge of empathy for the child. Even when she was very young, Jamie, too, had always hated the indignities heaped on the circus animals, and never could see why other children found them so hilarious.

"I liked the horses," little Kevin, on her other side, confided shyly. "They were all white, and they had feathers on their heads. They were so pretty."

Jamie smiled at the small boy and patted his thick dark hair, looking down at him thoughtfully. He was such a gentle, little fellow, just like Steven....

"Kevin," she said suddenly, "do you think you'd like to come home with me some Saturday, and play with Steven for the day?"

Kevin's eyes widened. "That's the little boy who lives in the big house?"

Jamie nodded. "He's just a couple of years older than you, and the two of you are a lot alike. I think you'd have all kinds of fun together."

Kevin's deep blue eyes flamed with excitement, and he began to bounce silently in his chair.

"Maybe in a couple of weeks, when summer holidays start," Jamie went on. "Steven's going to be really lonely once school's out, and he's all on his own every day."

"Aunt Jamie! Aunt Jamie!" the older children chorused in noisy outraged unison. "Me, too, Aunt Jamie! I want to go to the big house, too!"

Tears gathered in Kevin's eyes, trickling quietly down his plump cheeks. Never, ever, did he get any kind of treat just for himself, without his older brother and sister pushing in and taking it away from him.

But Jamie shook her head firmly. "Sorry. Just Kevin is invited, this time. If I take the whole crew, I'll get fired for sure."

She smiled, amused by the radiant glow on Kevin's small face, and the new dignity with which he ignored the older children and went calmly back to eating his mashed potatoes.

But, privately, she was concerned, knowing that even though her relationship with Daniel was much more relaxed that it had been at first, this was still a risky move. It amounted, in fact, to disobeying a direct order, and she hoped that there wouldn't be any unpleasant repercussions.

"How are things going over there, anyway?" Terry asked.

Jamie began to tell them about her job, about Hiro and Clara and Maria and the lavish house, trying to draw a picture for them of where and how she worked without compromising any of Daniel's privacy. The three adults listened, fascinated, while the children excused themselves one by one and slipped away from the table to watch their Saturday evening videos.

Kevin O'Rourke rose heavily from the table, extricated Dougie from his cozy nest in the high chair, and followed the children, turning to smile warmly at the young people around the table before leaving the room.

Terry, Doreen and Jamie relaxed in the sudden overwhelming peace and stillness while Doreen poured second cups of coffee all round.

"Look at you two," Jamie said cheerfully. "You look absolutely exhausted."

"Oh, Lord," Terry said with a deep sigh. "I'd rather take on a shift of riot control, any day, than take three kids to the circus."

Jamie laughed. "We should have done it the other way around," she said. "You two should have stayed home with the little ones, and let me go to the circus. I would have loved it."

"See?" Terry said to his wife, with a comical lift of his eyebrows. "Basically a crazy person. I keep telling you."

Doreen smiled and then sobered and turned to Jamie. "I hope," she said, her face troubled, "that you won't get into any trouble, taking Kevin over there. Didn't you say your boss doesn't want you to have any visitors?"

"Oh, well." Jamie shrugged. "He's mellowing quite a bit and one extra little boy shouldn't matter all that much. I don't think he'll really mind, as long as I'm careful to see that his own personal space isn't disrupted. He's kind of a fanatic about his privacy."

Terry and Doreen exchanged a quick troubled glance and Doreen looked down, absently pleating the edge of her napkin between her fingers.

Jamie turned slowly from one to the other.

"Hey," she said, "what is it? Is there something going on here?"

Terry cleared his throat and glanced reluctantly at his sister, his mild blue eyes distressed and uneasy. "Jamie, it's... it's Chad," he said.

"Chad?" she asked blankly. "What about him?"

Terry exchanged another look with his wife, and then went on. "He called last night, and asked me to stop by the gym when I came off shift. We went out for a coffee and talked a bit."

Terry paused, staring gloomily into the depths of his coffee cup, while Jamie watched him in growing uneasiness.

"And?" she prompted finally. "What did he say, Terry?"

Terry looked up, and met his sister's eyes. "He's really upset, Jamie. We're... Doreen and I... we're a little concerned about what he might do."

Jamie felt a quick stab of alarm, but ignored it. "Why should you be?" she asked. "What can he do? After all, it's not like the end of the world. People break off relationships all the time. And things haven't been good between us for a long time. In fact," she added, "they were *never* really good. I just tried to overlook all the problems, I guess, because I wanted..."

She paused, gazing absently out at the summer twilight while the other two watched her.

"Anyhow," she said finally, "it's over. What is there to be concerned about?"

Terry frowned, his normally cheerful face set in worried lines. "Chad's been my friend for a long time," he said. "Since school days. We usually get along fine, but I know there's a side to him that's... He doesn't like to be crossed. He wants what he wants."

"Don't I know it," Jamie said wryly.

"And he thinks," Terry went on, "that you've been taken away from him. He doesn't seem to understand that you might leave him because of something in himself. He thinks it was caused by...somebody else."

Jamie stared at her brother with mounting dread. "Who?" she asked. "Who does he blame?"

"Your boss," Terry said miserably.

"*Daniel?*"

"And he's planning to do something about it."

"Oh, my God," Jamie whispered. "What, Terry? Did he tell you?"

Terry nodded again. "He says he's going to go have a talk with Mr. Kelleher, tell him what he thinks of him."

Jamie stared at the other two, her face suddenly drained of color. "But that's... Oh, God, if he does that, Daniel will...Terry, can't you *stop* him?"

"How? Arrest him for threatening to talk to somebody?"

"No, no," Jamie said in confusion, "I mean, just tell him what Daniel's like and how foolish and useless it would be to—"

She broke off, knowing the futility of trying to tell Chad something like that.

"Maybe," Doreen said gently, "it would help if you talked to him, Jamie."

Jamie shook her head. "I don't want to talk to him again. It's too hard, because he's so... Besides, I couldn't do anything with him. We'd just wind up in another big fight and then he'd be more furious and resentful than ever."

"Sometimes," Terry suggested hopefully, "Chad's more talk than action. Maybe he's just letting off steam, and he won't actually go through with anything."

"Maybe," Jamie agreed with relief, although she knew she was grasping at straws. "It's been a couple of weeks already, and he hasn't done anything yet. Maybe it'll all just blow over. Anyway, let's not spoil our evening by talking about it anymore."

She got to her feet and began to clear the table, forcing herself to talk and laugh happily, bringing the conversation back to a light, cheerful plane and trying to ignore the nagging worries that haunted her mind.

CHAPTER SEVEN

ON MONDAY AFTERNOON Jamie was in her room, wearing an old black exercise leotard, tights and leg warmers, developing a new aerobic routine. She made a few experimental bends, frowned in concentration and jotted some notes in her workbook, then paused to rewind the tape on her stereo.

Planning and composing a new routine was a time-consuming job, requiring the combined talents of a physiotherapist, a gymnast and a choreographer. It was so important to get the proper moves in sequence and to find just the right music to go with them. Jamie spent many hours struggling to attain the perfect balance, the sort of flowing, varied routines that made her workouts so popular with her students.

She danced a few experimental steps, bent her long body gracefully at the waist and then swayed loosely from side to side in time to the music. Just then, a timid knock sounded at the door. Jamie straightened and took a few deep breaths.

"Yes?" she called. "Come in, it's open."

The door opened and Maria popped her head inside. "Jamie?" she said shyly. "Is this a good time?"

Jamie smiled. "This is a great time, Maria. Come in."

Still smiling, she tied a patterned wrap skirt over her leotard, sat in an armchair and indicated the other one for her friend.

Maria sank onto the extreme edge of the chair and held herself stiffly erect, her hands clutched tightly together, her dark eyes blazing with purpose.

"I'm ready," she announced.

Jamie looked at her intently. "You're sure, Maria? Absolutely sure? It has to be your decision, you know, or it won't be effective. You're the one who has to exercise all the willpower and do all the hard things."

"I know that. I've been thinking about it all weekend, and I know I don't want to go on like this. I'm expecting it to be hard, but I want to try."

Jamie beamed her approval. "That's the spirit. Now, there's nothing mysterious about this. First, you set your goal, and then there are a series of tasks that you have to perform to achieve it. Now, what's your goal?"

Maria gazed blankly at the tall woman opposite her. "Jamie, you know what my goal is. I just want to be able to go out again and not be so afraid."

"I know," Jamie said, "but in order for this to be most effective, you should have some specific goal. Some place you really want to go, or something you like to picture yourself doing outside the house, to keep you going when it gets tough and discouraging." Jamie paused. "It's like dieting," she explained. "It helps for people who are dieting to picture themselves—you know, on the beach in a bikini or dancing in a slinky little dress—that sort of thing."

"I see." Maria hesitated, thinking, and then said shyly, "I want to be able to go my high school reunion."

"Terrific! When is it and where?"

"It's going to be in a downtown hotel, in the fall. In October."

Something in Maria's voice, and in the warm glow of her face, caught Jamie's attention. "Maria, is there going to be somebody special at this reunion?"

Maria blushed scarlet and shook her head. "Not really. Just...just a boy I knew..." She laughed awkwardly. "But he's not a boy anymore. He's almost thirty, and he's an assistant manager at a supermarket across town."

Jamie smiled. "What's his name?"

"Tony," Maria said, with a faraway expression. "Tony Falco. We were going out in high school, and I really liked him. But then I came to work here, and my mother died and he went away to college for a couple of years. By the time he came back, it was already getting..."

Maria hesitated, casting Jamie a glance of anguished appeal.

"It was getting harder for you to leave the house," Jamie said gently.

Maria nodded miserably. "He kept calling, and I kept making excuses, and after a while he quit. He decided I just wasn't interested in him...that way, you know? But," she added, "he started calling again when they sent out the announcements last year about the reunion. He's just really casual, he calls once every couple of months or so, just to chat, and I know he's never married. I'd like...I'd like to see him again. I'd like to go to the reunion."

"Good," Jamie said briskly. "That's a really good goal and a reasonable time frame, too. We'll aim to have you able to go downtown to your reunion, and we'll shop for a pretty dress, and you'll get your hair done, and poor Tony will just be knocked right off his pins."

"Oh, Jamie..." Maria closed her eyes and drew in a long, wistful sigh. Jamie gazed at her, touched by her evident emotion and her shy prettiness. Because Maria's skin was never exposed to the sunlight, it was as soft and delicately white as a baby's, making her look as young as the dark-eyed high school girl that Tony Falco must remember.

"So," Maria said, opening her eyes and turning to Jamie with sudden determination, "what happens next? What do I have to do?"

Jamie chuckled. "You look like you're about to have a root canal or something. Don't worry, Maria. This is a program called 'behavior modification,' and it's arranged in easy steps, designed to start easily so you don't find the experience threatening, and then moving on to harder things when you feel you're ready."

She reached into a drawer in a nearby end table and took out another workbook, a bright red one.

Maria watched silently, her eyes half fascinated and half terrified.

"Now," Jamie said, "we've worked out a series of tasks for you. The first one is . . ."

"We?" Maria interrupted in sudden alarm. "Who's 'we'?"

Jamie met her eyes directly. "Mr. Kelleher and I."

Maria stared in wide-eyed horror. "Mr. *Kelleher?*" she whispered. "He . . . he knows about this?"

Jamie nodded gently. "He was the one who first drew it my attention, Maria. He suggested to me that he was afraid you might have a problem."

Maria blanched with horror and then flushed painfully. "I don't . . . I don't know what to say. I never thought he even took the slightest notice of me."

"Well, he does. In fact, he's aware of everybody in the house and concerned about them. He just finds it hard to express it, I think. He's gotten so in the habit of being distant and reserved."

Maria nodded. "I know. He used to be friendlier and even laugh and joke with us, before he..." She paused. "It's been good for him, Jamie, having you here. Already, he seems more... human, you know?"

Jamie grinned. "Well, that's good, all right. Because he sure didn't seem very human the day I first applied for the job."

Maria smiled, but then sobered. "I just... I hate the idea of Mr. Kelleher knowing about this," she murmured. "I feel so ashamed."

"Maria, don't feel that way. It's nothing to be ashamed of. I told you, thousands of people have this problem. It's not just you. In fact," Jamie added deliberately, "I think that watching you overcome your fears might be a really good thing for Mr. Kelleher."

"Why? What do you mean?"

"I think," Jamie said, "that he might have a similar problem, and not even realize it."

"Mr. *Kelleher?*" Maria asked, staring in amazement. "But he goes out. He drives himself to the hospital, and—"

"Sure," Jamie said. "But he doesn't travel anymore, does he, Maria? Has he left the city at all since his accident?"

Maria frowned in concentration, and then turned to Jamie. "No, not since he went to Ireland," she said slowly. "And I remember he cut that trip short. Is it...do you think it's the same thing, Jamie?"

"Not exactly the same. But I think it could be similar. And I think that if you can overcome this, and he sees you doing it, it might encourage him to do the same thing for himself."

Maria squared her shoulders, her eyes dark with resolve. "Okay. Then I'll really try. What did you say about these things you've planned?"

Jamie smiled at the look of grim determination on the housemaid's gentle face and opened the notebook.

"As I said, it's a series of tasks. You keep doing one until you feel absolutely comfortable with it, then you move up one step and master that one, and so on. All the way to the point where you can go downtown all by yourself."

Maria looked incredulous. "It's hard to believe that could really happen, Jamie. It sounds like a miracle. But I'll try. What's first?"

"First, you have to stand here by my window for two minutes and look out."

Maria glanced over at the broad, sweeping expanse of sky and city framed in the big window and shivered in terror.

"But," Jamie went on, consulting the notebook, "I'll stand right beside you at first. You can hold my hand, talk to me, do anything that helps."

"And after that?"

"Once you're comfortable by the window, then you do it without me. You learn to stand there alone."

"But will you still be somewhere nearby?"

"At first," Jamie said gently.

Maria nodded thoughtfully. "I see. Then, after I'm able to be near the window with you across the room, I'll try to do it when I'm all alone, and you're not even in the room."

"Exactly. And once you've done that a lot of times, we move from the window to something a little scarier and try it again."

"Doing what?" Maria asked hesitantly.

Jamie looked at the notebook again. "Standing by an open door for two minutes."

Maria paled, and her shoulders grew tense.

"But then," Jamie hastened to add, "we'll start all over. I mean, when you're beside the open door, I'll be with you at first, close enough to touch, until you start to get more comfortable."

"And this doesn't all have to happen right away, does it?" Maria said. "I mean, I'll have a little time to—"

"Maria, you'll have all the time you need. After all, we've got four months until your school reunion. And if you're really determined, you can accomplish an awful lot in four months, you know."

Maria nodded thoughtfully. Her eyes were still frightened, and Jamie could sense her reluctance.

"But," she said gently, "it has to be your decision, Maria. If you don't feel you're ready, then we won't—"

"I'm ready," Maria said abruptly. "If I'm not ready now, I never will be."

She got up and walked across the room toward the window, pulling aside the flimsy, transparent draperies and forcing herself, with obvious effort, to look outside. The view sprawled before her, miles of open space, and she paled and trembled, swaying a little on her feet.

"Jamie," she whispered in a small, choked voice.

Jamie hurried across the room, slipped her arm around Maria's trembling shoulders and held her close while Maria stared out at the broad expanse, biting her lip and moaning softly.

"How...how much longer, Jamie?"

"Ninety seconds," Jamie murmured, tightening her grip on the other woman's shoulders. "Are you going to be all right, Maria?"

Maria nodded, blinking back her tears and staring outside, her face stony with resolution.

"Yes," she said at last, in a small, strained voice. "Yes, I am. I'm going to be fine. I'm going to be just fine."

DANIEL SAT BY THE WINDOW of his study, gazing out at the grounds of his home and the western sky awash with sunset colors. There seemed to be an unusual amount of activity in the yard, and he leaned forward in his chair to pull the drapes aside, looking a little wistfully at the various members of his household moving about on the lawn below him.

Clara was in the dappled shade beneath the trees just at the edge of his vision, hung about with cameras that she was aiming and focusing one by one at the lacy expanses of rainbow-tinted sky framed by the trees.

Hiro, in jeans and an old Edmonton Eskimos T-shirt, knelt by the curving flower bed adjoining the drive, setting out bedding plants. Even from this distance Daniel could see the contented line of the small man's body and the gentle skill of his slender brown fingers as he probed at the soil and handled the delicate plants.

Jamie stood near him, chatting, leaning against the fender of her disreputable old Volkswagen. She wore a white exercise leotard and tights with a bright red wrap skirt, and her red-gold head gleamed in the fading light. She looked as rare and exotic as some lovely butterfly, gorgeous and graceful, fluttering magically down on a vagrant summer wind to brighten his world.

Daniel swallowed hard, watching the way she stood, taut and graceful as if poised for flight, and the way she threw her head back at something the gardener said and laughed her rich, hearty laugh.

He loved to hear her laugh.

In fact, he was growing to love a lot of things about her, and the idea frightened him. He had organized his life so carefully after his accident, deliberately shutting out the world to minimize his own pain. And he had been successful... at least until Jamie came along. But now, just by the very warmth and vibrancy of her nature, she was forcing him to reexamine his attitudes, to question his choices, to begin considering again, with reluctant dread, all the things that made him feel lonely and damaged and inadequate.

Daniel was sure that none of this was deliberate. As far as Jamie was concerned, she was just doing her job, following orders, performing her function to the best of her ability and training. She couldn't know what an overwhelming person she was, how profoundly she affected the lives of everyone she contacted, just by being a woman who rejoiced so fully in life, and insisted on drawing others into the glow of her own energy and happiness.

He saw her turn, say something to Hiro, and call to someone by the house. Hiro smiled, then stood and dusted off his knees, bending to say something to Steven, who came running up and joined them. Steven carried a small gym bag clutched tightly in his hands, and was fairly dancing with excitement. Two floors up, Daniel could see the flare of happiness in his son's eyes, and his austere face softened with gentleness and affection.

On Friday nights when Jamie instructed her class at the recreation centre, she took Steven with her. She had enrolled him in a beginner's swimming class at the pool in the complex, and Steven adored everything about the experience—the water, the lessons and games, the other children.

The three of them stood in a little group by the car, posing obediently for Clara, who hurried over to frame them in one of her lenses. Then they all turned once more, waving and calling to someone in the kitchen doorway.

The invisible person had to be Maria, Daniel realized. Jamie had been giving him regular bulletins on the housemaid's impressive progress in the two weeks since she had embarked on their carefully designed behavior modification program. Maria was now able to stand alone in an open door and wave to someone who was leaving the house, a remarkable improvement over her condition at the outset.

But Jamie had warned Daniel that she expected a setback before long, and was prepared for it. Maria couldn't keep advancing at the rate she was going, or she would soon have to venture all the way outside, and Jamie was certain Maria wasn't ready for that step.

Jamie and Steven climbed into her car and rattled off down the driveway, Hiro returned to his gardening, and Clara disappeared in the depths of the shrubbery. Feeling strangely bereft, Daniel wheeled his chair back across the room, positioned himself behind the computer monitor and returned to his work.

A knock sounded on the door. He looked up, puzzled, checked his watch, and switched on his intercom.

"Yes, Maria?"

"There's a gentleman to see you, Mr. Kelleher."

Still puzzled, Daniel flipped through his appointment book, almost all blank these days, and frowned at the intercom again.

"Send him in, Maria," he said, pressing the button that opened the big oak door.

The door slid aside and Maria appeared in the doorway, looking shy and terrified as she always did when required to approach this room.

"Mr. Kelleher," she said breathlessly, "this is...this is Mr. Bolton."

Abruptly she vanished, leaving Daniel to confront the tall man who now materialized in the opening and stepped into the room. He was a big blond young man with almost movie star good looks. He had a clean-cut face, shining hair a shade long for Daniel's taste, and a taut, hard-muscled body that moved across the carpeted office with silent, predatory grace.

"Chad," the blond man said abruptly, pausing in front of Daniel's desk and looking down at the man in the wheelchair. He extended his hand. "Chad Bolton."

"Hello, Mr. Bolton," Daniel said coolly. He shook the hand that was offered, but made no move to introduce himself or establish the interview on a more casual footing. "What can I do for you?"

Without invitation, the blond man sank into the leather chair opposite the desk and looked over at Daniel, his blue eyes challenging and defiant.

"I came to talk to you about Jamie," he said.

Ah, Daniel thought. The rejected suitor...

Daniel's mouth tightened, and the planes of his face hardened almost imperceptibly, but he gave no signs of recognition.

"Jamie?" he asked with deliberate vagueness. "I assume you mean Miss O'Rourke, my physiotherapist?"

Chad's bold facade cracked a little. "You know damn well who I mean," he said, leaning tensely forward, his voice low and furious. "And she may be your physiotherapist, but she's *my* girl."

"I believe," Daniel said mildly, his impassive expression belying the emotions raging within him, "that the proper verb in this case would be *was*. She *was* your girl, isn't that correct?"

"Oh, so she told you all about it, did she?" Chad said. "And the two of you had a good laugh about it, right?"

Daniel's tone hardened. "Mr. Bolton, the private relationships of my staff are not generally a source of amusement to me."

"Yeah, sure," Chad said, his face twisting unpleasantly with hurt and jealousy. "But Jamie's not just staff, is she, Mr. Kelleher? I'm sure that she's a *lot* more than just a physiotherapist by now, right?"

Daniel fought down a rising tide of hot anger that threatened to overcome his control and judgment. "What exactly do you mean, Mr. Bolton?"

"Hell, I know what Jamie's like. She's a sucker for a guy like you. I could never even get to first base with her, just because she knows I can look after myself. But a guy who's down, who's had bad luck and needs her help, that's just what Jamie's looking for."

Daniel stared at his visitor, his eyes flashing dangerously, but the man had something to say and an obvious need to say it.

"I've known Jamie's family a long time," Chad went on passionately. "And I know some of the guys she's been involved with. Losers, every one of them, Kelleher. Guys who needed her and used her and left her hurting. For some reason, that's the kind of guys that appeal to her. If you've got something going with Jamie, don't think it's because she cares about you or anything. It's just because she can't resist a loser."

Daniel's searing fury ebbed away as suddenly as it had come, leaving him with nothing but a great, miserable weariness.

"Look, Chad," he said quietly, "I know that what you're saying is true. I'm fully able to recognize that quality of sympathy and generosity in Jamie. What you don't realize is that I have absolutely no wish to take advantage of it.''

Daniel paused while the other man watched him, his blue eyes wide and startled.

''I think perhaps your unsavory behavior is motivated by some kind of concern for her. At least, I'd like to think so,'' Daniel went on. ''Let me assure you that whatever has happened between you and Jamie is exactly that…just between the two of you. I have no part whatever in Jamie's life or her emotions, nor do I intend to. Good evening, Mr. Bolton.''

''But…'' Chad began.

''Please leave,'' Daniel said quietly, ''before I lose my good manners, and I'm forced to treat you as you deserve.''

Chad bristled a little at this implied threat, and got to his feet in a menacing posture, his tall, muscular body towering above Daniel's.

But something in the demeanor of the man in the wheelchair—in those broad flat shoulders and relaxed tanned hands, the sculpted planes of the face and the piercing eyes—made Chad back away a little. He hesitated, puzzled and uncertain, and then plunged toward the door, pausing as it slid open before him.

''Look, I just wanted to say…'' he began, turning back to look at Daniel once more.

''Don't say anything,'' Daniel replied, so softly that his voice was barely above a whisper. ''Just go. Immediately.''

As if hypnotized by Daniel's brilliant, fathomless dark eyes, Chad backed away, turned and stepped through the door, which closed instantly behind him.

Alone in his quiet room, Daniel sat staring at the closed door, his face withdrawn and sad. Finally, he lowered his head onto his folded arms. For a long time he remained that way, silent and motionless, his face hidden, while the twilight shadows lengthened and filled the room with brooding darkness.

JAMIE WORKED OVER Daniel's long, still body, troubled by his silence. Usually the Monday morning therapy session was a companionable affair after their two days off, a time when each of them reported on weekend activities and thoughts and they laughed together, happy to be in one another's company again. But today, Daniel seemed different, as withdrawn as he had been in the very early stages of their relationship.

Jamie looked up at his austere features as he lay with his eyes closed, submitting himself to her touch. She wondered where his mind was and whether he was worrying or just daydreaming. She recalled the couple of times she had encountered him around the house over the weekend. He had seemed unusually reserved and distant on those occasions, too.

Maybe he was unhappy about something, she thought. Maybe his writing wasn't going well or his stocks had dropped in value, or some bad news had come in the mail.

But she couldn't shake the irrational feeling that his dark mood had something to do with her, that she had somehow upset or disappointed him.

She shook her head to clear the nagging thoughts and applied all her attention to the massage she was giving his motionless legs. Without thinking, she edged up the towel that covered his loins and applied pressure to the deep nerve areas in his hips, both to stimulate the feeling that remained to him and to increase the circulatory flow to his lower limbs.

As she worked, with her skilled hands performing almost independently of her thoughts, she gazed out the big windows of the sun-room, enjoying the beauty of the day and the sense of absolute privacy. Now that Daniel was comfortable enough with her to lie nude on the massage table with just the towel as a covering, they tended to close the doors that screened the sun-room from the house and pool area. The casement windows onto the patio were open, bringing the outdoor scents and sounds into the glass-enclosed space where Jamie and Daniel existed all alone, as cozy and secluded as if they were the only two people in all the world.

She continued to prod and stroke rhythmically, pressing deeply, panting a little with effort. Her eyes were closed and the light streamed through the open skylight onto her face, warming and soothing her. Birds sang their early morning chorus of joy at the new day and the sunny warmth, while bees buzzed drowsily in the banks of shrubbery outside the window. The June flowers were in bloom and the rich, heady scent of peonies and lilacs filled the world with a perfume that was almost intoxicating.

A breeze played gently through the open windows, cool and delicious on her bare arms and legs in the soft blue cotton sunsuit that she liked to wear for this morning session. Jamie was intensely conscious of the day, the sounds and scents, of her own body and that of the man on the table. She felt as if she were moving through some strange, dreamlike state where every sensation was heightened and sharpened to a pleasurable intensity, and every feeling was enhanced.

The hypnotic, rhythmic movements of her hands, the gentle symphony of morning sounds, the sweet perfumed flowers, the warm air and soft breezes all combined to create an atmosphere of physical delight that was almost erotic. Her mind wandered, creating images that she found absorbing, arousing, intensely stimulating.

She opened her eyes and looked down, realizing with detached surprise that her own feelings had somehow transmitted themselves to Daniel through her fingers. He was visibly aroused, thrusting up beneath the soft fabric of the towel that covered him. Fascinated, still in a dreamy trancelike state, Jamie gazed down at that obvious, jutting masculinity, wondering vaguely if it was just a reflexive response of some kind or if he was able to feel his own arousal.

Such spontaneous reactions were not unusual during a massage session, even with men with no sensation in the lower torso. Over the years, Jamie had learned to ignore these happenings tactfully or, depending on the patient, to treat them with calm good humor. But on this warm summer morning, looking down at Daniel's body, there was no way she could be casual....

He was silent, his face still and drawn in its fine, sculpted lines, and his eyes were closed. Jamie stared at his quiet features and felt a sudden flood of sexual desire that raced through her whole being, searing her with sweet warmth and leaving her feeling weak and hollow.

Automatically, barely able to breathe, she went on stroking him and stimulating him, coaxing his powerful male reaction. Although he held his body rigidly still and kept his eyes closed, she could tell by now that he was feeling it, too, that the range of sensation remaining to him allowed him to experience sexual arousal.

She was almost beyond awareness of what her hands were doing. All she knew was that she wanted to be here forever, in this place, touching this man, stroking his body while the sun streamed over them and the birds sang all around them....

Suddenly, without opening his eyes, he reached up a long arm and pulled her down close to him on the broad leather surface of the table.

Jamie gasped with pleasure and rising excitement as her body pressed against his and she felt his muscular arms close silently around her. His lips roamed over her face and his hands caressed her body, rough and demanding, stroking her breasts and her rounded hips, moving across her thighs, tugging impatiently at the fabric of her clothing.

Without hesitation, Jamie sat up and unfastened the snaps that closed the sunsuit, then pulled it off and cast it aside. She lay down beside him again, shivering in delight at the feeling of his hard, firm body and matted hairy chest against her bare skin. He began to kiss her, his mouth as rough and demanding as his hands, and she sighed, loving the feel of his lips, of the harshness and masculinity of his caresses.

He tugged at her lacy bikini panties, ripping the band that held them over her hips and casting them aside like a tattered cobweb. Jamie shuddered with joy as he lifted her above him and held her there, moving her body against his, stroking and caressing her torso as the sunlight flowed over her in a rich golden cascade. Then, abrupt with need, he lifted her and positioned her, entering her with a single warm thrust.

"Oh, God," she whispered, sinking down against him, swaying mindlessly, lost in her feelings. "Oh, God..."

Now, as she moved above him and their bodies were locked together, he was gentle. His hands played softly over her breasts, outlined the soft curve of her waist, reached up to touch her face and her hair with great tenderness. Jamie felt cherished, enriched, beautiful. She drifted on a wide, warm sea of eroticism and fulfillment, moaning softly with pleasure, watching rainbow colors play against her closed eyelids and flow richly through her body.

Once more, the mood and tempo changed. He began to move her against him with more urgency, and his still face became intent and sharply drawn. Jamie responded, with a rising crescendo of feeling that surged through her, mounting on waves of ecstasy that were almost unbearable, beating with a relentless, irresistible rhythm. Finally, she lost sight of his face, of the room, of their surroundings, of everything but the fiery flower of delight that grew and exploded within her, leaving her limp and flooded with deep joy.

Then she was drifting, far away, off among distant realms where the air was warm and fragrant, and soft music rippled, and her face and body were touched by gentle celestial breezes.

She opened her eyes, confused and disoriented, and realized that she was still in the sun-room, lying on the table in Daniel's arms, and the fragrant breeze was just the flower-laden wind blowing through the patio windows.

She stared up at the skylight, shaken and weak with emotion, still unable to think clearly. All she knew for certain was that this sexual experience had been unlike anything she had ever known in her life. The intensity of pleasure and desire and the richness of fulfillment far surpassed anything in her past...even in her dreams....

Tentatively, she looked at Daniel's face, so close to her own. She studied the line of his arrogant nose and full lower lip, the surprising soft fullness of his dark eyelashes against his tanned cheek, the small creases raying out from the corners of his closed eyes. All at once, she was flooded with smiling tenderness, and a desire to touch his face, to stroke his cheeks and run her fingers over his mouth.

Just at that moment, he opened his eyes and looked directly into hers. His dark eyes were brilliant and piercing, and there was no answering tenderness in them, just a quiet, unreadable expression that chilled her.

Her smile faded, and she met his gaze in silence for a moment before turning away.

She bit her lip and sat up, reaching for her sunsuit. With trembling hands, she pulled it on, fastened the snaps, and stuffed her abandoned panties into one pocket. Then she turned back to him, avoiding his eyes.

"Daniel . . ." she began finally, in a small voice.

"Please," he interrupted. "Don't say anything. Just bring me my chair."

"But I want to—"

"Please, Jamie," he said wearily. "My chair."

Still confused and bewildered, she brought his chair to the table, set the brake, and watched as he swung himself down into the seat and covered up with the towel again. His expression was distant and shuttered. It was impossible to tell what he was feeling . . . anger or disappointment with her or disgust at his own behavior.

He wheeled the chair silently toward the door, then paused and turned with sudden abruptness to face her. Now she could see his eyes clearly, and she was startled to read the emotion in them. It was not anger but a deep, deep pain, a kind of hurt and betrayal that went far beyond words.

"Daniel," she whispered, staring at him. "What's the matter?"

"I suppose," he said with tense, distant politeness, "that I really should thank you. You're very kind, Jamie. That was a generous service, indeed, to perform for a crippled man.''

Jamie continued to stare at him, her face suddenly drained of color. His cold expression and the implication of his words were almost more than she could bear.

''But you don't understand!'' she said desperately. ''I didn't... It wasn't...''

''Goodbye, Jamie.''

He turned again, wheeling himself rapidly through the door and across the plant-filled pool deck.

Jamie watched him go, her mind whirling. She knew what he was suggesting... that her wanton, unexpected behavior had been motivated only by pity.

No wonder he had been so deeply hurt.

She longed to run after him, to assure him that he was wrong, that she had wanted him sexually for his own sake, that she had found the whole experience marvelously fulfilling and satisfying in every way.

But she resisted the impulse, forcing herself instead to go automatically about the task of tidying the sun-room, putting away her equipment, trying to still her racing heart and her confused, spinning mind.

Because, in spite of her instant denial, she knew that there was a possibility he was right. Maybe she *had* been motivated by pity. She'd mistaken pity for love in the past, after all, more than once. Maybe it was happening all over again with Daniel. And this time, she'd actually gone so far as to make love.

And, if so, it was a terrible, unforgivable way to treat him.

Stiff with misery, her face bleak and drawn, Jamie finished cleaning the room, crossed the pool deck silently and crept away through the luxurious house to hide herself in the seclusion of her own room.

CHAPTER EIGHT

JAMIE SPENT the rest of the morning in her room,
drowning in misery and self-loathing. She made a cur-
sory attempt to work on the cool-down portion of her new
routine, but it was impossible to concentrate.

She found herself caught up in a strange, troubling
conflict. Part of her longed to go and talk with Daniel, to
apologize and seek reassurance from him and restore their
relationship to its old comfortable footing. But another,
more urgent part wanted to avoid him forever, to write a
letter of resignation, pack her things and creep from the
house unseen.

Most disturbing of all was her panicky inability to understand her own actions. Her behavior that morning in
the sun-room seemed so totally out of character, as if
some other wanton, lustful woman had occupied Jamie's
body for a brief, crazy time. She was not usually forward
or aggressive sexually. In fact, physical commitment
meant so much to Jamie that she hesitated to let any relationship get too serious. It had been a long, long time
since she had been intimate with anyone.

And yet this morning, out of the blue...

Jamie slumped onto the floor beside her stereo and
buried her head in her arms, quivering with humiliation.
She wasn't certain why she had behaved with such wild
abandon. There was something about Daniel that set him
apart, even above, any man she'd ever met before. But

still, she was grimly afraid that it was her old, treacherously sympathetic nature, allowing her to be carried away with pity for an unfortunate man and drawing her into a position where she could be the strong one, the one to offer warmth and comfort and emotional support.

And worst of all, she knew that Daniel knew it, too.

Never again she thought bitterly. *I'm not getting into another of those miserable one-sided relationships, not for anything.*

She ventured down to the kitchen at noon, trying to compose herself and appear as if nothing had happened. Maria was there, seated at the big sewing machine in a corner alcove, stitching a collar onto a new housedress. Clara stood at the table, methodically peeling hard-boiled eggs and scooping out the yolks to make deviled eggs, while Hiro sat nearby, his sensitive brown fingers working over a lawn mower carburetor placed carefully on a pad of newspaper.

"Hi, everybody," Jamie said, taking a couple of eggs from Clara's bowl and sitting down to help peel them.

"Here," Clara said briskly, "don't do that, you'll just make a mess of them. If you want to help, take the spoon there and start mixing the yolks in with this."

She handed Jamie a bowl of mayonnaise and seasonings, and Jamie began obediently to mash the yolks into the savory mixture.

"What's the problem, Hiro?" she asked, looking over at the greasy metal parts beneath his hands.

"I'm not sure. The motor's not getting enough gas, and something must be plugged, but I can't find it."

"Damn!" Maria burst out suddenly, startling the others. "Sorry," she said, looking over her shoulder with a sheepish grin. "It's just that I can't get the tension right, and the lower thread keeps breaking. It makes me so *mad!*"

"I'll look at it later, when I've cleaned up," Hiro promised.

"Come on, both of you, get out of my way," Clara said gruffly. "I have to set the table for lunch."

Jamie looked at her watch, reluctant to leave the comfort and security of the kitchen.

"Well," she said hesitantly, getting to her feet and pushing her chair in, "I guess it's time for my noon hour session."

"He's not coming down," Clara said.

Jamie's heart began to pound, and her cheeks turned pink. "He isn't? Did he call you?"

Clara nodded. "About half an hour ago. He asked for a tray in his room, said to tell you he'd be working straight through lunch and wouldn't be down until late afternoon."

Jamie felt a flood of emotion compounded partly of relief and partly of dismay.

She reasoned desperately that Daniel's decision to forgo the noon hour session wasn't necessarily related to what had happened between them that morning. After all, he had done this a number of times in the past, gotten caught up in his work and called down to let Jamie know that he intended to skip the noon hour massage. Maybe this was just another of those times.

She ate lunch with the rest of the staff, forcing herself to join in their laughter and conversation. She was irrationally surprised that they couldn't tell what had happened, that it wasn't somehow branded on her face for all the world to see.

After lunch she was confronted by the endless afternoon that must somehow be survived before she spoke with Daniel again and learned what her fate was to be. She drove downtown and shopped aimlessly for new exercise leotards and program tapes, arriving back at the house in time to change for her four o'clock session. Then she wandered out toward the pool, wondering whether Daniel would come down at all and what he would say to her if he did.

Her pulse quickened and her mouth went dry when she approached the deck and saw that he was already in the pool, methodically swimming laps, his sleek dark head and powerful arms knifing silently through the sparkling water. Jamie sank into one of the deck chairs, watching him as he finished his last lap and rested, panting, at the edge of the pool. Then he hauled himself out onto the deck and pulled his long body up onto the steel bench beside his parked wheelchair, lifting himself deftly into the chair and toweling off his wet hair.

Finally he glanced up, saw Jamie and wheeled himself over to stop near her. She dropped her eyes and looked down at her hands, nervously twisting and pleating the fabric of the sweater in her lap while the silence lengthened between them.

At last, unable to bear it any longer, Jamie forced herself to speak. "Do you . . . Would you like me to resign?" she asked in a low voice.

"Resign?" Daniel echoed in genuine surprise. "Why would you do that?"

She glanced up at him and then dropped her eyes again quickly, unable to meet that piercing dark gaze.

"Because," she murmured, "what I did was . . . was very wrong. I mean, it was completely unprofessional. I'm a therapist, and you're my patient, and the relationship isn't supposed to . . ."

Her voice trailed off and she continued to stare down miserably at her hands.

"Come on, Jamie," he said brusquely. "After all, you just considered that particular little experience to be part of the therapy, didn't you? Let the poor guy know he can still function, and all that?"

"No!" she burst out, looking at him directly for the first time, her face pale and strained. "No, that wasn't the reason. At least, not consciously. I mean," she added in embarrassed confusion, "I don't even know why..."

"Please, Jamie," he said. "I think we *both* know why you did it, and it doesn't make me feel a hell of a lot better to dwell on it. The fact remains, I still have to share the responsibility for what happened. What I'm saying," he added with a tight mirthless smile, "is that I don't feel that I was raped. Now do you think, for both our sakes, that we can just put it out of our minds and pretend it never happened?"

Jamie stared at him, her eyes wide and startled, groping to understand what he was telling her.

"Oh, yes," she whispered at last. "Please, let's just forget all about it. I'm really sorry, and I promise—"

"All right," he said harshly, his face shadowed with pain. "No apologies, and no promises. We'll just forget it, okay? Call it a touch of summer madness, and put it completely behind us."

Jamie smiled hesitantly. "That would be...would be wonderful. Well," she added, forcing herself to get briskly to her feet, trying to sound casual and cheerful, "let's get on with this session, shall we? There are a lot of things going on this evening, and we're going to be busy."

"What's going on?" he asked, wheeling his chair across the deck toward the sun-room.

"Well, the others will be eating early," Jamie began, enumerating the items on her fingers, "because Clara's going out into the country to film sunset scenes. But we won't be eating till later, at Steven's end-of-the-year picnic at his school. We both promised him we'd go."

"Oh, hell," Daniel muttered darkly. "I'd successfully repressed that thought."

"Oh, come on," Jamie said. "It'll be fun. Clara already packed a big picnic basket."

She stood by the massage table, watching him heave himself out of the chair and swing his body up onto the leather surface, almost lightheaded with happiness and relief.

It was going to be all right, after all. They were going to write it off as a moment of temporary insanity and return to their former comfortable relationship. She felt so light and free and wonderful, and so immensely grateful to him for his tact and understanding.

They had one bad moment, though, when he bent automatically to strip off his wet swim trunks after covering himself with the towel. He leaned up on one elbow, wrestling the trunks down over his immobile hips, and Jamie bent instinctively to help him. Their eyes met involuntarily and she flushed to the roots of her hair, while his face darkened with hurt, and with some other emotion that was less easy to read.

She looked away awkwardly, waiting for him to finish removing the swimsuit by himself. Finally he lay back and closed his eyes, his face silent and withdrawn as she began the massage.

"And," she said desperately, trying to keep her voice light and casual, "this is a really big night for another reason, too. I can't believe you've forgotten."

"What's that?" he murmured, his eyes still closed.

"Maria's ready to go outside tonight. She's going to step outside the kitchen door, after they've finished dinner and before we leave for the picnic."

Daniel's eyes flickered open and he looked at Jamie with sudden interest. "You're right, I *had* forgotten." He was silent a moment. "Do you think she's really ready for that? Are we moving her along too fast?"

Jamie frowned, considering. "I don't know," she said finally. "I've read all the books and given it a lot of thought, and I'm still not sure. The problem," she went on, squeezing more mineral oil onto her hands and rubbing it into the lifeless skin of his thighs, "is that there's not really an intermediate step between inside and outside."

"But isn't that what we've been concentrating on all this time, intermediate steps? I mean, looking out the window, standing by an open door, all that?"

"I know," Jamie said. "But that doesn't change the fact that it's still a huge, massive step to actually *go* outside. All those things help to bridge the gap, but they can't minimize the trauma of being out in the open air for the first time in years. It must be terrifying."

"Especially," Daniel said thoughtfully, "for someone whose worst fears are all centered around open spaces."

They were both silent for a moment, thinking about Maria.

"Does she still want us all to be there?" Daniel asked.

"Not necessarily *all* of us. But she feels it's important for you to be there. She doesn't think she can do it without you."

"That surprises me," Daniel said. "I mean, she's been here for years, but we've hardly exchanged more than a few words. She always seems terrified of me, for some reason."

"That's just it," Jamie said. "She's so in awe of you, and since you know about this therapy and are actually helping with it, Maria feels it would be more effective for her this first time if you're there. She's certain that she'll do better if you're watching her, because she'd be so humiliated to have you witness her failure."

"The poor girl. I hope she doesn't fail." He looked up at Jamie. "Any more word about the boyfriend? This young grocer she likes?"

Jamie shook her head. "She doesn't like to talk about him. I think it...it means an awful lot to her, you know?" she said softly.

He nodded, his eyes still thoughtful, while Jamie continued to work over his legs in silence and the warm afternoon sunlight fell in long golden bands across the floor and walls of their room.

MARIA STOOD BY the kitchen entry, clutching the door frame with desperate concentration and shrinking back in terror from the yawning opening. Not long ago, she wouldn't have been able to stand in the doorway like this at all, but Jamie's patient supervision had carried her along faster than she would have believed possible.

She stared fearfully at the waving branches and the patch of green lawn framed by the open door. The evening was mellow and lovely, with that rare, rich twilight softness that only comes in the early summer. It was a gentle, romantic, nostalgic time, and it made Maria feel suddenly wistful, full of deep nameless yearnings.

She closed her eyes and thought of Tony, of his gentle honest smile, his dark eyes and generous mouth and the dimple right in the centre of his chin, and the way a lock of curly black hair always fell down across his forehead.

All at once a dark, heavy wave of loneliness and longing swept over her, making her sway a little on her feet, leaving her feeling sad and empty. She opened her eyes, her face tense with determination, and looked out the open door once again.

They were all there, just outside the door on the edge of the drive, waiting for her in patient silence. She could see Jamie, whose warm golden features were soft with compassion and encouragement, and Steven, who held Jamie's hand and smiled eagerly, his dark eyes glowing. Even Hiro lent his support by working casually along the border nearby, trimming the hedge with his big hand shears, tactfully pretending that nothing unusual was going on.

But what Maria found most overwhelming was the presence of Mr. Kelleher himself, sitting quietly in his chair beside Steven and watching her with concern. His thick dark hair lifted softly in the evening breeze, and his fine arrogant features, usually so terrifying to Maria, showed nothing but kindness and warmth. She could never remember a time when Mr. Kelleher had taken such a direct interest in her. Maria was dizzied by the sense of family that wrapped around her, the warmth and caring and kindness that all these people were displaying. She couldn't bear to disappoint them, but it was so dreadfully hard.

She hesitated in the doorway, trying frantically to find the courage to step outside toward them, and wondered if they had any idea what it was like for her. How could they know her shivering terror of the wide unsheltered spaces, of the ominous shadows and lurking dangers in the massed shrubbery, of the treacherous open air that carried so many whispered threats?

Her throat constricted with the familiar clutching fear that had tormented her for years.

At first, in the early years, Maria had just begun to find it more and more scary to go downtown or out to social occasions. It had grown increasingly easy to stay at home, ordering things she needed through the catalogue and having her sisters and her friends come here to visit. But as the time passed, even the yard had become a terrifying place, full of hidden dangers. Because she never went out or paid return visits, people gradually stopped coming to see her. Her sisters moved away, and her friends got married, had babies and forgot about her. Eventually it was impossible even to step outside the door, and Maria became a lonely prisoner of her own fears.

But now they all waited outside, urging her to break her self-imposed bonds and take her first real step to freedom.

She moaned softly under her breath so they wouldn't hear. Her heart was thundering in her chest and her hands were clammy. Cold perspiration trickled down her body inside her dress, making her feel chilled and nauseated. Noises throbbed and hammered inside her head, where her terrors beat like dark hideous wings against the walls of her mind.

She looked out at the menacing stillness beyond the open door, and she knew she couldn't do it.

There was no way in the all the world that Maria could ever find the courage to step outside that door. Not for personal dignity, not for freedom and independence, not even for Tony.

She whimpered softly, wishing that she was dead. She wished she could just run and hide deep in the warm safety of her own room, where all the dangers were held at bay and muffled behind thick draperies. She wanted to climb into her bed, put her head under the pillows, and never, never again have to face the thought of going outside.

But Jamie was there, waiting. Jamie was so sweet and loving and good to her. Her friends Steven and Hiro were watching, too, urging her on, expecting her to succeed.

Most important, Mr. Kelleher was there.

A man like him, so rich and famous, so powerful and brilliant, was taking the time to watch her, Maria Santari, step out of a kitchen door onto a driveway. And the most incredible, bewildering thing, the thing that kept Maria standing in the doorway trembling with fear when she wanted only to run and hide, was the secret that Jamie had told her. Jamie had said that this man, almost godlike in Maria's eyes, had fears like her own. Jamie had said that if Maria was brave and overcame her fears, she might help Mr. Kelleher.

She drew an agonized breath, held the doorframe so tightly that her knuckles showed white as bone in her pale hands, and she took a tiny awkward step toward the opening.

Another step.

Maria sobbed in anguish as she felt the evening breeze play languidly over her face, and smelled the bewildering, dimly remembered scents of greenery and flowers. She hesitated, put her hand to her mouth to stifle her cry of terror and lifted her foot again.

One more step.

Now she was all the way through the door and her foot encountered the unfamiliar harshness of the concrete sidewalk. Waves of fear beat over her, threatening to drown her. She couldn't breathe. She felt herself choking and suffocating. The twilight air was cool and sinister on her face and her closed eyelids. She swayed, feeling sick and faint.

Then Jamie was beside her, hugging her, laughing aloud, heaping praise on her.

"Maria, you did it! You're terrific! You're so brave, Maria."

She felt a small, warm hand press into hers and knew that Steven was there, leaning against her in vibrant happiness.

"Well done, Maria," a deep voice said nearby. "Nobody will ever know how much courage that took."

She opened her eyes and looked down into Mr. Kelleher's quiet, tanned face and his dark eyes, warm and smiling with approval. Maria swallowed hard, feeling the warm salty tears begin to trickle down her cheeks. Jamie took a tissue from the pocket of her cardigan and tenderly wiped the tears away, whispering more words of praise.

"Can you stand it for a little while longer, Maria?" Jamie murmured.

Maria gulped and nodded, looking with a fearful wondering gaze at the unfamiliar world around her.

"Just...just a few more seconds, okay?" she whispered, holding tightly to Jamie's hand. "Tell me...tell me when it's been a whole minute."

"Thirty-five more seconds," Jamie said, consulting her watch.

Maria nodded again, feeling numb, while Steven continued to press against her on one side and Jamie's strong arm encircled her on the other.

Thirty-five seconds. It seemed like an eternity.

She looked timidly out at the trees swaying softly above the expanse of lawn, at the curving drive disappearing into the depths of shrubbery, at the tall fragrant masses of pe-

onies in the flower beds and the rich cascade of lilac near
the sun-room windows. Hiro was watching her, and he
smiled his gentle glowing smile, making her feel like crying again.

Mr. Kelleher, too, watched her quietly, and his dark
gaze was the only thing that kept Maria from bolting for
safety.

She knew, with weary resignation, that this was not the
end of the battle. In fact, it was just the beginning. Soon
she would have to stay outside for a longer time, even
learn to go out and sit on the lawn, far from the safety of
the house. And then later she would have to do it all
alone, without anyone nearby to give her support.

Her breath shortened and her mouth went dry with
terror, just thinking about it. Resolutely, she pushed the
menacing images from her mind. A step at a time, Jamie
always said. Just one step, leading to another. Two weeks
ago, she could hardly bear to be near an open window.
Now she was standing on the drive. If she took it a step at
a time, she could do it.

"I can do it," she aloud in a trembling voice. Her
glance fell on Mr. Kelleher, who nodded silently in agreement. Maria looked at him, startled, recognizing the expression on his face as one of admiration. She stood
quietly, stunned with amazement.

Mr. Kelleher *admired* her! He thought she was brave!

"Okay, kid," Jamie murmured. "Time's up."

Maria turned and hurried gratefully back toward the
open kitchen door, still savoring a warm, wondering glow
of happiness.

She had done it. She had actually gone outside and
stayed there for a full minute. And Hiro and Steven had
been happy for her, and Jamie had praised her, and Mr.
Kelleher had looked at her with admiration.

Maria felt wonderful. The terrifying reality of the experience still drained and sickened her, but over it all she felt a warm glimmer of triumph, a sense of courage and invincibility that was new and rich and satisfying.

She sighed with pleasure in the safety of the kitchen and smiled hesitantly at Jamie, unaware of the tears that streamed down her face.

"Are you going to be all right?" Jamie asked with concern, looking at Maria's tense, radiant, tear-streaked face. "Do you mind us leaving you alone now?"

Maria shook her head, wiping her eyes and blowing her nose, then smiled awkwardly. "Sorry for being such a baby," she said. "It's just... Jamie, I'm so happy. You can't imagine how happy I am. Jamie, thank you."

"Oh, come on. Why are you thanking me? You're the one who did all the hard things. You're doing this for yourself, Maria, and you deserve all the credit in the world."

Maria nodded. "I just feel so happy," she repeated. She looked over at Jamie and then reached for a piece of her fabric draped on the sewing machine. "Go on," she said shakily. "You'll be late for the picnic."

Jamie stood by the window, watching as Hiro backed the Lincoln from the garage, helped Daniel into the driver's seat and then folded the chair to tuck it away in the trunk. Steven danced with excitement on the drive until Daniel smiled at him and leaned out the window to say something. Obediently, Steven hopped into the back seat and they both looked at the house, waiting.

"This is nice for Steven," Maria said gently. "He's so happy that you're both going with him."

Jamie smiled. "His father wasn't too pleased with the idea, but he knows it's important to Steven." She glanced at Maria with concern. "Maria, are you absolutely certain that—"

"Go!" Maria said with a mischievous grin. "Jamie, I'm never scared to be *inside* the house."

Jamie grinned back. "I guess not. Okay, we'll go, but Hiro will be here, and we'll be back in just a couple of hours. Maria," she added impulsively, "I really mean it. I think you're just wonderful."

She bent to give the smaller woman another warm hug, grabbed the big picnic hamper and ran out the door and down the drive to the waiting car.

Maria walked over to the window, marveling at how easy and natural it now seemed to look outside, when even this simple action had so recently been impossible for her.

She watched while Jamie folded her long body gracefully into the passenger seat and turned to exchange some laughing remark with Steven in the back while Daniel slid the big car into gear and rolled off out of sight down the curving drive.

Finally alone with her thoughts, Maria moved back across the room toward the sewing machine and frowned at the piece of fabric. But her face glowed with joy, and her thoughts were not on the work in her hands. They were far away, across town, in a supermarket where she could see a dark-haired man working quietly, his kind thoughtful face as dear and familiar to her as if she had been with him only yesterday.

DANIEL SAT in his wheelchair under a spreading poplar tree on the school grounds. People were all around— shouting, tumbling children and cheerfully harried parents sat on blankets and lawn chairs while they exchanged gossip, laughter and food. Daniel kept himself aloof, responding in curt monosyllables when spoken to, and his neighbors looked at him with fear and respect, knowing his reputation for enormous wealth and his reclusive tendencies.

They would have been surprised to know his thoughts as he sat quietly in the dappled shade of the school yard. Daniel was watching the kids-and-ladies' three-legged race, in which Jamie and Steven were entered, and his mind was in turmoil.

Nothing else existed for him in all that varied, busy, colorful scene...all he could see was Jamie. He looked at her tall, lithe body as she stood at the starting line of the race, laughing with joyous excitement, her wild red hair gleaming like fire in the slanting evening light. She had an arm laid affectionately around Steven's shoulders, and she was teasing and talking with the other women around her, making jokes as the scarves were tied around their legs, tethering each of them to a wriggling child.

She blazed like the sun in Daniel's world, lighting his universe with fiery brilliance. He yearned for her, hungered for her, longed to feel her touch and draw her close to him again.

His grim mouth curved upward in an involuntary smile as the race began and the clumsy three-legged teams surged forward across the grass. Many of the young mothers were plump and short of breath, some of them falling immediately with their children into an awkward tumble of arms and legs and laughter. But Jamie and Steven were different. Steven had a natural athleticism inherited from his father, and Jamie's tall splendid body was designed for physical competition. She and Steven immediately adopted a swinging stride that carried them forward with amazing speed while the onlookers roared their approval.

Daniel watched, his eyes delighting in her, in the rich, shapely curves of her long body in soft faded blue jeans and T-shirt, in her vivid buoyant energy and her brilliant rebellious head of hair. She and Steven crossed the finish line far ahead of the others and were carried off in the midst of a laughing crowd to the refreshment tent to receive their prize.

As soon as they were out of sight, Daniel slumped in weary dejection, his mind flooding once again with sadness.

He had told Jamie that they would forget about the incident of the morning, and she had agreed with evident relief. But how could he forget it, when the sight and feel and taste of her were branded so indelibly on his memory? How could he keep himself from recalling the rich taut lines of her wonderful body, the delightful warm spontaneity of her response, the glorious happiness that had flooded him when they were joined by their pounding desire?

He had to forget it. He had promised, and it wasn't fair to her to break that promise. Because Daniel knew that she shared none of his feelings. She had admitted through her own silence that the incident that morning had been motivated by pity, and he couldn't bear the idea that she should feel pity for him. He remembered her rejected boyfriend, Chad, with his handsome body and his powerful athletic grace, saying bitterly that Jamie couldn't resist a loser.

Daniel scowled, and shifted awkwardly in his wheelchair.

The unfairness of life was almost overwhelming, so brutally painful that he couldn't bear to contemplate it. He had never felt this warmth of love and desire for his vain and shallow wife... had not even known he was capable of such feelings.

And now, of all times in his life, he had found the woman of his dreams, the woman he needed and wanted and hungered for, only to realize that in her eyes he could never be anything but a damaged excuse for a man, someone to be pitied.

With dispassionate objectivity, Daniel remembered himself as he had been before his accident. Then, he had been tall and swift-moving, immensely strong. Women in those days didn't find his body something to inspire sympathy or revulsion.

If only, he thought desperately, he could have found Jamie then, while he was still able to stand on his own two feet and woo her properly, to give her the kind of love and physical fulfillment that she deserved.

But those thoughts were futile. The past was gone, and the present reality could never be changed. He was doomed to live forever with this poor damaged hulk of a body, these useless legs that kept him trapped, unable to travel or do his own research, unable to offer anything to the woman he yearned for.

His gloomy thoughts were interrupted by the arrival of Jamie and Steven, both of them bubbling with fun and triumph.

"We won!" Steven announced, leaning against the arm of his father's chair, his dark eyes glowing. "We beat everybody!"

Daniel looked down at his son, stabbed by the look of shining joy in the little boy's face. "You certainly did," he said, forcing his voice to sound cheerful. "You just blew them away."

He looked up at Jamie, who smiled back at him anxiously.

"Are you all right?" she asked. "Not too cool, here in the shade?"

Daniel waved his hand impatiently, irritated by the implication that he needed special treatment. "I'm fine. What was the prize?"

"Chocolate sundaes," Steven said blissfully. "With nuts on. I ate mine, but Jamie gave hers away to Matthew. He was crying 'cause they came in second."

"Typical," Daniel said dryly. "Jamie has great sympathy for losers."

He saw the sudden flood of color that mounted her cheeks, and the pain in her eyes, and instantly regretted his words.

"Well, I didn't have a sundae, and I'm getting hungry," he said with forced heartiness. "Shall we see what Clara packed in that basket?"

Happily, Steven hauled the basket out into the middle of their blanket and burrowed inside it. Jamie sat cross-legged beside the small boy, carefully filling plastic mugs with coffee from the thermos and passing one up to Daniel in his chair.

He looked down at her as she sat below him spreading out their food, enjoying the way damp tendrils of hair curled against her warm cheeks and forehead. She chatted easily with Steven and his friends while Daniel listened in silence, looking out at the bustle of activity across the grounds.

Eventually Steven became involved in complex negotiations that involved trading a number of Clara's deviled eggs and two pieces of fried chicken for some cupcakes from another picnic basket, and went off with a friend to conclude the deal. Daniel and Jamie were left alone, sipping the last of their coffee in the fading light and gazing up at the glowing bands of pastel colors that illuminated the western horizon.

"This is lovely, isn't it?" Jamie said with a blissful sigh, stretching languidly on the blanket. "I just love picnics."

In spite of himself, Daniel smiled at her childlike enjoyment. "*You're* certainly an easy girl to please," he observed. "Not very elegant tastes at all."

Jamie rolled onto her back, resting her head on her folded arms, and looked up at him with a small teasing grimace. "Oh, sure," she said. "Make fun of me, just because I'm not a world traveler like you, all cosmopolitan and sophisticated."

"I'm not a world traveler, Jamie," he said quietly. "Not anymore."

"Well, you used to be," she said. "And I'm sure that you will be again."

Silence fell abruptly between them. Jamie got up, her face shadowed, and began to pack the remains of their lunch back into the picnic basket while Daniel sat in brooding silence, gazing at the glorious sunset that arched above them, flooding the world with radiance.

CHAPTER NINE

KEVIN SAT BESIDE JAMIE in the front seat of her old Volkswagen, gripping a bright new Mickey Mouse backpack in his small hands. He gazed silently out the window at the yards and houses flowing past, tense and breathless with excitement. Unlike his older sister and brother, Kevin never got noisy when he was excited. Instead, he grew intensely quiet, his small face pale, his blue eyes dark and brilliant.

Jamie glanced over at his taut body in clean jeans and T-shirt, and his black hair, still damp and slick from Terry's comb.

"You're awfully quiet," she said cheerfully.

He turned to gaze at her, his blue eyes wide with appeal. "Aunt Jamie, what if Steven doesn't like me?"

"He'll like you." Jamie frowned briefly, easing past a stalled van at an intersection. "He's really excited about you coming. He can hardly wait."

"But what about the man? Steven's daddy? What if he gets mad?"

"Well," Jamie said thoughtfully, frowning above the steering wheel, "that's another story. We do have to be careful about that."

She thought about Daniel and about their strange, uneasy relationship since that fateful morning in the sunroom. They had agreed to forget the encounter, to carry on as if nothing had happened, and at first, they had even seemed to be successful. But Jamie was beginning to realize that the situation was much more complicated than it appeared. She didn't seem capable of forgetting the sensation of lying in his arms, stunned and shaken with passion, and sometimes she was afraid that her thoughts and feelings showed on her face.

She wondered often if he remembered, too. Was that morning branded on his mind the way it was on hers? Was that the explanation for the moments of strain and awkwardness that fell suddenly between them from time to time.

"Does he know I'm coming to play with Steven?" Kevin asked, interrupting her thoughts.

"Oh, goodness, no!" Jamie said hastily. "If we *asked* him to let you come and visit, he'd just say no, so we didn't ask. We thought that if you came this first time and you and Steven had fun together and stayed out of his way so he could see that it won't be any bother to him, then he wouldn't mind letting you come back."

Kevin nodded solemnly, his face so pale that the dusting of freckles stood out sharply on his cheekbones.

"So what you have to do," Jamie went on earnestly, "is play very quietly and don't make any kind of noise or mess. Just show him how good two little boys can be. Here we are," she added, turning up the winding drive and stopping in front of the huge garage.

Kevin looked around in awe at the spacious silent house and grounds. "It looks like a castle or something," he said.

"Well, it isn't. It's just a house where people live."

"Where's Steven's room?" the little boy asked, peering out at the banks of windows.

"You can't see his room from here. It's on the other side, like mine."

Jamie glanced in concern at her nephew's terrified face and his small hands, spasmodically gripping the little backpack.

"Hey, Kevin, push this button and see what happens," she said.

He peered at the remote control in her hand. "This one?" he asked, glancing up at her nervously.

Jamie nodded.

Tentatively, he extended a small forefinger and pushed the button, then watched in amazement as the garage door rolled silently upward.

"Wow," he breathed, his eyes shining. "Can we close it and do it again?"

"Better not," Jamie said with a grin. "Steven's daddy might be watching at the window, and he'll get suspicious if he sees the garage door whipping up and down, won't he, now?"

Kevin nodded solemnly, still hushed with awe.

Jamie parked the car, scooped Kevin out of the passenger seat and slipped through the side door and into the house, gripping him tightly by the hand.

In the big kitchen, Maria looked up from the table where she sat sipping coffee with Clara and smiled at them warmly.

"Hello, Kevin," she said in her soft, sweet voice. "It's nice to meet you at last. We've heard so much about you."

Kevin smiled shyly, warmed by the gentleness of her tone. Clara, meanwhile, examined him intently, and he returned her gaze with the calm steady curiosity of childhood.

"Are you a good little boy?" Clara asked abruptly.

Kevin nodded. "Yes," he said. "My mother says that if my brother and sister were as good as me, her life would be lots easier."

Clara glanced at him sharply, and then, seeing the quiet earnestness of his face, she laughed a sudden sharp bark of amusement that was alarming in its unexpectedness.

"Well, I just hope you know what you're doing," she said, turning to Jamie.

"So do I," Jamie said fervently. "So do I, Clara. I suppose he's decided to work all day today, and he's buried behind his computer already," she added gloomily.

Clara nodded. "Even worse. I took him a tray for breakfast. He's been working most of the night, and he looks like death, but he says he's going to work straight through till he's finished, and the house is to be kept absolutely quiet."

"Oh, great," Jamie muttered. "Just great. Well," she added, drawing herself together and forcing a smile, "we're not going to be any bother to him, are we? These boys are just going to play outside and be as quiet as little mice. Right, Kevin?"

Kevin nodded again, munching in wide-eyed pleasure on a huge chocolate chip cookie that Maria handed him.

"Where's Steven now?" Jamie asked, helping herself to a cookie.

"He's already out in the yard, waiting," Maria said. "Hiro helped him carry his dolls and doll house out there, and almost every other toy he owns, so he'd be ready when Kevin came."

Jamie smiled fondly and took Kevin's hand. "Okay," she said. "Let's go."

Kevin trotted beside her through the house, looking around him in stunned amazement. "They have a *swimming pool*," he breathed. "Right inside their house. And a *forest*," he added.

Jamie chuckled. "Shh," she whispered. "Don't talk out loud, sweetie. Wait till we get outside."

They emerged through the door by the pool that opened onto the patio, and crept silently over the flagstones and into the grassy expanse of the yard. Knowing Steven's habits and hiding places, Jamie made her way rapidly across the rich sea of emerald green to a small sheltered glade amid a stand of graceful birch trees.

Steven was there, kneeling on the grass, busily arranging his doll family on a picnic blanket in front of their house. He was unaware of their approach, and Jamie looked at him for a moment, moved almost unbearably by his thin jutting shoulder blades under the soft fabric of his shirt and the fragile look of his small body.

"Hi, Steven," she said finally. "Look who's here."

The little boy leaped to his feet, his eyes lighting with joy as he caught sight of Kevin, who stood clinging shyly to Jamie's hand.

"Hi, Kevin," he said.

"Hi," Kevin said briefly, and then hesitated. "Can you swim in the pool any time you want to?" he asked with childlike directness.

Steven nodded. "As long as my daddy or Jamie or somebody's there."

"You're lucky," Kevin said.

"I think *you're* lucky," Steven said with surprising tact. "Jamie says you have brothers and sisters who live right in the same house, so you always have somebody to play with."

Kevin considered this, thinking about his older brother and sister. "You can have them," he said grimly, "if you want them."

Jamie chuckled. "Look, you two," she said, "are you going to be all right out here? Because if you are, I'll leave you alone to play. Hiro's got the lawn tractor downtown being serviced, and Clara's taken off for the day, and

Maria and I are going to be around the other side working in the garden. If you need anything, just . . ."

"We'll be fine," Steven assured her comfortably, smiling at the smaller boy. "We've got everything we need."

Jamie hesitated. "And you'll be very, very quiet?" she asked anxiously. "You won't go into the house or up to your room or anything, Steven? Because your father is . . ."

"I know. He's working, and he's really grumpy today. We'll be quiet," he assured Jamie. "We won't even go near the house."

Jamie hesitated a moment longer, watching as the two little boys squatted in front of the doll house while Steven introduced the members of the plump cloth family.

"And this is the baby. . . ."

Kevin examined the dolls with interest. Younger and much gentler than his rowdy siblings, Kevin would have loved a doll to play with, but he was also wise enough to know that he would be teased to death if his parents ever bought him one.

"What's his name?" he asked, touching the cloth baby doll with his gentle small hand.

"Her. The baby's a girl. Her name is Alexandra."

"Our baby's a boy," Kevin said. "His name's Dougie."

"Is he a *real* baby?" Steven asked, fascinated. "Does he cry and wet his diaper and all that?"

"All the time," Kevin said briefly.

Jamie grinned again, and swallowed a sudden lump in her throat as the two boys began, with the instantaneous understanding of children, to dress the doll family for an outing.

"Well, I guess I'll get back and start helping Maria," she said. "Come around and get us if you need anything."

Already deeply absorbed, they nodded amiably, barely noticing her departure. Jamie turned and started back across the lawn with her long lithe stride, feeling all at once deeply happy, and as light as air.

DANIEL RAN a distracted hand through his rumpled hair and frowned at the screen of his computer, then turned aside to leaf impatiently through a thick leather binder of notes and information.

"It's *got* to be here," he muttered aloud. "I remember reading the data on the Austrian parliament in here just the other day."

Once again, he cursed the necessity to employ a research staff and have his facts gathered and compiled by others. In the old days, when he was still a whole man, he had done all his own research, organized his own data, arranged it in logical sequence so he could find anything at a moment's notice. In those days, writing had been a joy, not a chore, because a study of his research notes would recall the places he had traveled and the experiences he had enjoyed while he was gathering his information.

Wearily, he rubbed at his red-rimmed eyes and leaned back in the depths of his wheelchair, stretching and flexing his tired back muscles. He longed suddenly for a massage and thought wistfully of ringing to see if Jamie was available. Then he remembered that it was Saturday, and paused, slumped with disappointment.

Instead he buzzed the kitchen, hoping to find somebody who would bring him a cup of hot coffee. But there was no response. Absently, he recalled seeing a good deal of coming and going that morning, of vehicles leaving the big garage, and supposed that the household was busy with weekend activities.

Even Maria was busy these days. She was able to go outside now, and she forced herself to spend a good deal of time in the yard and garden, though always in the company of another member of the household.

That *was* one disadvantage of Maria's recovery program, Daniel thought with a flicker of wry amusement. At least, in the old days, he could always be sure of finding someone in the kitchen.

He flipped restlessly through the notebook again. Finally he closed it in disgust and turned aside, wheeling his chair from behind his desk and across the room to the big window. He reached out a lean brown hand to draw the heavy drapes and then positioned himself where he could look down into the grounds below.

The summer day was rich and golden, already drowsy with the approaching heat of midday. But the lawns and shrubbery, lovingly tended by Hiro, were cool and green, full of inviting depths and shady glades. Daniel gazed wistfully downward, wondering what Jamie was doing this morning. He thought how delightful it would be to find her, to surprise her and take her hand and stroll with her into one of those leafy sheltered glades and then, in those green private depths, fold her into his arms and cover her face with kisses.

His body ached with painful yearning, and he scowled, angered by his wayward thoughts. He was dreaming like a schoolboy, he thought. And worse, whenever he indulged in these fantasies, they involved an image of himself as a whole man walking beside her, standing taller than her, quick and strong and athletic. In his dreams he was never a battered wreck of a man trundling along at her side in a wheelchair.

Daniel was flooded all at once with a desperate sadness that darkened the world and threatened to engulf his soul.

He sat for a moment in weary silence, his head bowed. Then with characteristic self-discipline, he set his jaw and turned away from the window, preparing to move back behind his desk and bury himself in his work.

But just as he began to wheel himself into position at his computer screen, he was startled by a burst of noise that chilled him with sudden fear.

Hastily he swung the chair back around and opened the casement window. The noise filled his quiet study, screams of sheer animal terror that obviously issued from the mouth of a child.

Daniel thought of Steven, playing all alone down in the yard, and his face paled beneath its tan. Recklessly he propelled his chair across the room, out into the hallway, and down to his elevator.

He hurtled across the silent rooms on the lower floor, heading in the direction of the terrified screams, looking frantically around for help. But there was nobody at all in the vast silent house that lay still and shaded against the summer heat.

Daniel wheeled himself through the patio doors, barely pausing to think, and started across the lawn toward his son. The surface was rough and uneven in patches near the shrubbery, and his chair bounced precariously because of his speed. And all the time he shivered at the sound of those frantic screams.

By now the cries of panic were so loud that it seemed impossible for one small boy to be making such an uproar. Daniel wheeled himself into a little glade of birch trees, cursing angrily as he tried to find a path between the trunks wide enough to accommodate the wheels of his chair.

Finally, sweating and panting with effort, he wrenched himself into the opening that, he saw at a glance, was filled with Steven's familiar toys neatly set out on the grass.

And then, with a chill of horror, he saw his son.

Steven was hanging from the middle branches of one of the birch trees about ten feet off the ground. A rope was tied around his midsection, but was slipping relentlessly upward, digging in beneath the little boy's armpits, holding him tightly as he swayed upright above the grass below. His eyes were squeezed shut in terror and his mouth was open, his face red with exertion as he bellowed in fear and panic.

The whole scene seemed to be happening in stereo. Suddenly Daniel saw why. A second little boy was also dangling amongst the branches, even higher up. Daniel gazed up at him, startled, and took the situation in at a glance.

They had one rope that they had tied around both their bodies, one at each end. Obviously they had been climbing the tree and one boy had slipped, pulling the other from his perch as well. The rope, Daniel could see, had lodged tightly into a crook in a branch, holding them both suspended, one above the other, like a pair of clock weights.

He swallowed a brief hysterical chuckle and sobered instantly. At first glance their predicament looked amusing, but Daniel could see that there was nothing funny about this. It would take only one abrupt movement on the part of either little boy to dislodge both of them, and send them hurtling through the rough branches and down to the ground with crushing force.

The thing to do, he realized, was to hold Steven's body, since he was the lowest, and ease him downward, drawing the other child, whoever he was, gently upward so he could grasp the branch above him and cling to it until he could be rescued as well.

I'll need a ladder, he thought quickly, running his mind over the situation. *And I'll need to find some way to brace myself so I can balance Steven while I help the other boy up into—*

Then, with dreadful, shattering desolation, he remembered that there was nothing at all he could do. He was alone here, and the boys were both beyond his reach. He couldn't do a thing to help his son. If either boy moved abruptly, or if the rope gave way or one of their clumsy knots opened, he could only sit and watch in utter helplessness as his son fell.

A darkness closed over him, deep drowning waves of frustrated rage at the fate that had done this to him, rendered him so useless to the people he loved. He beat on the arm of his chair, shouting aloud for help, adding his voice to the noisy clamor of the frightened children.

Jamie and Maria burst suddenly into the clearing, their faces pale with alarm.

"Daniel!" Jamie shouted. "What is it? We heard—"

She followed the direction of his gaze and stopped short, her hand to her mouth, her eyes wide with horror.

"Oh, God," she whispered, staring up at the hanging, gently swinging bodies of the two little boys. "Oh, my God. Are they . . . are they all right?"

"They appear to be," Daniel said dryly, trying to hide the grim intensity of the emotions that he was suffering. "They're certainly making a healthy amount of noise."

"Maria . . ." Jamie began. But when she turned, the smaller woman was already gone, running back across the lawn toward the garage.

"I'm getting the ladder!" Maria shouted over her shoulder without breaking stride.

Jamie nodded briefly and moved over to stand beneath the tree, bracing herself to catch either little body if one of them slipped before Maria could get there with the ladder.

Daniel sat with his hands resting on the arms of his chair and watched her, his dark face quiet and tense with fear.

Soon Maria panted back across the lawn, dragging the aluminum stepladder, and Jamie took it from her gratefully and positioned it beneath Steven's body. She climbed up and braced herself at the top, her bare brown legs flexing with muscles, her strong upper body in its skimpy tank top, firm and knotted with tension.

"Steven," Jamie said gently, "stop yelling and listen to me. Can you hear me?"

The little boy suspended his shouts of panic, hiccuped, and opened his eyes cautiously, peering down at Jamie as she stood just beneath him gripping him around the waist.

"Can you hear me?" Jamie repeated.

He gulped and nodded.

"All right," Jamie said. "Now, listen to me. I can't untie you right away, or Kevin will fall. What I have to do is pull you down so you can stand on the very top of the ladder. Then I'll untie you and lower Kevin to the ground. Okay?"

He nodded, a little calmed by her practical, matter-of-fact tone. Firmly, Jamie gripped him and tugged on the rope, drawing him down toward the upper step of the ladder while Kevin's small body rose upward into the branches. Finally, she had Steven in position and was holding tightly to the rope to keep the other child's body weight from pulling him aloft once more.

"You'll have to be careful untying him," Daniel said quietly below her. "If you get him loose and then lose your grip on the rope, even for second, the other kid will fall.''

Jamie nodded tightly, examining the knots and pondering. But, before she could decide how to approach her task, Maria had climbed the ladder beside her, negotiating the steep rungs with surprising agility, and was wedged beside her at the top.

"You hold the rope tight," Maria said calmly, "while I untie Steven."

Jamie nodded gratefully, and braced herself to throw all her weight on the rope that balanced Kevin's little body while Maria tugged at the bulky knots around Steven's thin chest.

"All right," Maria panted. "It's going to be loose in a minute. Ready, Jamie?"

"Ready," Jamie muttered. "Hold him, Maria, and be ready to help him down. He's going to be really shaky."

Jamie grasped the rope and leaned out away from the ladder, still bracing herself against the trunk of the tree and watching as Maria freed the quivering, sobbing little boy, gathered him in, and half-carried him down the ladder. Only when they were safely on the ground did Jamie begin, with great care, to play out the free end of her rope and lower Kevin gently to the grass.

When he finally dropped onto the green surface, Jamie leaped down from the ladder and gathered her small nephew up into her arms, murmuring and cuddling him, kissing his hot, tear-streaked cheeks.

At last his sobbing subsided and he rested in her arms, burrowing against her breast, his small hands still gripping her with painful strength. Jamie felt Daniel's eyes resting on her and looked up. Steven was in his father's lap, also sobbing and burrowing, and Daniel stroked the boy's dark head as he looked over at Jamie thoughtfully.

"I take it," he said finally, "that you are acquainted with that child?"

"Yes...yes I am," Jamie faltered. "He's my brother's little boy. His name's Kevin. I'll...I'll take him home, now, I think..."

Unable to endure Daniel's quiet scrutiny any longer, she suited actions to words and got to her feet, still holding the trembling child in her arms. Silently, Maria moved over beside her, carrying Kevin's Mickey Mouse backpack, and they started off across the green sweep of lawn in the direction of the garage. Daniel held his son's small shivering body and watched them go, his face silent and cold in the dappled noonday light.

JAMIE SAT IN Daniel's office, looking at him across the polished oak expanse of his desk. It was early evening, and the cool bands of shadow fell long and muted in the dim stillness of the room. Jamie got up abruptly to switch on the overhead light, then sat again and faced her employer with a touch of defiance.

"What I can't forget," Daniel was saying calmly, "is the fact that you disobeyed a direct order, Jamie, without bothering to tell me or ask my permission."

"We knew that you'd just refuse if we asked permission," Jamie said, avoiding his eyes. "We thought...we thought that if Kevin came, and the two of them had a good time, and you could see that he was no problem, you might be more likely to agree to a visit in the future."

A brief, mirthless smile flickered across Daniel's powerful sculpted features.

"And do you really expect me to feel, at this point, that your nephew was 'no problem,' as you put it?"

Jamie flushed. "Daniel, they're just little boys. They were playing. It was an accident. It wasn't...I mean, Kevin didn't do it on purpose, or anything, you know."

She glanced up at him, but it was impossible to read his expression. He sat looking down at the surface of his desk, his strong brown fingers riffling through an untidy pile of computer printouts. Despite her unhappiness and concern, Jamie was still moved by the line of his tanned cheek, and the way his eyelashes swept dark and soft along the hard plane of his cheekbones. She gripped the arms of the big leather chair and sighed.

It was always this way. She was vulnerable to so many little things about this man, irrational tiny things like the line of his profile, the curve of his lower lip, the way his hair grew at the nape of his neck. Without warning, she would catch a glimpse of him, or hear the sound of his voice unexpectedly, and her mind and body would turn to jelly, robbing her completely of reason and strength. The wayward physical attraction was so all-pervading, so violent and unpredictable, that she could never be entirely certain of her own reactions....

Daniel glanced up at her sharply, raising his eyebrows in question.

Her flush deepened, and she shifted awkwardly in her chair, trying to recapture the thread of their earlier conversation.

"I mean," she went on finally, "I don't think you should forbid him to come back, just because—"

"Does he actually want to come back?" Daniel interrupted. "He looked like a pretty unhappy little boy when you carried him away. I can't believe he'd ever want to come near the place again."

Jamie smiled suddenly, her wide grin lighting up the somber room. "He goes through a lot, you know, with his older brother and sister. Kevin's a quiet, shy little boy, a lot like Steven, but he's much more used to trauma. The other kids are always using him for their experiments and getting him into things that he doesn't understand. Today was really just par for the course, even though it seemed terrifying at the time."

Daniel studied her in disbelief. "He's sufficiently accustomed to trauma, you mean, that he wouldn't be averse to coming back here, even after that horrible experience?"

Jamie nodded. "He's already almost gotten over it. He's even pleased to have a story to impress his brother with. He wasn't scarred for life or anything. And," she added softly, "I think he and Steven really did have fun together. They seemed to warm to each other right away. I know Kevin would like the chance to play with him again."

Daniel looked up suddenly, his piercing dark eyes seeming, as always, to look right into her soul. Jamie summoned all her courage and met his gaze in steady silence, waiting.

"Well," he said finally, "it appears that Steven feels the same way. He was terrified by the accident, but he got over it a lot quicker than I thought he would. And he really liked this kid. I suppose now that they've actually met, I really have no option. I'm going to be in big trouble if I say he can't come back."

Jamie stared at him, wide-eyed. "You mean—" she began in wonder "—you mean you'll let them play together again? Kevin can come back here?"

"Yes," Daniel said wearily. "He can come back. As I said, I have no choice. It's obvious that it means a tremendous amount to Steven, and I'd have to be a real ogre to deny him the company of this one friend, wouldn't I?"

Jamie's eyes shone. "Daniel, that's wonderful! That's just so—"

"Just this one kid, Jamie," he said abruptly. "Don't break the rules again and start smuggling your whole army of nieces and nephews onto my property, please."

Jamie ignored the coldness of his tone and leaned forward impulsively to grasp his hand in both her own and squeeze it warmly, beaming at him. "Daniel, quit pretending you're so mean," she said cheerfully. "Actually, you're a really nice man, and everybody knows it."

He glanced up sharply, his eyes fixed on hers with a strange expression that made her feel weak and confused again. Awkwardly, she released his hand and settled back in her chair, trembling a little.

Daniel watched her a moment longer and then turned aside to gaze out the window, his arrogant features thoughtful and distant.

"What were they doing anyway?" he asked casually. "I couldn't get Steven to tell me. He kept saying they were just playing, and the rope slipped, but he wouldn't tell me why they were up in the damned tree in the first place. Do you know?"

Jamie nodded. "Kevin said they were playing 'tree house,' and they tied the rope around them to be safe, like mountain climbers, so that if one slipped he could hold the other one."

Daniel grinned unexpectedly. "Not a bad plan, except that they failed to consider what would happen if they *both* slipped."

"Yes," Jamie said, and shivered a little. "They didn't think of that."

Daniel was silent a moment longer, still gazing out the window. "Why 'tree house,' anyhow?" he asked, turning to face Jamie again. "Whose idea was that?"

"Oh, that was Steven's idea," Jamie said promptly. "Steven's obsessed with tree houses. Didn't you know that?"

Daniel shook his head. "It appears there's a lot of things Steven doesn't tell me."

"One of the little boys at his school has a tree house," Jamie said. "Steven thinks it's just absolutely the most wonderful thing in the whole world, even though he's never seen it. He's just heard descriptions of it, but he'd give anything to have a real tree house, with a ladder, you know, and a little door, and all that."

Daniel smiled again, his rare, shining boyish smile that transformed his whole face. "I had one," he said. "When I was a boy, I had a tree house, and it *was* wonderful. As a matter of fact, I wrote my first novel in my tree house," he added, his grin widening.

Jamie smiled back at him, warmed by his change of mood. "Really, Daniel? How old were you?"

"Nine. It was awful—my novel, I mean."

Jamie chuckled, and then peeped over at him, watching as his smile faded and his guarded, remote expression returned.

"God, I wish *I* could build him a tree house," he muttered, almost to himself. "I'd give anything if I could just—"

He broke off and stared out the window again, while Jamie watched him in troubled silence.

"What about Hiro?" Daniel asked abruptly. "Why can't he build a tree house for Steven? He's pretty handy with tools, isn't he?"

"Daniel, Hiro doesn't *have* any tools."

He waved his hand impatiently. "Of course the man has tools. He has the use of all the tools on the property."

"There aren't any tools on the property, Daniel," Jamie said patiently. "There's just lawn and garden equipment, and a few essentials that he uses for basic repairs, like a hammer and screwdrivers and an old hand saw. Hiro doesn't have any power equipment at all."

"How did you come to know that?"

"Well, because it happens to be his dream. Hiro's obsessed with woodworking. His father is a carpenter in Japan, apparently, and Hiro spent a lot of time working in the family shop when he was younger, before he emigrated. Now, he goes to all the carpentry and woodworking shows in the city and uses his free time to look through tool shops and work out patterns for jewelry boxes and things."

Jamie paused, and then grinned.

"You should see his rooms, behind the garage. Maria and I were invited over there the other day for tea. Where other single men have pinups tacked on the walls, Hiro has pictures of drill presses and table saws."

Daniel stared at her, astounded. "If the man is so wild about woodworking," he asked slowly, "why doesn't he buy some tools? I think I pay him generously enough that he could afford to buy what he needs."

Jamie leaned forward earnestly, telling Daniel the story of Hiro's family in Japan, and of the paycheck that was sent away every month, and the fifty dollars that Hiro allowed himself for all his personal needs.

"My God," Daniel muttered, appalled. "*Fifty dollars.* That's not even enough to..."

He looked up at Jamie abruptly, fixing her with that unsettling dark gaze. "How do you *do* it, Jamie? These people have worked for me for years and years. You've been here about two months, and you already know all the secrets of their souls. How does this happen?"

"I don't know," Jamie said simply. "People just tell me things, I guess."

Daniel gave her a wan smile. "I guess," he said, looking down at his desk and paging idly through the sheaf of computer printouts again while Jamie watched him.

"What are you doing tomorrow?" he asked finally.

"It's Sunday. I'm staying overnight tonight at my brother's house and baby-sitting while they take my father to a baseball game in Edmonton."

"Then on Monday morning," he said slowly, "before my massage, could you bring Hiro up here to see me, please?"

Jamie glanced at him in surprise and then nodded. "Certainly."

She hesitated, looking at her watch, and got up.

"Well, I'd better go," she said. "I promised Terry and Doreen I'd be there before eight o'clock."

She smiled again at the dark, quiet man behind the desk, and walked across the room. At the door she paused and turned back to look at him.

"Daniel," she said softly, "it really is nice of you to let Kevin come back again. I appreciate it so much, and I think it's a good thing for both boys."

He waved his hand abruptly in dismissal and looked up. Jamie met his gaze, stunned by the depths of misery and pain revealed suddenly in his dark eyes.

"Daniel . . ." she whispered.

"Jamie . . . can you imagine how I felt, today?" he asked, his handsome face twisting passionately. "Can you even begin to fathom how it felt to be a man in that situation, with my child in danger, and be so absolutely, totally helpless to do anything about it? *Can you?*"

Jamie hesitated in the doorway, moved almost unbearably by his words and by his obvious agony.

"Yes, Daniel", she said slowly. "I can imagine. It must have been terrible for you."

"And you think I should travel again," he went on bitterly. "You think I should be able to forget my disability and do the things normal people do. For God's sake, Jamie, I can't even lift my hand to save my child! How can I live like a normal man?"

Jamie stared at him, seared by his pain, searching for the right words. "Daniel, you're right. You have a disability. There are a lot of things you can't do, that other men can. But that doesn't change the fact," she went on with rising conviction, "that there are a lot of things you *can* do. More things than you allow yourself to consider. There's no point in pretending that your life can ever be completely normal again. But I do think you owe it to yourself to do as much as you're able to do."

He stared at her in brooding silence. Her cheeks were flushed with emotion, her ample bosom was heaving, and her fiery red hair stood out in a bright curly halo around her head. She shone in the doorway like a tall candle flame, glowing vividly with life and color and strength, so warm and lovely that his soul ached for her.

But he knew that he could never tell her how he felt. He turned aside, his face shuttered and remote, and flipped on his computer monitor.

"Goodbye, Jamie," he said curtly. "I'll see you Monday morning."

She paused in the doorway a moment longer, looking unhappily at his dark head as he bent over the pile of papers. At last she turned, closed the door gently behind her and walked away down the silent, carpeted hallway.

CHAPTER TEN

A LONG CRYSTAL PRISM hung in the kitchen window, revolving slowly in the morning breeze that lifted and stirred the fluffy white curtains. As the prism rotated, broken fragments of rainbows danced and fluttered on the walls and floor, and glimmered warmly on the faces of the people around the table.

Clara sat sipping her coffee, deeply absorbed in a photography magazine propped against the syrup jug.

"Did you know," she announced suddenly to the room in general, "that they're now making autofocus telephoto lenses with a *five-to-one* zoom ratio?"

The others glanced up at her, startled. Nobody answered, and she went on reading.

"Come here, Steven," Jamie murmured. "Your sneaker is untied again."

The little boy rounded the table to lean beside Jamie, lifting his foot obediently onto the edge of her chair and continuing his own conversation. "He could live in the garage," Steven said earnestly to Jamie, "and Hiro and I would look after him, all the time. Daddy wouldn't even know he was around. Right, Hiro?"

Hiro, paging through a tattered second-hand magazine called *Woodcrafter's Monthly*, looked up, startled at the sound of his name, and nodded absently, returning at once to his reading.

"Can I?" Steven asked Jamie. "Can I, Jamie? *Please*?"

"Steven . . ." Jamie began helplessly, tying a firm knot in his shoelace and lifting his foot gently from her chair, "it's not *my* decision, you know. I'm not the one to decide if you can have a puppy. Your daddy has to make that decision, not any of us."

"But you can ask him," Steven argued, with the dogged persistence of childhood. "He'll do it if you ask him. He always does. He likes you lots."

Jamie glanced in startled silence at the little boy's earnest face, and a warm flush crept up her cheeks.

"Well, Maria," she said heartily, turning toward the sink, where the slender woman stood running water over the bacon grill. "All set? Looking forward to our outing this afternoon?"

Maria turned to face the others, dark eyes filled with terror. "Oh, Jamie . . ." she whispered.

Jamie studied her friend in thoughtful silence. "Maybe it's too soon," she said finally. "You don't have to go yet, Maria. You can spend some more time outside, if you like, before we—"

"No!" Maria said. "We planned it, and I'm going to do it. Putting it off will just make it harder."

"Good girl!" Clara said unexpectedly. "I'll have to get a couple of shots of you before you leave," she added. "After all, it's a momentous occasion. Your first trip downtown in ten years. As a matter of fact," Clara added, struck by the thought, "I should really have been filming the whole thing. It would make a very strong photo-documentary, wouldn't it?"

Maria's face paled and her eyes widened in panic.

"Never mind, Maria," Jamie said soothingly. "Clara isn't going to be allowed to film your trip downtown. She knows I won't stand for it."

Clara grinned amiably, closed her magazine and got up. "Marketing day," she announced briskly, and strode from the kitchen, crisp and businesslike in her neat gray dress.

"Can I, Jamie?" Steven continued. "I'll brush him and feed him and take him for walks all the time, and then when Kevin comes over, we can..."

"Steven, I *told* you," Jamie said with a distracted air, "I really don't know."

"But will you ask? Will you tell him that I said I'd—"

"If I think of it," Jamie said helplessly. "Hiro!" she added, as the slender young man got up quietly to leave.

"Yes, Jamie?"

"Hiro, don't go for a minute, all right? There's something...something we have to do this morning."

"Yes?" he asked again, pausing by the table with his usual quiet courtesy.

"We have to...Mr. Kelleher wanted us to go up and see him for a few minutes this morning. He wants to talk with you about something."

Hiro's smooth golden face turned ashen, and he stared at Jamie in sudden panic. "Why?" he whispered, gripping the edge of his chair. "Have I done something wrong?"

"Of course not. At least, not that I know of," Jamie amended. "He just asked that I bring you up to his office this morning for a few minutes before his massage. I don't know what it's about."

Clara came back into the kitchen, and she and Maria stood tensely silent, staring at Hiro with alarm. He looked down in dismay at his shabby coveralls, and then glanced up at Jamie with a ghastly smile.

"Well," he said unsteadily, "we might as well go, then."

She nodded and walked beside him from the kitchen, through the luxurious foyer and into Daniel's small private elevator. She noticed with concern as they neared Daniel's office that Hiro's hands were trembling. He clenched them tightly into fists and held them rigid at his sides while Jamie knocked and spoke with Daniel through the intercom.

"Don't be scared, Hiro," Jamie whispered as the door slid open. "I'm sure it's..."

Before she could finish they were inside the room, and she saw Daniel sitting quietly in his chair by the long mullioned windows, exactly as he had been the first time she ever met him. Memory washed over her, and all the other emotions, so strong and unmanageable, that assailed her these days whenever she was with him.

She smiled awkwardly and held Hiro's arm to draw him forward. "Well, here he is," she said with forced heartiness, "present as requested."

Daniel smiled at them, his white teeth flashing warmly in his tanned face.

"Sit down, Jamie," he said, indicating one of the big leather chairs. "You too, Hiro. I hope I'm not interrupting your work?"

Hiro cleared his throat nervously and sat on the edge of the chair Daniel indicated, gripping his hands tightly together between his knees. "No, sir," he whispered.

"What are you doing these days, anyhow?" Daniel asked pleasantly.

Hiro cast Jamie a frightened glance and licked his lips. "Just...just the usual yard work," he murmured in his soft musical voice. "The lawn and garden need much attention now, and I am . . . I am repairing the chain link fence at the back of the property, on the cliff edge."

Daniel nodded thoughtfully, listening to the man with quiet attention. Sunshine poured through the window behind his wheelchair, gilding his dark head with light and glinting on the planes of his strong handsome face.

"I see," he said quietly. "Do you have any free time at all? Would you be able to find time, for instance, to do some extra work for me, do you think?"

Hiro stared at him, astounded. "Of course," he said simply. "If you want something done, I will *make* time. Always."

"Steven wants a tree house," Daniel said. "I wonder if you'd be able to find a suitable tree on the property, and design and build something that would be safe and adequate for him."

Hiro's eyes flicked over to Jamie with quick desperate appeal, and he was silent for a moment. Finally, his shoulders slumped in resignation. "Yes," he said in a low strained voice. "I can do that, sir."

Daniel's eyes sparkled with sudden amusement, but he kept his face solemn. "Can you really, Hiro? With a hammer and an old handsaw?"

Hiro flushed, but replied with his customary politeness. "Yes, sir," he said quietly. "I can do it, if you want me to."

"Well, actually I was thinking more along the lines of making a deal with you," Daniel said cheerfully.

Hiro looked up at him, startled, and said nothing.

"You see," Daniel went on, "I don't feel that something like this is within your actual job description. I mean, if you build something for me, as a personal request, then it's above and beyond the call of duty, and I'd like to pay you extra, or else work out a trade, if that's all right with you."

"A trade?" Hiro asked cautiously, glancing into the other man's brilliant dark eyes.

Daniel nodded. "You came after my father died," he said in a casual conversational tone, "and so you never knew him. He was a fanatic about woodwork, and really quite skilled at it."

Hiro's black eyes kindled with surprise and interest, but he held himself silent in the chair, waiting.

"His shop is still in the basement, fully equipped. After he died my mother could never bring herself to dispose of his tools, because he'd loved them so much. She hoped that someday they'd be of use to someone in the household. I think maybe this is that time."

Jamie gazed at Daniel in stunned silence, and then stole a quick look at Hiro. His eyes were wide with wonder, and he gripped the arms of the chair so tightly that his knuckles were white in his thin, callused hands.

"What I'm proposing," Daniel went on calmly, "is a kind of mutual accommodation. If you'll be good enough to build a tree house for Steven, and a few other things that I'd like for the household, including," he added with an engaging smile, "a few more bookshelves for my ever-expanding personal library. . . ."

Hiro glanced briefly around him at the walls of the office, his eyes lighting with pleasure and delight, and faced his employer again in breathless silence.

"In that case," Daniel concluded simply, "I'd be willing to work out a deal. You build the things I want, on your own time or mine, whatever you can manage, and I'll give you full use of the workshop and the tools for your own personal projects, as well. Does that sound fair?"

Jamie could see that Hiro wasn't going to be able to answer. "I think it sounds fair," she murmured, to save him embarrassment. "*Very* fair, right Hiro?"

The little man swallowed hard, gulped, and looked over at her, his dark eyes eloquent with emotion. Jamie understood at once.

"Do you think," she whispered to Daniel, "that you could show him the shop right now?"

Daniel grinned, and took a set of keys from the pocket of his polo shirt, leaning forward to hand it to the thin young man across from him. "Let's go," he said cheerfully.

They made their way in silent procession through the levels of the house to the basement. In the cool depths of the lower floor, Jamie stepped out of the elevator and looked around curiously. She had only been down here a couple of times, to fetch supplies for Clara when the cook was busy, and she barely recalled what it was like.

The basement rooms, though not as luxurious as the rest of the house, were large, neat and well maintained, comfortably ventilated and practical in design. Daniel wheeled himself rapidly down a tiled corridor and paused in front of a solid oak door, turning to nod to Hiro.

"Well, here's your shop," he said. "And you're the man with the key."

Hiro reached out a shaky hand to turn the key in the lock. The door swung open, and he stepped into the huge dim room, followed by Daniel, who reached up to flip the switch, flooding the room with light. He looked over his shoulder at Jamie, grinning and jerking his head in Hiro's direction.

Jamie followed his glance, and gave him a misty smile in return.

Hiro stood stock-still in the middle of the room, gazing around him in hushed awe at a workshop that was equipped with everything a woodworker could dream of having. From a lifetime spent with a father and a group of older brothers, Jamie was able to recognize a number of pieces of equipment—routers and drill presses, scroll saws and lathes—all expensive, gleaming, beautifully maintained. But there were other tools that she couldn't even identify, although Hiro was already moving reverently among them, reaching out his hands to stroke and caress the shining oiled surfaces.

On shelves and pegboard walls numerous small tools hung, and neatly labeled cabinets held a vast array of nails, screws, bolts and washers. The room almost looked as if Daniel's father had just stepped away in the middle of a project and would be coming back through the door any moment to carry on with his work.

Jamie glanced at Daniel's powerful shoulders and his calm sculpted profile as he sat watching the gardener, and wondered briefly what his father had been like. There were so many things she didn't know about Daniel, and her curiosity was endless. She hungered to know where he had gone to school, what he had looked like as child, how he had felt about his parents, what his favorite games had been when he was little.

Alarmed by her reactions, she reined in her runaway thoughts and wondered for the hundredth time just what on earth was happening to her.

"So, is this all right with you, Hiro?" Daniel was saying. "Do you think we have a deal?"

Hiro glanced up at his employer. He was standing near the band saw, running a gentle hand over the shining metal surface, his straight black hair falling unheeded across his forehead.

"I can't... I can't use these things," he murmured in anguish. "They are so beautiful... the best of all tools. Such quality.... I can't possibly..."

"Of course you can," Daniel said comfortably. "Nobody else is ever going to use them. And if you won't use them, then how will Steven ever get a tree house? How will I get the bookshelves I need?"

Hiro hesitated, staring at the big man in the wheelchair, his hand still clenched automatically on the control knob of the band saw.

"This room is yours to use as you wish," Daniel concluded firmly, "and as your employer, I expect you to agree with that decision, without a lot of argument. Now, it's time for my massage, and then I have work to do. Ready, Jamie?"

"Ready," Jamie agreed briskly, smiling at Hiro's stunned expression.

"You can keep that set of keys," Daniel said casually. "I have duplicates, but it'll be understood that this is your private domain, Hiro, and nobody enters without your permission. I think they're adequately labeled—some of them lock the big cabinets over there, as well."

Hiro gulped and nodded, looking first at Daniel's face and then down at the ring of keys in his hand. Finally he straightened his shoulders, drew a deep breath, and took one last look around the room.

"I have work to do, too," he said with a sudden luminous smile. "So much work."

Jamie and Daniel grinned at one another as Hiro followed them out into the hall and paused to lock the door to the workshop, putting the key carefully away in the breast pocket of his coveralls and then patting it anxiously. He gave them another shy smile and hurried off down the corridor to the outside basement entrance, his dark head high, his step buoyant and joyous.

SOON AFTERWARDS, Jamie and Daniel were in their customary place on the patio for his full morning therapy. The summer day was hot and still, with that astonishing sharp clarity in the air that is only encountered on the prairie in the early morning. The tree branches all around them dipped and lifted in the soft wind like dancers in a stately minuet, and a pair of nesting robins in the massive elm tree overhead made constant trips to gather food for their noisy brood of young.

"God, what a job," Daniel observed idly, lying with his hands behind his head and watching the busy pair of birds as Jamie worked over his legs. "Look at them go, Jamie. They have to work that hard, all summer, and then find the strength somehow to fly thousands of miles south as soon as autumn comes. How do they ever manage it?"

"It's nature," she said comfortably, lifting and flexing his left knee. "They've done it since time began, and I'm sure they'll still be doing it long after we've all gone."

They were both silent for a moment, enjoying the warmth of the day and the caressing softness of the morning breeze.

"Are you getting too warm?" Daniel asked.

Jamie shook her head. "The air feels so nice. But," she added, "I think it'll be too warm, by noon, to be out here at all."

She paused thoughtfully, then moved around to begin work on his other leg. Her expression altered a little, and he glanced up at her quickly. "What is it, Jamie?"

She shook her head and met his eyes with an awkward little smile, biting her lip. "I just can't get over... Daniel, did you see his *face?* He was just in seventh heaven.

Every time I think of it, I just feel warm all over, and it's all I can do to keep from bursting into tears."

Daniel smiled, and reached out to grasp her hand. "I know," he said. "I've just been thinking the same thing. You know—how it seems that sometimes the means to make someone else blissfully happy is right in our grasp, and we're just too self-absorbed and preoccupied to realize it."

Jamie nodded and looked down at him, painfully conscious of the grip of his strong brown hand on hers, and his gleaming, heavily muscled upper body so close to her own. She felt a flow of gratitude for his generosity, and pure affection for him because of his warmth and kindness toward the gardener, accompanied by a hot flood of the same disturbing, urgent passion that tormented her so often these days.

She swayed unsteadily on her feet and leaned down toward him, drawn irresistibly by that glistening tanned body, the wide powerful mouth, wanting only to be closer and closer to him, within him, surrounding him.

His dark eyes stared into hers suddenly, and she caught a look that chilled her. His look was one of caution, almost of warning.

Stung, she pulled back and turned aside, flushing painfully, to carry on with her massage.

"One other thing," she said, struggling to keep her voice light and casual, "since you're so much into making people happy today."

"And what's that?" he asked, his face once more calm and unreadable.

"Steven," Jamie said, squeezing more mineral oil onto the palms of her hands and beginning, with great energy, to massage his thighs. "Steven wants a puppy."

"Oh, God," Daniel groaned in mock horror, flinging an outstretched arm over his eyes.

"I'm supposed to tell you," Jamie went on, "that he'll keep it in the garage all the time, and feed it and brush it and take it for walks."

"In the garage all the time!" Daniel scoffed. "I'll bet. The very first night, mark my words, it would be up in his room right next to me, howling and scratching and keeping me awake."

"He says Hiro will help him look after it," Jamie reported. "He swears it'll stay in the garage."

"Give it up, Jamie," Daniel said amiably. "Rest on your laurels. You got Hiro a workshop, and you got Steven a friend and a tree house. You'll all just have to be satisfied with that for now, I'm afraid."

"No puppy?"

"No puppy," Daniel said.

They smiled at one another, both relieved that another dangerous moment had been safely passed and that their relationship was back on its old cheerful footing. Daniel closed his eyes and relaxed in the beaming warmth of the sun, while Jamie continued to rub and flex his long motionless legs.

JAMIE AND MARIA stood by the bus stop at the end of their driveway, peering anxiously down the shaded street. They were both dressed for the afternoon heat in cool light skirts, cotton blouses and sandals. Maria, though, shivered in the sunlight, looking pale and terrified.

"I wish we could go in your car," she whispered, her face ashen. "I wish it didn't have to be on the bus."

"But it does, Maria," Jamie said patiently. "We've been through all this. You've been out for drives in my car, quite a few of them, and it's wonderful that you can do that now, but you have to be able to go on the bus, too, if you're going to keep progressing. You know that, don't you?''

Maria nodded. ''Yes, I know. I don't drive, so if I'm ever going to go downtown by myself it'll have to be on the bus.''

''And I'll go with you,'' Jamie said, ''as often as you want me to, and then when you feel you can manage, you'll go by yourself.''

Maria shuddered and gripped her handbag, hugging it to her chest in panic. ''This is so hard,'' she murmured. ''The hardest of all, I think. Jamie...''

She looked up at the tall woman beside her, wondering how Jamie always managed to look so cool and comfortable, even on the hottest days. It must have something to do with how self-possessed Jamie was. She seemed to be so cheerful and accepting of life as it happened, never flustered or angry or anxious.

Today, Jamie wore her red patterned wrap skirt and a cool white camisole top held up with little lacy straps over her strong tanned shoulders. Her face was golden and beautiful, her generous mouth lifting slightly at the memory of some private amusement. She looked, Maria thought, as if she could do anything, face anything without fear, go anywhere in the world that she chose to.

''Jamie, aren't you ever scared?'' Maria whispered in anguish. ''Of anything?''

Jamie looked down at her friend in surprise. ''All the time, Maria. Lots of things scare me.''

''But you never show it. You always look so...so brave and capable and happy....''

Jamie paused thoughtfully, searching for words. ''Maria,'' she began, ''we all have different fears, and they affect us in different ways. Yours are much more visible, because they're so crippling, you know, and it's difficult to hide them. The rest of us have fears, too, lots of them, but we're just more able to keep them hidden, that's all.''

Maria thought this over, still clutching her handbag in tense fingers. "What...what kind of things are you afraid of, Jamie?''

Jamie gazed unseeingly at a car gliding past them on the opposite side of the street and did not answer. But her beautiful mobile face showed, to Maria's surprise, a rapid series of emotions—of tension and wistful longing and sudden, quickly suppressed pain that was startling and deeply upsetting to the small woman beside her.

"Jamie?'' Maria urged anxiously.

"What? Oh . . . frogs,'' Jamie said helplessly. "I'm terrified of frogs. Absolute blind horror.''

Maria stared. "*Frogs*?'' she asked. "Really?''

Jamie nodded, her normal cheerfulness restored. "Terrified,'' she repeated. "If I had to be alone in the same room with a frog that wasn't in a cage or something, I think I'd die. No kidding, Maria. That's why I admire you so much. I know what it's like when something is frightening to *me*, even though it's something that other people might not find scary at all. Because it's always our own fears that we have to deal with, not other people's, and it's a hard, hard thing to fight them.''

Maria giggled, her dark eyes dancing.

"Frogs!'' she repeated in a voice choked with laughter, and looked, all at once, girlish and lovely, her face sparkling with impish humor. "And have you had a lot to do with frogs, Jamie? Have they been a . . . a regular part of your life, would you say?''

Jamie looked sadly towards the heavens. "See how they turn on you,'' she mourned to nobody in particular.

"Even your best friends. Confide your secret fears and what happens? They laugh at you."

"I'm not laughing," Maria said, instantly contrite. "Well," she corrected herself quickly, "Maybe only a little. It's just that I'm trying to picture..."

"Remember, Maria, I had three older brothers," Jamie told her. "And when they discovered this fear they were just merciless. For a certain period of my life there were frogs in my bed, frogs in my dresser drawers, frogs in my schoolbag...."

Jamie shuddered, remembering.

"What happened?" Maria asked, her laughter stilled, her pretty, dark face gentle with sympathy.

"My father found out what was going on," Jamie said, "and threatened them with such terrible punishments if it happened again that they didn't have the nerve."

She sighed, still clearly overwhelmed by the memory of that terrible time, and the wonderful relief of having her father finally intervene on her behalf and put an end to her agony.

Maria watched her friend's expressive golden face, moved by the emotions that showed there, and so absorbed in Jamie's story that she hardly noticed when the bus ground to a stop beside them and they clambered aboard.

Maria followed Jamie tensely down the aisle and watched as the tall woman folded herself gracefully into a seat near the back. Closing her eyes in sudden panic, Maria followed suit, grateful for Jamie's warm supportive presence.

She kept her eyes squeezed shut for a moment, then opened them and peeped cautiously around, feeling like a time traveler who suddenly finds herself transported into the future. There were sights all around her that she had only read about or seen on television. A girl with her hair dyed red and green in a wild brush cut...a working girl in miniskirt that was dangerously short...a sober young man in the seat opposite them reading a calculus textbook, his head shaved completely bald and a cross in one earlobe. Maria stared at them all in wondering, fearful silence.

Then, without warning, the old crippling terror came flooding back, the cold icy dread that crept along her spine and clutched at her heart and hammered in her ears. She was drowning in fear, unable to breathe, about to scream or faint.

"Jamie," she whispered, her voice low and choked. "Jamie!"

"Shh," Jamie murmured beside her, gripping Maria's small, callused palm in her own strong and capable hand. "Shh. It's all right, Maria. It's just fine. I'm right here, and nobody's going to hurt you. You're going to be fine. You're going to be just fine. We're going to get off the bus downtown, right by the park, and we're going to walk to the..."

Her voice flowed on, gentle and soothing, whispering steadily while the dark wings beating inside Maria's mind gradually fluttered and stilled, and her heart began to beat more normally, and she was able at last to breathe again.

She squeezed Jamie's hand in embarrassment, avoiding her friend's eyes. "Sorry," she panted. "I'm so sorry."

"Sorry?" Jamie asked in surprise. "What for?"

"For this," Maria muttered unhappily. "For being such a baby."

Jamie chuckled and gave her friend a little push. "Oh, go on. I just confided to you that I'm terrified of frogs, and *you're* apologizing for being a baby?"

Maria giggled shakily and looked around again. She felt painfully exposed and conspicuous, as if everybody on the bus—everybody in the *whole world*—knew about her, and they were all watching her with avid interest, waiting for her to fall apart and make a complete fool of herself.

But in actual fact, nobody took the slightest notice of her. The green-haired girl gazed darkly out the window, thinking her own thoughts, the mini-skirted woman filed her nails with concentrated attention, and the bald young man remained serenely buried in the depths of his calculus book.

"They look so *strange,* Jamie," Maria whispered.

Jamie chuckled. "Kid, you ain't seen nothin' yet," she muttered, gangsterlike, from the corner of her mouth. "Wait'll we get to the mall!"

Maria stared up at her friend in alarm, and then glanced furtively around again. Finally, she sighed and retreated to safer ground.

"Hiro's not sure what he's going to start on after the tree house and the bookshelves," she said, picking up the thread of an earlier conversation. "He thinks he'd like to make some small curio boxes that he could sell at the craft sales in the fall and earn extra money to send to his family."

"I wish," Jamie said absently, "that he'd keep some money for himself. All that sacrifice tends to make me a little uncomfortable, you know?"

Maria nodded. "I know. I feel the same way. It's just not...part of our culture. But it seems perfectly natural to him. He says that after his family is looked after, once they're all safely over here and settled, then he can think of himself."

Jamie nodded thoughtfully, gazing out the window at the jagged downtown skyline that rose to meet them.

"He's not going to tell Steven anything at all about the tree house," Maria went on, chattering determinedly to hold her fears at bay. "He's going to build it in sections, down in the workroom, and he wants you to ask everybody not to tell Steven anything about it until it's all ready to go up in the tree."

Jamie smiled fondly, her face reflecting her pleasure at the thought of how overjoyed Steven would be on that day.

"You should see his plans," Maria said. "You weren't there, you were giving Mr. Kelleher his noon hour massage when Hiro showed us some of his ideas. It's going to have a table and chairs inside, and a window that really opens and closes, and a little porch."

Maria sighed in childlike bliss at the picture, and Jamie gave her a warm, quick smile.

Silence fell briefly between them. Maria glanced out the window at the narrowing streets, choked with afternoon traffic and darkened into tunnels by the high buildings rising on both sides. Her breath quickened and she clutched Jamie's hand, talking with desperate earnestness to hold the panic at bay.

"I'm going to buy a sewing pattern and some material," she panted. "I want to make something really dressy for the afternoon part of the reunion. I thought a tailored suit would be nice, with a long jacket and a pin, you know, Jamie? Maybe in black or gray. What do you think?"

Jamie considered. "I agree that a tailored suit would be nice," she said. "But I think it should have a short jacket to show off your figure. You've got such a fantastic shape, Maria. And I think it should be a brighter color. Get a nice bright red or paisley, or something. You wear black and gray all the time."

Maria considered, her face pink with excitement and fear. "Then I'd have to buy new shoes, and a handbag and—"

"Terrific," Jamie said comfortably. "More things to shop for. You have to make regular trips downtown, so it's nice to have lots of things to buy. Besides, think of your bank account, Maria," she added with a teasing sidelong glance. "All these years you haven't gone anywhere or done anything, and the cash has just been piling up in there."

Maria nodded in agreement. "It certainly has," she said. "You're right, it's time I started spending some of it." Unexpectedly, she dimpled and her creamy features turned a deeper pink. "Tony always loved the way I looked in red," she confided shyly. "He said once that when I got married, I should have a bright red wedding gown because red was my color."

"Tony sounds like a terrific fellow," Jamie said. "Has he called lately, Maria?"

The housemaid shook her head, her eyes suddenly troubled. "I think he's waiting, you know?" she whispered. "He knows the reunion is coming up, and he's not going to call anymore, he's just going to wait and see if I..." She was silent for a moment. "Oh, Jamie," she wailed suddenly, "I hope I can go!"

"Of course you can go," Jamie said calmly, putting an arm around her friend's trembling shoulders. "You're halfway there already."

Maria shivered and gulped, then gathered herself together with an effort, trying not to look out at the terrifying alien vistas beyond the bus window. "What...what are you going to shop for today, Jamie,?" she asked desperately.

"Yarn," Jamie said cheerfully. "Tons of it, remember? I've finished that silly little afghan, and now I'm ready to start crocheting my bedspread. I like *big* projects."

Maria giggled. In the fun of Jamie's company, she even forgot for a moment that she was undertaking one of the most terrifying experiences of her life.

CHAPTER ELEVEN

JAMIE SAT IN partial shade on her little patio, wearing white cotton shorts, pink T-shirt and sun hat, surrounded by masses of crocheted squares that flowed over the wrought iron table and chairs in a pool of cream and buttery yellow. She frowned thoughtfully as she threaded her crochet hook into the last loop on another square, secured the yarn, searched under a pile of yellow wool for her scissors and snipped the end.

Then she held up the finished square in front of her and grinned suddenly, a bright warm smile that illuminated her face and briefly smoothed out the tired, strained shadows around her flower blue eyes. But almost as soon as it appeared the smile faded, and the shadows crept back again.

In the month since Jamie had begun her bedspread, she had often experienced the strange and confusing feeling that nothing was happening, but everything was changing. The subtle shifts and alterations within Daniel's household were measured, it seemed, by her steadily mounting pile of crocheted squares. Jamie had calculated at the outset that she would need over a hundred of these ten-inch squares to finish a whole bedspread, and she now had almost forty of them.

And all the time she had been working, the mood and attitude of the household had been altering, widening, warming in all kinds of barely perceptible ways.

Hiro was rarely visible anymore, spending all of his free time in the basement workshop, sometimes in secret consultation with his employer, who made frequent visits to the tool room. After Daniel left, though, Hiro often labored until the small hours of the morning and then woke, seemingly tireless, to attend to his daily caretaking duties. His face was growing more and more deeply contented, with the quiet rich glow of a man who is living his life exactly as he wishes and has found absolute fulfillment.

Maria, too, was growing happier and more confident with each passing day. After a number of trips with Jamie on the bus, marred by just a few small setbacks, she was now able to travel partway downtown all by herself and then get off and wait by the bus stop for Jamie to come and pick her up. She had not yet managed the whole trip, including shopping alone, dealing with strangers, and handling a bus transfer to get her safely home again, but that would come soon. It was the final step necessary in preparation for her high school reunion, which was now just six weeks away.

And Steven... Jamie picked up a ball of cream-colored wool, turning it absently in her hands and smiling to herself.

Steven was a joy to behold, a little boy so happy and full of fun and high spirits that it was hard to believe he was the same sad-eyed child Jamie had encountered on her first visit to this house back in the spring. He had spent his long, sun-drenched summer holidays laughing and romping with little Kevin, who was now allowed to come over several days a week, and both boys had benefited enormously from their friendship. And when Kevin wasn't visiting, Steven spent more time with Daniel, enriching the lives of both father and son with games and laughter, with instruction and chatter and outings.

Jamie's smile faded, and the shadows darkened her blue eyes again.

Life was turning out well for everyone, she thought. Everyone but her...

She shifted restlessly in the lounge chair, moving her bare legs into the sunlight and pulling her floppy straw hat lower over her eyes. Her hands fell loosely into her lap and she leaned back, gazing up through the lacy veil of leaves overhead, still thinking about her life and trying to analyze the source of her growing discontentment.

Maybe, she thought, squinting at the brightness that rayed through the masses of greenery, maybe she was just a born crusader, a real do-gooder, and now that everybody seemed happy and had no further need of her she was ready to move on.

But she knew that wasn't true. Daniel still needed her, depended more on her skilled hands and the warmth of her company all the time. He had no qualms at all these days about letting her know how valuable the therapy sessions had become to him. And besides the actual physical treatments, Daniel and Jamie tended to spend a great deal of time in comfortable conversation, chatting easily about everything...the other members of the household, Jamie's family, Daniel's work, the fascinating people and places he had seen in his travels, Jamie's workout programs.

She shook her head, closing her eyes and tipping her hat back to let the golden sunlight fall warmly onto her face.

It wasn't true that they talked about everything.

There were a few things they never mentioned at all, and it seemed to Jamie that these omissions spoke more loudly than their words.

For instance, after that first time they had never again discussed Daniel's refusal to pick up the broken thread of his life, to resume the travels and personal research that had always been so enjoyable to him and so important to his career. And they never, never mentioned that balmy spring morning, now almost two months ago, when Jamie had climbed into his arms and abandoned herself to her passion, carrying both of them to crashing heights of physical sensation and fulfillment....

Jamie rubbed her temples wearily, trying to push the thoughts away from her mind. She could never quite forget that morning interlude. The memory haunted her dreams frequently in the lonely moon-washed nights and tormented her at odd hours during the day, particularly when she was with Daniel. She would be working on his body, warm and passive beneath her hands, and she would suddenly remember how it had felt to be in his arms, to feel his thrusting male strength, to experience the passionate joy of being lifted out of herself and carried so far, far away....

She sighed and stirred in the chair, her face bleak with unhappiness.

She knew that her motives were all wrong, that she was just being tormented by her old familiar weakness. Daniel's dangerous attraction for her had to lie in his helplessness, in his absolute need of her strength and warmth. The others, Hiro and Maria and Steven, were all beginning to find their own way, to create their own interests and find fulfillment in their own fashion. Only Daniel remained dependent on Jamie for her physical help and her warm encouraging company.

And yet she sometimes wondered if her admitted craving to be the strong and giving partner in a relationship could really explain *everything* she felt for Daniel. Could it account completely for the wild, passionate feelings that this man aroused in her, the erotic fantasies that plagued her incessantly, the urgent longing she felt to be intimately near him?

Was she, perhaps, just hypnotized by the strength of his personality or driven by her own craving for power over an undeniably powerful man?

Endlessly, relentlessly, her thoughts circled and whirled and nagged at her, until she was almost desperate with weariness. She knew, in her moments of complete honesty, that she should leave this position. She was becoming too emotionally involved to be an effective therapist. And although Daniel had given no sign, after that one passionate sexual encounter, of being physically drawn to her in return, he was still her patient and therefore in danger of being damaged at some time by her lack of control.

The others here had no further need of her. They were all doing very well, and could manage on their own. And, although Daniel might miss her at first, he would be better off ultimately with a different therapist, one whose motivations were not so troubled and confused.

But somehow Jamie couldn't bring herself to leave. She loved the house and the people in it and the comfortable daily routine of work and relaxation. The thought of resigning, of going away and leaving everything behind, and looking for another job somewhere, was just too hard to contemplate.

Jamie frowned suddenly and picked up the ball of wool again, studying it in thoughtful silence. She realized that she was waiting. Something, she sensed, was going to happen, something that would bring the situation to a head, force her to take action, remove the decision from her hands.

She knew that it was coming, and that it was going to happen soon.

With a strange mixture of apprehension and relief, she picked up her crochet hook, pulled a length of yarn into a loop, and began, methodically, to work a new square.

LATER THAT SAME DAY, still in her shorts and T-shirt, Jamie pulled her Volkswagen to a stop by the curb in a midtown residential area and leaned over to flip the lock on the passenger door. Maria sat on the bench beside the bus stop, so deep in conversation with an elderly lady that Jamie finally had to toot the horn to get her attention.

Maria turned, beamed at Jamie, and spoke to her new friend as she jumped to her feet and gathered up her handbag. Then, after a final word to the woman on the bench, she hurried over and climbed into the passenger seat, flashing Jamie an incandescent smile.

"Well, that's some change," Jamie observed, trying to sound indignant. "When I first started to do this, you were always waiting for me on pins and needles, looking like you'd die if I was one minute late. Now, you don't even notice me."

Unruffled, Maria giggled. "She was such a nice lady. She has three sons, and they're all chefs."

"No kidding," Jamie said with interest. "At Christmas and Thanksgiving, do they all come to her house and cook the turkey for her?"

"Do you know, I asked her that, and you know what she said?"

"What did she say?" Jamie asked, peering into her rear view mirror as she backed up to pull away from the curb.

"She says that they all take her *out* for holiday dinners. Three chefs, and nobody cooks!"

Jamie chuckled, and glanced over at Maria's glowing face. "You look so pretty," she said sincerely. "You look just beautiful, Maria. You should see yourself."

Maria dimpled with pleasure and waved her hand in dismissal, blushing faintly.

"Well, how did it go?" Jamie asked.

"Just fine. No problem at all. Tomorrow, I'm going to do the whole thing."

Jamie tensed suddenly, and tightened her grip on the wheel. "Maria," she began slowly, "are you sure that's a good idea? All the way downtown, all by yourself, and changing buses and everything?"

"Don't worry, Jamie. We agreed that would be the next step. I've done this lots of times, coming this far by myself and having you pick me up. I think I'm ready."

"I don't know," Jamie said, still concerned. "I really think it would be better to do it this way a few more times."

"Jamie, there's only *six weeks* until the reunion! And I have to be confident about traveling by myself. I have to get started now, so I can do it a lot of times before then and feel completely comfortable. I can't afford to take things so slowly!"

Jamie was silent. As a trained therapist she knew that taking things slowly was the only way to achieve most goals, and that Maria's new haste could be dangerous. But she also knew that the patient's motivation was always the strongest factor, and there was no doubt that Maria was motivated. Her passionate desire to be fully cured and independent showed in every line of her face, every inflection of her voice.

"Okay," Jamie said finally. "If you feel that strongly about it, I guess you're ready."

They pulled into the curving drive, parked in the garage and hurried, laughing, into the big kitchen where a small ceremony seemed about to get under way.

In fact Daniel, Clara, Hiro and Steven were all there, grouped solemnly around the kitchen table, clearly waiting for their arrival. Jamie hesitated, struck by the unusual sight of Daniel in the kitchen. Then her eyes widened.

"Oh," she faltered. "Oh, my goodness, is it that time?"

Daniel nodded solemnly, his dark eyes sparkling with fun. Jamie stared at him, still trying to adjust to the image of him in this casual, comfortable room where the staff spent so much of their free time. He looked so imperious, so handsome and arrogant and aristocratic, with his finely sculpted features, his powerful body and the brilliant fire of intelligence in his eyes.

Jamie felt, as she almost always did when she saw him these days, a helpless overpowering surge of physical warmth and desire that flowed like rich liquid fire through her whole body, leaving her feeling limp and shaky. And then, as usual, the initial shock of desire was followed by a melancholy stab of emptiness and sadness and a vast, painful yearning.

I wish... she thought, gazing down at the floor and struggling to collect herself. *Oh, God, I wish...*

Always her mind stopped here, because she could never allow herself to pursue the thought and find out what she wished for. She realized that she was afraid to know. But today, because she was tired and sad, Jamie was no longer able to hold her emotions at bay and the truth surged into her mind with ruthless clarity.

I wish he weren't in that chair, she thought. *I wish he were a whole man, so I could love him freely, without pity.*

Shame and self-loathing washed over her, hot and agonizing, and she forced herself to look up at him again, biting her lips and forcing her voice to sound cheerful.

"Well, I guess we'd better get on with it, then. Are you sure you're ready, Hiro?"

Hiro sat beside Daniel at the table, dressed for the occasion in his best pair of jeans and an old dress shirt of dazzling whiteness. His hair was carefully brushed, and he was so tense with emotion that his thin hands shook badly. But he looked at Jamie with luminous excitement and nodded.

"I finished this afternoon."

"You mean it's up there and everything?" Jamie asked cryptically.

Hiro nodded again, his face pale, his black eyes blazing.

Steven swallowed a huge mouthful of peanut butter-and-jelly sandwich, and twisted around in his chair to gaze up at Jamie. "What's up where?" he asked. "Daddy said I had to come in here because Hiro had something to show me, but he won't say what it is. He said we had to wait for you and Maria."

"Well, it's nice that you waited," Jamie said, smiling down at him. "I'd hate to miss this."

"Miss *what?*" Steven asked helplessly.

Jamie sat beside him while the others looked on with knowing, secretive smiles. The little boy wore faded cutoffs and an orange Mickey Mouse T-shirt, his thin arms and legs tanned nut brown by his long summer in the sun. His small body vibrated with curiosity and his eyes were bright with the excitement of a surprise, and the unaccustomed fun of having all the adults gathered together in the kitchen sharing a secret.

Jamie reached over to hug him. He nestled against her briefly before pulling back and returning, with newfound boyish dignity, to his sandwich.

"What did you do this afternoon?" Jamie asked him. "Where were you while Hiro was...while he was working?"

"Daddy took me to the aquarium. He said we had to get out of the way, or we'd spoil the surprise. But he wouldn't tell me what it *is*. What is it, Jamie? What's the surprise?"

Jamie glanced over at Daniel with a smile. His eyes, dark and full of laughter, caught hers and they gazed at one another for a moment while his smile slowly faded and his face grew serious and intent. Jamie was the first to look away, flushing a little and turning back to the small boy beside her who had climbed up to kneel on his chair and was bouncing with impatience.

"I think we'd better let your Daddy and Hiro tell you," she said gently. "After all, this was your Daddy's idea, and Hiro did all the work."

Steven turned to his father, who nodded briefly, his eyes dancing again. "All right," Daniel said cheerfully. "I guess we can go have a look at this. Clara, is that camera loaded?"

Clara looked down at the camera in her hand, and then threw her employer a startled glance. "Certainly it is," she said with dignity.

Daniel grinned. "Good. Let's go."

He wheeled his chair around and headed for the door, followed by the rest of the group, while Steven danced among them and bombarded them all with questions.

"Just wait, dear," Jamie murmured to him as they trooped across the drive and down into the grounds, still following Daniel who led the way in his chair. "Just wait, and you'll see in a minute."

Jamie felt her own excitement mounting. By the time they reached the large elm tree deep in the shaded acres beyond the house where Hiro had chosen to mount the tree house, her heart was pounding and she felt warm with pleasurable anticipation.

Still bewildered, Steven gazed from one adult to another as the little procession paused beneath the spreading, low-hanging branches and Clara began to mount a lens and prepare her camera.

"What *is* it?" he asked his father. "Why are we stopping here, Daddy? Is this the surprise? What is it?"

Daniel smiled tenderly at his son and turned to Hiro, who stood tense and silent by the gnarled trunk of the big tree.

"Show him, Hiro."

Hiro gazed at his employer for a moment with an expression of admiration and respect that was close to worship. Then he reached out a thin brown hand and tugged at the end of a rope tied around a low-hanging branch, barely visible amongst the leaves. As he pulled, a sturdy wooden ladder began to appear through the foliage, unfolding itself in sections with ghostly clocklike precision until it swayed, silent and inviting, just a few inches off the ground.

A hush fell over the gathering beneath the tree. Steven clutched the metal rail on the back of his father's wheelchair, his small hands white with tension beneath the summer tan. He bit his lip and stared, wide-eyed, at the little wooden ladder.

"Daddy..." he whispered, unable to take his eyes from those wooden rungs that disappeared so enchantingly into the leafy cloud above. "Daddy, what is it? Where does it go?"

Daniel twisted in his chair and looked up at the child, gripping the little hand closest to him, his eyes warm with a depth of emotion that he seldom revealed.

"Why don't you climb up and check it out, son?" he said. "Find out for yourself where it goes."

Steven's mouth dropped open. He looked around at the adult faces above him, his eyes full of wonder and a slowly dawning joy. Tentatively, he gripped the rungs and began to climb, slowly at first, and then with increasing speed so that his thin body was soon just a flash of orange amongst the vivid green of the leaves.

"Oh, wow!" he shouted suddenly. "Oh, *neat!* This is so neat! Look, there's a little . . . and there's a . . ."

Abruptly, the awed voice from within the tree stilled, and they could hear the small rustlings of Steven's body, and the quick patter of his feet on boards overhead as he explored.

Jamie gazed upwards finding herself just able to discern the shape of the structure that was concealed so cleverly amongst the leaves. There was the slope of a wall, and the overhang of a little roof edge.

"It's more visible from the other side," Daniel said beside her. "Hiro put a window on that side, too, that gives Steven a view out over the city."

"It's . . . it's just beautiful Daniel. I saw the plans, and I knew it was going to be impressive, but this is just so—"

She broke off and shaded her eyes with her hand, gazing wistfully up into the branches again while Daniel cast her a keen sidelong glance.

"I understand," he said casually, "that's there's lots of room for two, Jamie. Why don't you climb up and have a look?"

She stared down at him, wide-eyed, and then shook her head reluctantly. "I'd better not. I'm so big..."

"Go ahead," Hiro said unexpectedly, with a new pride and confidence that illuminated his entire small body. "Mr. Kelleher is right, Jamie. There's lots of room for you and Steven both."

Jamie looked from one face to the other, still hesitant.

"Hey, there's a little *porch* up here!" Steven shouted suddenly from overhead. "With a railing! And there's little *cupboards*, and they've got crayons in them, and cookies and stuff, too. Oh, this is just so *neat!*"

"Okay," Jamie said with a chuckle. "That does it. I've got to see this."

She gripped the small wooden ladder and braced one foot tentatively on the lowest rung, swaying lightly while she tested its strength. Then, with lithe athletic grace, she began to climb, her bare tanned legs flexing as she mounted slowly into the leafy cloud overhead.

The tree house was about eight feet off the ground, with the ladder opening comfortably onto the little railed porch that Steven had described, and so well positioned among the branches that Jamie was almost able to stand erect when she stepped from the topmost rung. She paused on the child-size veranda, enchanted by the magical feeling of being hidden amongst the soft rustling leaves, and then stooped to edge her way through the tiny front door.

She found herself in a surprisingly substantial space about eight feet square and furnished with charming little benches and foldout tables. Jamie sniffed with pleasure at the warm, rich smell of fresh lumber and paint, and the fragrance of sun-warmed leaves that drifted in through the opened casement window made of real glass. Along one wall were the miniature cupboards where Steven knelt, the muted light from the window playing over his finely drawn childish features as he explored in hushed silence the contents of a lower cabinet.

He glanced up at Jamie, his eyes so wide that they seemed to fill his whole face.

"Jamie," he whispered.

"Hi, Steven," she said with a smile. "I think I'm too big for those little benches," she added cheerfully. "I'll just curl up right here on the floor. Do you think I could have a cookie," she added, "since I'm your first houseguest?"

He hurried to fetch a little plate and cup, to put out the cookies and a cardboard carton of juice on the tiny carved table. But he was silent, still unable to speak.

"Is it all right, Steven?" Jamie asked anxiously. "Do you like it?"

He gazed at her. "It's... it's beautiful," he murmured at last. "It's just the best... the very best." His face crumpled suddenly and he began to cry, brushing awkwardly with the back of his hand at the tears that trickled down his thin brown cheeks.

Jamie reached out and drew him close, cuddling him and stroking his smooth dark hair while he sobbed briefly against her breast.

At last he drew away and looked up at her. "Did anything ever make you so happy that you just had to cry?" he whispered.

Jamie smiled. "Lots of times," she said. "When you're just really, really happy, sometimes there's nothing you can do but cry a little."

He smiled gratefully through his tears and began, with great dignity, to pour the juice and serve the cookies. "I'm going to live up here forever," he announced. "I'm going to have a sleeping bag, and sleep up here, and do my schoolwork, and..."

"Oh, no, you're not," Jamie said firmly. "Not a chance. Playtime only."

He grinned cheerfully, and then gave Jamie another wistful glance. "Jamie, I wish Daddy could come up here."

Jamie looked down at him, feeling a wave of the old hopeless sadness. "So do I, darling," she whispered, turning away to gaze blindly out the little window. "So do I."

MARIA STARED AHEAD at the back of the bus driver's shaggy gray head, warmed by her buoyant feelings of confidence and success. Although she had made a number of trips on the bus by herself, this was definitely a different sensation. Before, she had always known that when she stopped she would just have a brief wait before Jamie arrived to take her home again, and the meeting places had always been carefully prearranged.

But today there were no plans at all for meetings with Jamie. Maria was on her own, from beginning to end. She would ride downtown, buy a couple of spools of thread and some more yellow wool for Jamie, and then get on the bus to come home again, just like any normal woman out running a few errands.

Maria took a deep breath and smiled to herself as she watched the trees and houses flow past the window. Her sense of exhilaration and independence was almost dizzying in its intensity. All the colors looked brighter, and the sounds were clearer. Every time the bus door was opened, the fresh afternoon breeze with its tangy hint of autumn came rushing in, cool and bracing on her skin.

And always at the back of her mind was the joyous lift of optimism that she felt whenever she looked ahead to her school reunion. She imagined herself, trim and pretty in her new red suit, meeting and chatting with old classmates and teachers. And then, from the back of the room came Tony, smiling at her with his warm shy smile, and she moved toward him and took his hand. . . .

Maria smiled again and moved a little on the hard vinyl bench, almost overcome by her daydreams.

She thought of Jamie, and of how the tall woman's warm, patient friendship had transformed Maria's life.

A little cloud drifted across Maria's face when she thought about her friend. Jamie didn't seem as happy these days as she used to, but she would never talk about what she was troubling her. Maria suspected that it had something to do with Mr. Kelleher, who also seemed distant and preoccupied lately, although he was never as brusque and harsh anymore as he been so often in the days before Jamie arrived.

Maria's mind continued to wander, remembering the tender warmth of her employer's handsome dark face when he witnessed Steven's joy over his tree house, and the fun that sparkled in his eyes when he teased Clara about her photography.

He was really a very nice man in a lot of ways, Maria thought, and not nearly as scary to be around as she had always assumed he would be. He even cared about *her*, and frequently asked her how she was progressing, taking the time to show her articles from his library on agoraphobia and gravely discussing the condition with her just as if she were one of his peers.

Maria wondered why, when two people were both as nice as Jamie and Mr. Kelleher, they seemed to find it so hard to get along with each other. Maybe it was because they were both such strong personalities or maybe they just had to spend so much time together and that made it too—

Maria's thoughts were interrupted by a lurch and grind as the bus slowed to stop, swinging clumsily in to rest by the curb. She looked out again, realizing in surprise that they were already downtown, right by the stores where she had planned to get off.

Her heart began to thud a little and her palms grew moist with anxiety, but she reminded herself sternly that this was no different from all the other times she had come downtown with Jamie. There was nothing to threaten her, and nothing to hurt her. All these other women were doing the very same thing, and none of them were afraid.

Reluctantly she got out of her seat, edged to the front, and gave the bus driver a shy, anxious little smile as she stepped down to the curb. The bus door slid shut behind her and the big vehicle pulled away, leaving Maria feeling utterly alone and exposed on the bustling city street.

She hesitated, peering around her with a sense of growing uneasiness. Things looked different downtown, somehow, than they had when she was with Jamie. The air was stale, and the buildings were tall and impersonal, and the people's faces looked cold and distant as they pushed their way along the sidewalk.

Maria felt a brief clutch of panic, and looked around desperately for a telephone.

"Call me," Jamie had said. "Make sure you have the right change and if you feel the slightest bit uneasy, get to a phone and call me. I'll be right here waiting in case you need me."

Maria bitterly regretted her own haste. She knew that Jamie had been reluctant about this, had thought that she was moving too fast and missing vital steps in her therapy, and she was right. Maria should have come downtown by herself and had Jamie meet her here a few more times before she tried to do it all alone. But she had been doing so well, and she was so tired of waiting for her life to begin . . . for Tony. . . .

Maria shuddered and clutched her handbag, standing very pale and silent in the middle of the sidewalk as the afternoon crowds streamed around her, jostling and pushing at her.

A hand closed on her arm, and she whimpered in terror. A voice was speaking in her ear, but she could barely hear it over the pounding inside her head. She turned, gazing blindly into a face, very close to hers, a broad red face surrounded by harshly dyed blonde curls. . . .

But the woman's blue eyes were kind, Maria realized, and she was just showing concern.

"Are you all right, dear?" the woman asked, in a husky heavily accented voice. "Can I help you?"

Maria gave her a small shaky smile. "No . . . no . . . I'm fine. I was just feeling . . . a little dizzy," she whispered. "But I'm fine now."

The woman hesitated, peering into Maria's face with shrewd worldly eyes.

"You're sure? You don't look well. Maybe I should—"

"Really," Maria assured her, warmed and strengthened by this small display of human caring and concern. "Really, I'll be fine. Thank you so much."

Finally the woman moved away, swept off by the passing throng. Maria began hesitantly to fall into step with them, allowing herself to be carried toward the huge entry doors of the department store.

All at once a hard body lurched against hers, and she felt a hot breath on her neck, a hand clutching at her bag. She tensed, too terrified to scream, staring around her in horror. But the man was gone, swallowed up in the crowd, and she couldn't even have said who it was. Shaking violently, she looked down at her handbag. It was intact, the flap still closed, the handle gripped tight in her hands.

Maybe she had just imagined it....

But now the people looked different. Their faces were cold and hostile, full of veiled dangers. Their eyes passed over her with hatred, and noises began to rise all around her, of sirens and pursuit, of screams and sighs and sheer animal terror. The noises mounted to a shrill pitch, mingling with the pounding rush of her own pulse that hammered against her skull. She felt nauseated, sick with terror, unable to breathe.

Another hand clutched at her, and a voice shouted. Maria broke away and ran, clumsy in her high heels, wanting only to escape, to get away from the masses of people and the noisy snarls of traffic and the menacing danger of towering buildings against the wide, terrifying autumn sky.

She heard shouts, felt more hands, saw ranks of staring faces. Her long black hair fell into her eyes and her breath came in great ragged gasps. Hot tears flowed, streaming down her cheeks so that she couldn't see where she was going. She heard the grinding of brakes and the sharp angry blare of horns, and felt the searing exhaust fumes from passing cars that burned against her legs.

Suddenly the texture of the pavement beneath her feet changed, became bumpy and uneven. She slipped on a patch of loose gravel and sprawled headlong, sharply conscious of a sudden burst of pain in her temple, of gritty stones that dug into her palms and a burning agony in both knees.

Then, at last, a merciful cloud of oblivion settled over her terrified mind and she knew no more.

CHAPTER TWELVE

MOONLIGHT WASHED THROUGH the big mullioned windows, splashing the walls and floor with slanted silvery blocks and outlining the sleek gleaming furniture in soft fingers of light.

Daniel lay wide-eyed in the darkness, his hands clenched at his sides, his face rigid. He arched his back and shifted a little in his huge bed, trying to find a position that would ease the pain. But it continued to burn like a fiery rotating wheel of agony, centered near the base of his spine and raying out, it seemed, all the way to his fingertips.

Desperately, he glanced over at the luminous dial of the bedside clock. It was just a few minutes after one o'clock. Far too late, he thought miserably, to bother Jamie. She'd be sound asleep, and it had been such a terrible day for her.

He flipped on the bedside lamp and tried to distract himself by gazing around at his surroundings. He loved this room, which had been all his own ever since his boyhood and which he had furnished himself, entirely to his own taste. The furniture was mostly teak with fine clean lines, and the colors were the earth and jewel tones that he loved, bronze and dark green and amber. A big curly goatskin rug covered most of the shining hardwood floor, scattered here and there with colorful velvet throw cushions. The bed in which Daniel lay was the only ornate piece of furniture in the room. Its massive headboard, hand-carved from dark mahogany and inlaid with pearl, was a treasure that he had bought years ago in Pakistan.

In fact, this room contained all the treasures, small and large, that he had collected during his life. There were mementos from his school days, caps and pennants and trophies, side by side with rare leather-bound first editions, fine pieces of porcelain and small sculptures and exotic souvenirs from his travels. A pair of Haida masks from the British Columbia coast hung next to a finely woven Persian tapestry, while camel bells from Iran lay across the hull of a beautifully carved jade Chinese junk almost three feet long.

Daniel looked wistfully at the things he had gathered from the far corners of the world, trying to ease his pain by concentrating on each object, remembering where he had acquired it and under what circumstances.

But even this distraction no longer helped him much. These days, thinking about the past and his travels only tended to make him feel worse, especially since Jamie was so relentless in her gentle, unspoken conviction that he should just resume his old busy far-flung life as if he were any normal man.

He gritted his teeth and reached behind him to grasp the headboard, trying to ease his body into a more comfortable position. The pain ripped at him, knotting and clenching his muscles like a fist of iron. He moaned and brushed his damp forehead.

In desperation, he brought Jamie's face into his mind, concentrating on the generous warmth of her wide, sweet mouth, the breadth of her cheekbones, the calm depth of her brow, the gentle tenderness of her flower blue eyes.

Dear God, he thought, *how I love her.*

Instantly ashamed, he dismissed the thought. Love for Jamie was an indulgence that he could never allow himself, especially not when he knew so clearly how she felt about him.

Daniel was an intelligent man, and his natural keen insights were abnormally heightened by his disability. He could always sense when anyone felt pity or condescension toward him. And all too often he saw the warm flame of sympathy that Jamie tried to hide when she looked at him, saw how she was drawn to him and how clearly she yearned to give him her warmth and physical comfort.

And, always, he saw the angry jealousy on the face of her rejected boyfriend, heard him saying that Jamie could never resist a loser.

Daniel's mouth set in a cold bitter line.

I'll be damned, he thought, *if I'll have her giving me anything out of pity. I have nothing to offer her but a wrecked body, and she knows it, so I'll take nothing from her in return. Nothing!*

But still he yearned for her, hungered for her soothing touch, saw her lovely face glimmering in the moonlight, heard her sweet laughter whispering on the prairie breeze.

Daniel sighed and gripped the headboard again to pull himself over onto his side. Pain washed through him, a molten pool of agony that seemed to flow from his back and spill over his whole upper torso, so excruciating that it was all he could do to keep from shouting aloud.

He reached for the house phone, hesitated and then dialed Jamie's number.

She answered after three rings, her words sleepy and muffled. "Hel-hello? What is it?"

"Jamie, it's me. I'm sorry to—"

"Daniel," she said, sounding instantly alert and wide awake. "What's the matter? Are you in pain?"

"Yes," he said with a small rueful grin. "I'm in terrible pain, Jamie. Do you think I'd bother you otherwise, at this hour?"

"Is it your back again?"

"The same thing. But this is the worst it's ever been. I can hardly bear it."

"I'm coming right away. Don't try to move until I get there."

Limp with relief, he hung the phone up and rolled carefully onto his back, staring blindly at the ceiling and waiting for her.

In just a few minutes she was there, padding quickly into his room, her arms laden with towels, heating pad and liniment tubes. Daniel glanced up at her and tried to smile.

"An angel of mercy," he said, "in Donald Duck pajamas."

Jamie grinned and glanced briefly down at herself. She wore heavy, pale blue knitted socks and a pair of fleecy blue polo pajamas with cuffs at wrist and ankle and a huge decal of Donald Duck on the front.

"So, I wasn't exactly planning on doing any socializing tonight, okay?" she said. "You stop making fun of me."

"I might have known," he said, gritting his teeth against the pain as she tugged his shirt over his head and rolled him gently on his side, "that you wouldn't wear lace and feathers to bed. You're just not the type."

"Lace is itchy," Jamie agreed cheerfully. "And feathers make me sneeze. I like Donald Duck. Roll over onto your stomach please, Daniel. Easy, now..."

He obeyed, cradling his head on his folded arms and concentrating on not shouting aloud as her long sensitive fingers probed gently along his spine.

"Here," she said finally, stopping at a tight knot of muscle and rolling it lightly under her hand. "This is it, right?"

He drew his breath in sharply, with a harsh involuntary gasp of pain.

"Sorry," she murmured. "It's a bad one, all right. But I think we can fix it. Just try to relax, Daniel, while I..."

She shifted a little on the mattress beside him, making herself comfortable while she began with exquisite skill and gentleness to massage the knotted, tensed muscles. Her hands moved slowly, with that rare sureness and firmness that always seemed magical to him, and after awhile the pain began to ease, to ebb and subside into a dull throbbing.

"Oh, God," he sighed in bliss, rolling his head on his arms. "That's wonderful, Jamie. You're a marvel. Never, never stop."

She chuckled. "Not for a while, anyway. I'll keep massaging until I'm sure the tension is eased, and then we'll put the heating pad on it for a while. It must have been terrible," she went on. "This is the first time you've ever called me at night, you know that? You said at the outset that you might have to, but you've never done it till now."

He nodded, his face still hidden from her. "I hated to do it. Especially after—"

Her hands paused suddenly, and then resumed their slow probing circular motion.

"I know," she said. "It took me hours to get to sleep. I just lay there, thinking and thinking about her."

"What do you think? Is it a total relapse? Will Maria be all right, do you think?"

"I don't know. I really don't know, Daniel."

He couldn't see Jamie's face, but he could hear the misery in her voice and his heart ached for her. She was so loving and generous, always wanting everyone around her to be happy, no matter what she had to do personally to ensure it.

"I'm glad," she went on, "that the police were kind enough to bring her home, like she wanted, instead of insisting on taking her to the hospital. I don't know what shape she'd be in tonight if she were in a strange place somewhere."

"You're sure she shouldn't have gone in overnight, just for observation?"

"I'm sure. She banged her head against that lamppost, but it's not a concussion or anything. And she skinned her knees badly when she fell, but I've disinfected them and cleaned and bandaged them. I think they'll heal soon."

They were silent for a moment, both thinking about the other, hidden wounds that might take much longer to heal.

"Damn!" Jamie burst out abruptly, her hands stilled again. "It's my fault, you know, Daniel. I *knew* she wasn't ready to do that much, but she was so anxious, and I gave in...."

"Jamie, come on." He lifted his head and turned to look up at her. "You can't take all the blame for everything. Other people have some responsibility for their own actions, you know. It's *not* all your fault."

"But I—"

"You did all you could. You've done so much for her...for all of us, in fact. I won't have you blaming yourself whenever anything goes wrong."

Jamie sat on the edge of the bed, gazing down at him in grateful surprise. He leaned up on his elbows and rolled over onto his back, wincing a little and then smiling up at her.

"There, that's better. The pain's almost gone already."

She smiled back at him. "Good. Lift up a bit, while I just slip the heating pad under here...." Suiting actions to words, she slid the pad under the small of his back and adjusted the control. "And," she went on, "I'll wait here for few minutes to be sure it's not going to knot up again."

"Okay. Here, keep warm."

He pulled out an edge of the bedspread and wrapped it companionably over her legs while she sat beside him, tailor-fashion, in her fleecy blue pajamas. Jamie smiled, tucking the spread cozily up around her waist.

"That's nice. My, aren't we getting casual?" she observed. "We've come a long way since that first day, when you interviewed me."

He grinned. "Don't remind me. You said I was a bastard."

"Well, you were, you know. You even agreed!"

They smiled warmly at one another. Their eyes met and held and gradually their smiles faded into a slow, charged intensity of feeling. Finally, they both looked away and retreated hastily to safer ground.

"So," Daniel asked, "what do you think? Is it a permanent setback? Will she have to start over at the beginning, or will she never be able to leave the house again, or what?"

Jamie shook her head thoughtfully. "I really don't know, Daniel. It all depends on her. She was absolutely terrified, but if it matters enough to her, and she's sufficiently strongly motivated, she might be willing to try again. We'll just have to wait and see."

Daniel stared up at the ceiling, his dark sculpted features silent and withdrawn as he thought about Maria's terror and about himself—about airport terminals and customs officials, about restaurants and service wickets and washrooms and all the myriad small but dreadful obstacles that a disabled person had to confront every day, out there in the world of impatient able-bodied people.

"It must be awful," he said softly. "An experience like that, I mean. When you haven't done it for years, and you finally get up the courage to tackle it, and then all your very worst fears are realized."

Jamie glanced down at him quickly, and he wondered how much his voice had given away.

He looked up, met her eyes, and drew his breath in sharply. She was gazing at him, her clear blue eyes warm and full of sympathy, her lovely face glowing with tenderness.

"Daniel..." she murmured. "Daniel, you know it's not—"

He reached up, touching her lips gently with his fingers, not wanting to hear what she was going to say. But the small action, the soft fullness of her lips against his fingers and the look in her wide, startled eyes were suddenly too much for his overtaxed self-control.

With a low moan of anguish and desire, he pulled himself up in the bed and drew her toward him. Jamie resisted, trying to pull away from him, trying to slip from his embrace and climb out of the bed, but his arms were too powerful. She stiffened against him for a moment and then relaxed with an incoherent whisper, hiding her face against his broad, naked chest.

"Jamie..." he whispered into the warm fragrant masses of her red-gold hair. "Oh, Jamie, I love you.... I want you so much..."

She drew her breath in and shifted against him, her face still hidden. He sensed an answering warmth in her, an unspoken acquiescence that made his heart pound with excitement.

"Jamie," he murmured again, kissing her hair and the nape of her neck, running his hands over her slender curving body.

Daniel felt her tension mount as he reached gently beneath her soft pajama top and began, with exquisite tenderness, to explore the lines of her body, of her back and shoulders. Gently, gently he ran his hand around her waist and then higher to cup her full breast, feeling her shiver as he brushed his fingertips lightly across the small firm nipple.

"Daniel," she protested softly, her face still hidden, her voice slow and dreamy. "Please don't. Daniel, we mustn't...."

"Shh," he whispered. "Don't say anything, Jamie. Just let me..."

He said no more, but continued his gentle caresses, fondling and stroking her lovely breasts, then pulling her shirt aside and bending his dark head to kiss them and run his lips gently over their rounded firmness while she trembled in his arms.

Jamie kept her face hidden, but again he sensed a softening in her, a warmth and gradual yielding that made his pulse race, and gave an added tenderness and purpose to his movements.

With that same slow gentleness, Daniel reached beneath the waistband of her pajamas and caressed the silken skin of her rounded hip, holding his breath as he felt the beautiful muscular firmness of her body. He palmed her taut, flat abdomen, then ran his hand gently downward, drawn irresistibly to the welcoming, womanly warmth that he knew was there.

Jamie shifted in his arms, murmuring broken inaudible words, and he could feel the rising passion in her, the heat of desire she was so often barely able to control. Daniel's own need rushed to meet hers, with the thrusting male urgency that was always so intensely gratifying and amazing to him. He marveled at the arrogant firmness that could still rise almost magically from his damaged body. And even in the white heat of his desire, his soul thanked the woman in his arms and blessed her for calling it forth.

Jamie moved against him, her body obeying its own urging, her movements slow, languid, and intoxicating in their unconscious eroticism. He held her with increasing strength, his muscular arms tightening around her, his mouth no longer gentle but harsh and demanding. Jamie responded just as hungrily, raising her face to meet his, and he crushed her lips beneath his own as if he wanted to drown himself in the warm, rich nectar of sexuality that was part of the essence of her.

Daniel felt her tongue moving slowly against his, thrilled to the sinuous clinging movements of her curving womanly body, gasped at the electric currents of passion that surged powerfully through him, leaving him shuddering and on fire with need.

Then, suddenly, he felt a change in her, a gradual purposeful shift in mood. She was like a swimmer, carried away by a raging current, who makes one last desperate attempt to rally his strength and save himself.

He could feel her trying to muster her own defenses, to deny the clamorous urging of her body and pull herself back from the brink of total abandon. Searing disappointment gripped him, and a sense of loss and hurt that was crushing in its intensity.

"Jamie," he murmured against her hair. "What's wrong, dear? What are you afraid of?"

"Oh, Daniel . . ." She drew back, and raised her face briefly to his. Her cheeks were flushed, and her eyes so haunted and unhappy that he felt a quick stab of guilty remorse.

Daniel looked steadily at her until she dropped her eyes, drawing away to adjust her rumpled clothing and then clenching her hands tightly together in her lap. In the soft shaded light, her downcast eyelashes threw dark sweeping fans of shadow on her warm cheeks. Daniel could see her breasts rising and falling, hear her rapid shallow breathing as she struggled to regain control of her emotions.

"What's wrong, Jamie?" he asked again.

"It's . . . not right," she murmured almost inaudibly, her face still turned away from him.

"Why not? We're both grown-ups, aren't we? And you want it as much as I do, Jamie. I can see it in your eyes, and feel it when I hold you. I don't think I'm such a poor judge of character that I could be wrong about a thing like that."

She looked up at last, meeting his gaze directly. Her face was tense and unhappy, but her eyes were filled with a clear, uncompromising honesty that made him feel, all at once, deeply troubled.

"Yes," she said steadily. "I want it, Daniel. I want it almost all the time, and I don't seem to be able to help myself, even though I know it's wrong and terribly unprofessional of me when I'm in a therapist-patient relationship. But I have to try to control my feelings, because of the consequences if I don't."

"What consequences?" he argued. "After all, it wouldn't even be the first time for us, Jamie."

She continued to look at him with that penetrating clarity that made him so uncomfortable and defenceless.

"Right," she agreed. "It's happened before. And it was awful for both of us, Daniel. Not while it was happening," she added with a brief faraway smile. "We seem, sexually at least, to be pretty good for each other. The problem was afterwards, when we both started brooding about . . . about things. That was terrible for both of us, and you know it."

His handsome dark face was still flushed with passion and frustrated desire, but he was unable to deny the truth of what she said.

"What you mean," he said slowly, "is that we make love and it's great, but then afterward we start questioning our motives and that's not so good, right?"

Jamie nodded, still gazing straight into his eyes, willing him to understand.

"Not *my* motives," he went on, trying to smile at her. "After all, I'm just a normal man, after a fashion, with a lot of normal desires that don't really have much of an outlet."

"Daniel," she murmured in anguish. "Please, don't—"

"It's *your* motivations that we're concerned about, right, Jamie?" he went on, interrupting her calmly. "Because we're not at all sure why you want to do this, are we? Is it genuine feeling for me, or is it just sympathy for a poor disabled guy, since disabled guys need love, too?"

She gazed up at him, her eyes full of pain, unable to find words.

"And," he continued, "we all know where Jamie's weakness lies. She's full of sympathy for the poor and needy, emotionally speaking. And it always leads her to grief. Right, Jamie?"

"Right," she agreed tonelessly, gazing down again at the rumpled mass of blankets around them. "It always leads me to grief."

"So, which is it this time, Jamie? Do you have any genuine feelings for me, besides pity for my disability? Am I a man to you in any other way?"

She avoided his eyes. He leaned forward, unable to hear the words she murmured.

"Pardon, Jamie? I didn't catch your answer."

"I said," she began, her head still lowered, "that I don't know, Daniel. I really don't know. I keep trying, all the time, to figure out whether I..." Her voice caught, and she was unable to continue.

He looked at her, his dark arrogant face softening a little.

"Never mind, Jamie," he said. "It's not fair to put you on the spot. There's no fault in you. You're just a warm, sweet, generous woman, and you're not doing anything wrong. The fault is in me, for wanting and demanding something from you that I don't deserve. I'm sorry, sweetheart. I won't do it anymore."

Stung by his words and his tone, she threw her head up to stare at him. "Daniel, I never said..."

"Please, Jamie. It's all right." He met her eyes, his face set once more into its customary withdrawn lines, and smiled politely. "This won't happen again. Thank you for helping with my back. It's much better now."

"Daniel, I didn't mean that I—"

"I think you'd better go back to bed now, and get some rest," he interrupted in that same quiet, polite tone. "You've been looking tired lately. You need your sleep."

She nodded miserably and slipped from the bed, padding quietly around the room to gather her equipment. Then, without looking at him, she bent to tidy the rumpled bedclothes and plump his pillows for him while he watched her in steady silence.

Jamie turned to go, pausing in the doorway to look back at him. His eyes were dark with suppressed emotion, his wide mouth set in a firm bitter line.

"Daniel . . ." she began hesitantly.

"Good night, Jamie. Thank you again for getting up at this hour."

She inclined her head, in acknowledgment both of his calm courteous words and his tone of dismissal. Then she closed the door softly behind her and vanished into the night.

After she was gone, Daniel lay very still in the pool of lamplight, his head resting against the wide carved headboard as he gazed up at the ceiling. His mobile face reflected the emotions that he had been unable to share with her—the bewildered pain, the frustration and resentment and impatience with himself and his own fate that haunted so much of his life.

But there was something else there in his face, too, an elusive, slowly growing conviction that was difficult to put a name to, even for someone with a mind as incisive as Daniel's. He knew only that it had something to do with the look in Jamie's eyes just before she left him, and the stern unyielding honesty that was so much a part of her.

Once you met and acknowledged something like that, Daniel thought, truly acknowledged it, then you were forever changed.

He wasn't really sure just how he was changing, or even if he was going to be strong enough to follow the transformation through to some kind of conclusion.

But he knew that, after this night when he had looked into Jamie's clear blue eyes and seen the truth about him-

self, he would never again be the same man he had been
in the past.

JAMIE LAY IN THE LONELY silence of her bed, staring wide-
eyed at the shadows on the ceiling. She had long ago given
up any attempt to sleep, knowing that her mind was far
too crowded and tormented to release her into merciful
blankness.

She watched the hours creep by on the lighted face of
her bedside clock and fought the raging tide of emotion
within her that threatened to sweep her away into a deep
sad ocean of misery. She felt hopeless, terribly alone, unable to understand her own feelings, barely even able to
control them. Her body ached with sexual longing, and
her mind was haunted by Daniel's words and her own re-
plies.

Was he right? Was she really drawn to him so intensely, with such passionate and heated desire, just out
of her own generosity? Was she about to give in to the old
treacherous feelings that had caused her so much pain in
the past?

She moaned and rolled over onto her stomach, burying her face in her hot pillow and clutching the sides of the
bed. For a long time she huddled in silence while the
moonlight washed over her tense, still body.

Finally she got up in weary defeat, pulled on a robe and
a pair of slippers and went out into her small sitting room.
She pulled an armchair around to face the huge windows, drew the sheer drapes aside and curled up in the
chair, hugging her knees and resting her chin on them in
brooding silence as she gazed at the lightening sky to the
east.

A shining clarity, as pale and delicate as a shimmer of
light on the edge of a seashell, marked the place on the

horizon where the sun would soon be rising. Apart from this, there was nothing to separate land from sky. Like the two halves of a shell, they remained closed in upon one another, silver-gray and silent. The sky reflected the rippling expanse of misted grass, and the land was as hazy and diffuse as a billowing mass of leaden clouds. The world was endless and unfathomable, an opaque sphere suspended in time, hushed and expectant.

Suddenly, in utter silence, the sun slid above the horizon and glory spilled across the prairie. A crimson pathway of light rolled over the silvered grass, glittering in the prisms of frost that clung to each slender stem. The clouds caught fire and beamed rainbow colors onto the sleeping earth. A breeze sprang up with the sunrise and swept lightly across the ground, and the jeweled grasses swayed and lifted, while the buildings of the city, still silent and hushed in the dawn, glowed in soft pastel colors, their windows flashing dusky gold against the luminous skyline.

Jamie gazed at the wondrous spectacle of the prairie sunrise, feeling unutterably lonely and sad. The glowing pale light seemed to shine into her very soul, highlighting her confusion and the miserable disarray of her weary thoughts.

She had no idea what was happening to her, where these feelings were leading her or what was going to happen. The only clear impression she had was one of real and imminent danger. She sensed that, unless she could somehow take control of herself and turn things around, she was going to find herself deeply and inextricably involved in Daniel's life. She would be in his bed, in his arms, using her physical warmth and emotional strength to help and comfort him, to shield him from the world he dreaded.

Oh, no, not that. Never again, Jamie told herself, her face as set and cold as stone.

She had resolved that from now on she would only involve herself with men who could help themselves. And she had no intention of breaking that vow to herself. Not even for someone as irresistible as Daniel Kelleher.

All at once her mind was filled with light, as clear and revealing as the sunlit path that rolled across the sleeping prairie. She knew what she must do, and she understood that she had to do it immediately.

Moving slowly, numb with pain, Jamie pushed herself out of the chair and made her way back into her bedroom, dressing silently in jeans, moccasins, a fleece-lined pullover and a warm denim jacket. She packed a few things in her carry-on bag, barely pausing to think, anxious only to have this over with. Then she took a sheet of notepaper, sat at her desk to compose a brief letter and sealed it in an envelope.

Taking the envelope and her bag, she stole from her room and out through the hushed stillness of the big sleeping house. In the foyer she paused, dropped the sealed envelope on a gleaming rosewood table and looked down at it for a few moments in strained silence. Her face tightened in an agony of indecision and her hand hovered briefly above the envelope.

At last she stuffed her hand grimly in her pocket, slipped through the kitchen, let herself out the side door and crept into the garage to get her car.

CHAPTER THIRTEEN

DOREEN'S KITCHEN was just a few miles from Knightsbridge Heights, but light-years away in appearance and atmosphere. It was like dropping into a completely different world, Jamie thought. In fact, you could get a bad case of jet lag just crossing the city.

But at least, she told herself wryly, in this kitchen you didn't have much of a chance to sit around feeling sorry for yourself.

Her thoughts were interrupted by a substantial blob of oatmeal that sailed past her cheek and landed with a damp splatter on the table in front of her plate. Jamie stared down at the spreading, oozing mass, and then over at Dougie who clutched his curved baby spoon and returned her gaze with great sweetness. He looked at the spoon in his plump fist with considerable satisfaction and then at the blob of oatmeal. His mouth opened in an enchanting smile that showed off all his new teeth and he chuckled aloud, banging his spoon energetically on the tray of his high chair.

"All right, my little man," Kevin O'Rourke said to his merry grandson. "If it's throwing it about that you're planning, then you're not very hungry anymore, are you? Gramp will take you and clean you up then."

He lifted the squirming baby from the depths of the chair and carried him off, still crowing with delight, to have his face washed and his bib removed.

Jamie grinned wanly as they vanished from the room, and turned her attention to a fierce altercation between Sean and Teresa, the two oldest children, apparently centered on metaphysical considerations.

"They are *not!*" Sean shouted, beside himself with rage.

"They are so, dummy," Teresa told him serenely. "*Everybody* knows that. You see it all the time, on TV and movies and everything. I can't believe you're so stupid."

"Yeah?" Sean said belligerently. "Then how come when they're haunting houses, they carry *chains* and stuff, huh? How come? How come?"

Intrigued in spite of herself, Jamie looked at the two of them. They were seated at the other end of the table, eating waffles drowned in syrup and glaring fiercely at one another. Red-haired Teresa, who had eccentric tastes in clothing, wore an old, blue satin ruffled blouse scrounged from her mother's discard pile, coupled with high-top runners and a ragged pair of gray sweatpants with a large hole in one knee. Because it was Saturday, Sean still wore nighttime attire, an old Star Trek outfit that was far too small for him and gaped alarmingly at stomach and back.

"Right, Aunt Jamie?" he asked, turning to her with a look of desperate appeal on his round freckled face. "I'm right, aren't I?"

"He's stupid," Teresa said calmly, pouring another stream of syrup onto her waffle. Diplomacy was never Teresa's strong suit. She believed in calling a spade a spade.

"Not so much syrup, Tessie," Jamie said automatically. "It's not good for you. What's the argument about?"

"She says," Sean began indignantly, "that ghosts are invisible like wind, and they can't do anything but scare people."

"Well, isn't that true?" Jamie asked, bewildered. "That's what I always thought."

"See?" Teresa said smugly. "Aunt Jamie says so, too."

"But they move stuff around!" Sean said. "They carry stuff and throw things and push people and everything. How can they do all that if they're just air, or something?"

Jamie, who frequently found herself drawn into these discussions amongst her nieces and nephews just because they were so interesting, frowned thoughtfully now and considered the matter.

"Well, what do *you* think they are, Sean?" she asked finally. "Ghosts, I mean?"

"I think they're like real people, only invisible. Like, if you bumped into a ghost, you'd be able to feel him."

"If I bumped into a ghost," little Kevin announced unexpectedly from his place beside Jamie, "I'd just die. I wouldn't feel *anything*."

In spite of herself, Jamie gave a shout of laughter and gathered the small boy onto her lap, fork and all, to give him a loving cuddle.

"Where's Miriam?" she asked suddenly, pausing to count noses.

"Here I am," Miriam's gentle voice said from somewhere very near the floor.

Jamie bent to peer under the table and saw her shy dark-haired niece sitting in her favorite place, sheltered by her family's feet and legs and their vigorous loud voices while she solemnly dressed her little army of Barbie dolls in a bewildering array of finery.

Jamie smiled and sat erect again, absently stroking Kevin's cowlick.

"Aunt Jamie," he said, twisting in her lap so he could look up at her face, "can I go over to play with Steven today? I haven't been there for a whole week, and we have something we want to do in the tree house. It's a secret."

"Not today, dear," Jamie said. "It's . . . it's my day off today, and I wanted to stay here and visit, and then I'm—"

Her voice caught suddenly. She turned aside to take a hasty sip of coffee, but not fast enough to escape Doreen's shrewd glance from across the table.

"All right," Doreen said suddenly. "Out, all of you. Teresa, help Miriam to get dressed. Sean, you take Kevin and go clean up your room. Then you can all watch cartoons downstairs until it's time for Daddy to wake up and take us to the mall. Hurry, now, no dawdling!"

Magically, the kitchen emptied and peace descended over the two women at the table, who smiled at one another and lifted their coffee mugs in a silent, eloquent toast.

"I don't know how you do it, Doreen," Jamie said with admiration. "You're a wonder. You just open your mouth, and the whole world changes."

"Maybe I'm a ghost," Doreen said dryly. "God knows, some days I feel like one."

Jamie chuckled and then sobered, gazing out the kitchen window.

"So, spill it," Doreen said brusquely. "What's up?"

Jamie looked over at her sister-in-law, and then dropped her eyes quickly and began tracing the pattern in her place mat with a careful trembling finger.

"Oh, nothing special," she said, trying to keep her voice light. "Just a regular Saturday."

"You don't look all that good, Jamie."

"I just . . . I didn't sleep well, that's all," Jamie said.

"Come on, Jamie. It's just you and me now. No men, no kids. Tell me what's the matter. Quick, before they invade again."

Jamie kept her face lowered. Biting her lip to control her voice which threatened to betray her, she said, "Well, I think I'm going to quit my job, Doreen. In fact, I guess I already have. I left a letter of resignation this morning before I came over here."

She looked up, her blue eyes desperate with appeal and unhappiness. Doreen returned her gaze in steady silence, waiting.

"It was just . . . It was getting . . ."

"I thought you loved the job," Doreen said.

"I did! But things are getting so . . . complicated," Jamie said awkwardly.

"Is Mr. Kelleher being rude again? Is he still bullying you?"

"No, not at all. On the contrary," Jamie said, "I just seem to be . . . making all the same mistakes again, you know?"

Doreen looked at her thoughtfully for a moment. "Jamie, does all of this have anything to do with Chad?"

"Chad?" Jamie asked blankly. "Why would it? I haven't seen him or even thought of him for ages."

Doreen hesitated, looking down at her work-worn hands in troubled silence. "You remember how we told you, a long time ago, that Chad said he was going to go and talk with Mr. Kelleher? Well, I guess he did. He bragged to Terry that he really told him off—Mr. Kelleher, I mean."

Jamie stared at the other woman, her face white. "Chad said that?" she whispered. "He talked to *Daniel?* Oh, God."

She dropped her face into her hands, and sat for a long time in silence, trying to gather her miserable scattered thoughts. At last she looked up, blinking to hold back the flood of warm tears that was perilously near to overflowing.

Doreen met her gaze, her face warm with sympathy and understanding.

"Jamie, don't look like that. I just wanted to mention it, in case this all had something to do with your problems, but it was ages ago that Chad did this, you know. It wasn't recent or anything."

"I suppose so," Jamie said. "And I doubt that it's done any permanent damage. But I—"

"I think you've probably just been stretching yourself too thin," Doreen interrupted her comfortably. "You've been worrying so much about Mr. Kelleher and about little Steven and poor Maria and even the handyman... what's his name?"

"Hiro," Jamie said with a wan smile.

"That's right. Well, I think you just need a little holiday. Why don't you take off somewhere all by yourself for a few days, and think things through and then decide what you want to do about your job?"

Jamie stared at Doreen's round, sweet face, feeling a quick surge of hope. Then her spirits plummeted again.

"But, Doreen, I already resigned. I left a letter for him...."

"I'll call him," Doreen said cheerfully. "I'll tell him that you're just feeling really tired and not yourself and that you need a rest from everything for a little while and that you'll get in touch with him again in a week or so."

"But, I don't know..." Jamie whispered, and paused. "I don't know if I can go back there again," she said, looking up at her sister-in-law with her heart in her eyes.

Doreen returned Jamie's pleading gaze in thoughtful, measured silence, with a depth of understanding that came from listening all the time to the troubles and problems of others. Finally she nodded briskly and got up to begin clearing the table.

"Okay," she said, apparently in agreement with some unspoken decision of her own. "Then it's all settled. You can go away for a few days' rest, and I'll give Mr. Kelleher a call later in the day after you've gone, just to explain what's happening. Then, when you get back, that'll be soon enough to talk with him if you want to and decide how you feel about your job and... and everything."

Jamie felt as if she were about Miriam's age, being picked up in capable hands and dusted off, having her hurts soothed and her world made all better again.

In her ragged and jangled state, it was an enormously soothing sensation.

"Where should I go?" she asked humbly. "I haven't... I've never had much experience with taking holidays all by myself," she added with a brief, shaky smile.

"You can go to the cabin," Doreen said matter-of-factly. "Nobody's using it right now, and it's just lovely up there in the mountains this time of year, with all the fall colors."

Immediately, Jamie saw the wisdom of Doreen's words. She pictured the family cabin set snugly amid silent towering pines, and gave a small involuntary sigh of bliss.

The O'Rourke men, Kevin and his sons, had bought this rustic cabin in the mountains near Banff a number of

years earlier, and they took turns using it as a family retreat in the summer and a ski lodge in the winter. All of
Jamie's older brothers planned their holidays around
times when the cabin would be free, and it was usually
occupied more or less continuously throughout the holiday season.

Jamie herself, though she didn't hold a share in the
property, was frequently invited to stay there and enjoy
the skiing and hiking with one family group or another.
But she had never been at the cabin alone, and in her
present overwrought state she found the thought of having the place all to herself for a whole stretch of days almost unbearably inviting.

"Oh, Doreen..." she began, her tired face warm with
grateful affection.

But Doreen waved her words aside airily. "There's
dishes and cutlery there all the time," she said briskly,
"and tinned goods and firewood and bedding, and the
Flemings are still there, just down the road, if you need
anything else. All you have to do is stop on your way out
of town and pick up a few things like milk and greens. I'll
go right now and get the key."

She bustled out, her plump body full of energy and
purpose, leaving Jamie alone in the silent kitchen. Jamie
sat at the table, sipping her coffee and gazing in weary
thankfulness at the empty doorway.

In a few moments Doreen returned with the cabin key,
attached to a miniature wooden totem pole hand-carved
by one of Jamie's elder brothers during some long-ago
holiday. Behind Doreen came Terry, padding sleepily into
the kitchen in a dark blue sweatsuit with a Calgary City
Police logo on the breast pocket.

Jamie wasn't sure what Doreen had said to Terry, but he smiled at his sister with gruff affection and dropped a big hand on her shoulder.

"So, Jamie-girl, Doreen tells me you're having a little holiday."

"Just a few days. You're sure it's okay for me to use the cabin?"

"It's great. Somebody's got to do the last cleanup and put the storm shutters on. Might as well be you, kid."

Jamie smiled up at his cheerful freckled face, so much like Sean's. She felt surrounded by love and family warmth, by caring and concern, and her raw, over-wrought emotions threatened to betray her once more.

Swallowing the lump in her throat, she pushed her chair back, took the key from Doreen's hand, and shrugged into her denim jacket.

"Well, if I'm going to have a holiday," she said, trying to keep her voice steady, "I'd better not waste a minute of it. Thanks for everything, you two. Give Da and the kids a big kiss for me, okay? And, Doreen, if you talk to Daniel, tell him . . . tell him that I—"

"I'll tell him," Doreen said comfortably. "You just go and have a good time."

Jamie looked at the two of them for a moment longer, began to speak, and thought better of it. Finally, she just waved and fled through the side door and down the walk to her battered little car, unaware of the long, troubled look that Terry and Doreen exchanged as they stood by the window and watched her cloud of bright red-gold hair disappearing into the busy clamor of Saturday morning traffic.

NEXT MORNING, Jamie sat on the rustic front veranda of the cabin and raised her face to the sun, luxuriating in the peace and solitude. The air was heavy with the scent of pine, the stillness broken only by the busy chatter of squirrels and the lovely melancholy song of a pair of loons that carried far across the lake.

Oh, yes, she thought, stretching her long legs and folding her hands behind her head in drowsy contentment. *Oh, yes, Doreen, you were so right about this. This is just what I needed.*

She smiled to herself, thinking about the delightful healing solitude of the past twenty-four hours. Already she felt stronger, more in control of her life, more able to deal with everything.

Everything except Daniel, she thought, with a quick troubled frown, and then shook off the thought. Daniel was still a problem, but one that she would think about later when she had to, not now.

Now she was going for a walk along the lakeshore, and she wasn't going to think about anything but sun and sand, about shorebirds and pine trees and rich, sweet solitude.

Jamie smiled and swung gracefully to her feet, slipping into her old sneakers and grabbing her sweater from a hook by the door. She went inside briefly to bank the fire in the big stone hearth in the main room and push the logs well back. She checked to make sure the rear door was locked, sniffed the aromatic bouquet of cedar that she had gathered the day before and arranged in a milk carton on the table, and then ran out across the veranda and down to the lakeshore.

She wandered for a couple of hours along the water's edge, pausing to skim rocks out over the water and to make brief excursions into the woods to look at the birds and squirrels. Her mind drifted and wandered, lost in sunshine. She hummed to herself, breaking occasionally into snatches of song.

The air was tangy with autumn, clear and sparkled with gold, and so silent that she could hear the water lapping softly against the rocks along the shoreline and the gentle murmur of the wind in the pine branches overhead.

When the sun was nearing the middle of the sky, Jamie turned and started back to the cabin, thinking idly about the long solitary afternoon and evening ahead, wondering with lazy pleasure whether she should have a nap or find a rod and do some fishing or just build a fire, make a big bowl of popcorn and read all afternoon.

She sighed in anticipation, and postponed the pleasure of the decision by sinking down onto a big flat rock just around the bend from the cabin and gazing out across the glimmering water. The warm rays of midday light shone upon her, lying softly across her body as she stretched out on the smooth surface. Silence expanded all around her, pressed close to her with an intensity and warmth that was richly soothing. She had the odd sensation that she was the only person in all the world, but somehow not alone, and that her thoughts and emotions were just a small part of some vast intricate design.

The feeling was comforting and pleasurable, especially after her long period of loneliness and weary soul-searching. Jamie lay back on the rock with her eyes still closed, letting the sunshine wash over her as she sank deeper and deeper into the peaceful stillness that cradled her. Her thoughts drifted in warm golden streams, flowed together, began to take form.

Suddenly, with a brilliant clarity that startled her, Jamie saw Daniel's face. He was laughing, his wide arrogant mouth curved upward in humor, his dark eyes flashing, his hair falling casually across his tanned forehead. He reached his arms toward her, and she smiled and ran to him, sinking down into that warm strong embrace, breathing in the familiar scent of him, feeling the warmth and closeness of the big, hard-muscled body that always thrilled her and stirred her with such rich desire.

Jamie opened her eyes and stared up at the lacy fragment of blue sky caught among the treetops. Her eyes were wide and surprised, her mind reeling with the dazzling diamond bright certainty that all at once flooded her being.

"I love him," she whispered aloud to the wind and the water. *"I love him."*

Jamie knew irrevocably that it was true. She loved Daniel Kelleher as she had never loved any man. She loved him with all her heart and soul. It had nothing, *nothing* to do with pity, with the fact that his body was damaged. Her love was far deeper than that. Her love sprang from the depths of her soul and flew straight to the center of his. A love that would outlast time and eternity.

Jamie continued to gaze up at the sky. Her soul felt as if it had been washed clean. She wondered how she could have taken so long to recognize her feelings, how she could have kept on struggling and denying and confusing her love with pity.

Because I didn't want to face this, she thought. *I knew that as soon as I did, I'd have to make a decision....*

Now she was able at last to be honest with herself, but that didn't make her position any simpler. She couldn't get in her car, drive straight to his house as she longed to, and tell Daniel that she loved him. Because as soon as she confessed her love, other considerations would come rushing in, flooding the world with miserable reality.

She finally understood that Daniel's damaged body didn't matter to her at all. But his soul was damaged as well, and that was something that Jamie knew she couldn't risk getting involved with.

But I can help! she thought passionately. *With my help, he can learn to travel again, to face life with courage, to take his place in the world. I'll go with him, and I'll—*

And in that thought, she realized, lay the great and terrible danger to her own happiness.

It was all so clear now that she wondered how she could have missed it all these months. She had denied her love, insisted on confusing it with pity, because as soon as she acknowledged her feelings she was forced to deal with this dilemma.

If she left Daniel's life, she turned her back on the deepest, truest love she would ever know. But if she stayed, she would be cast into her old role of burden bearer, problem solver, giver of strength and comfort—a role that never failed to crush her, to destroy relationships and leave her miserable. In the new, bright clarity that flooded her mind, there was only one possible choice.

"Goodbye, Daniel," she murmured silently to the wind and the shining waves. "I love you more than you'll ever know, but I won't see you again, not ever."

Warm tears gathered in her eyes and slipped softly down her cheeks. She brushed at them and squared her shoulders, throwing her head back to face the world and the life that must be lived.

She knew that she would muster new strength and carry on, find some kind of meaning and happiness in life, because that was just the kind of person she was. And if Daniel ever recovered, if he could find the courage to change his life and return to claim his place in the world, then she would be waiting for him. But she wouldn't be the one to help, not this time. That was something he had to do alone.

She climbed down from the rock, her face drawn and remote, reflecting the new maturity and firmness that had come with her momentous revelation. Silent and thoughtful, but nevertheless feeling more at peace with herself and the world than she had been for a long time, she rounded the bend in the lakeshore and started up the bank toward the sheltered log cabin.

Suddenly she stopped short and stared, then shaded her eyes with her hand to look more carefully.

A vehicle stood by the side of the cabin, just off the entry road beneath the trees. It was unfamiliar to Jamie, a large silver van, its flat sides flashing in the afternoon light.

Her heart thudded briefly with alarm. She approached the veranda cautiously, looking for signs of life, but nobody seemed to be around, just that expensive silver van, large and conspicuous, parked beside the cabin. Jamie's nervousness mounted. She hesitated by the lower step of the veranda, poised for flight.

A sudden movement at the edge of the cabin startled her, and she swung around, then stared, speechless with shock.

Daniel Kelleher sat there in his wheelchair, wearing his black sweatpants and a cherry red fleece-lined jacket, looking at her in steady silence.

"Hello, Jamie," he said quietly. "Sorry if I frightened you."

"D-Daniel..." Jamie floundered, searching for words, trying to compose herself. She could hardly hear herself speak over the pounding of her heart, and the drumming in her ears.

"Hey, come on," he said with a grin. "I'm not *that* terrifying, am I?"

"I just... I didn't expect..." Jamie looked around helplessly. "Who brought you? Was it Hiro? Where... where is he?"

Daniel's face clouded with sudden pain, but he met her eyes steadily. "He isn't here, Jamie. I brought myself. That van—" he waved his hand in the direction of the big silver vehicle "—is quite a piece of equipment. It has all kinds of gadgets. Swivel seats and ramps and things, you know, to make life easier for guys in wheelchairs."

"Where did you get it?" Jamie asked, still feeling stunned and foolish with shock.

"I rented it," he said cheerfully. "But after today, I think I'm going to just write a cheque for it and take it home. I love it."

"That's... Daniel, that's so good..."

He continued to gaze at her with that same thoughtful, penetrating calm, and Jamie felt a slow revealing flush mount her cheeks. She turned aside in confusion.

"Jamie," he said gently, "I think we have a few things to talk about."

"Yes," she whispered. "I guess we do."

"Do you think you could find a piece of board somewhere to make a ramp, so I can get up these steps and into the cabin? I thought there might be something in the shed around back, but it's got a huge padlock on it...."

Jamie clutched gratefully at the chance for something to do. She ran around the cabin, unlocked the shed and hurried back dragging a heavy slab of plywood left over from last summer's construction of a small family wharf down on the lakefront.

Puffing with exertion, she installed the makeshift ramp and helped Daniel wrestle his chair up the incline and onto the veranda. Then she unlocked the cabin, brought out coffee for both of them from the pot simmering on the back of the wood stove, and sank into one of the old cane chairs on the veranda, clutching her tin mug in trembling hands.

Daniel wheeled his chair around so he was facing her and leaned forward to look at her intently.

"Jamie," he said softly.

She couldn't look up, couldn't even trust her voice. She stared down at the mug held tightly in her hands and concentrated on not giving way to emotion.

"Jamie, why did you leave? Was it just because I was so out of line the other night? I want you to know I'm sorry, Jamie. I had no right to put that kind of pressure on you. It was a rotten thing for me to do."

"Daniel...please... I don't want to talk about...about all that. Not yet. Please?"

She gazed up at him, her blue eyes full of anguished pleading. After a moment he nodded. "Okay, Jamie. Whatever you say. What would you like to talk about?"

"How...how did you find out where I was?" she asked.

"Well, Maria brought me your letter yesterday morning, and I was just recovering from the shock and trying to decide how to track you down when your sister-in-law called. A very nice lady, your sister-in-law, by the way."

"That's Doreen," Jamie said with a brief smile. "She's everybody's mother."

"That's what I thought when I met her."

"You *met* Doreen?" Jamie asked, staring at him. "How? I thought you said she just called you."

"She did," Daniel said cheerfully. "But then we all went over there for supper. We had a barbecue in the backyard."

Jamie felt that her world was reeling and falling apart into strange disconnected little pieces. She continued to stare at Daniel, speechless with shock.

"Jamie," he said with grin, "your mouth is hanging open."

"I... Daniel, I can't imagine... Why did you go over to my brother's house?"

His smile faded, and he returned her stunned look with quiet steadiness. "I felt just terrible when I read that letter, Jamie. I wanted to find you right away, to apologize to you and bring you home again. Your sister-in-law wouldn't tell me where you were, but she said she might be willing to discuss things with me face-to-face. Then she invited us over for the evening, and we all went."

"All?" Jamie asked, still blank with astonishment. "What do you mean by 'all'?"

"I mean everybody. Steven and Maria and Hiro and Clara and me. We all went."

"Oh my," Jamie breathed helplessly, trying to visualize this scene. She saw the battered, trampled grass in Terry's backyard, their old gas-fired barbecue with the ketchup stains on the cutting board, the picnic table with its plastic tablecloth, the lively mass of noisy children....

"It was fun," Daniel said calmly, as if he were reading her mind.

"Fun!" Jamie exclaimed, astounded. "Daniel, I can't even imagine—"

"The steaks were delicious," he went on. "Your brother has a real touch. And that secret barbecue sauce he invented is just a dream. Clara tried hard to get the recipe out of him, but he wouldn't budge."

Jamie grinned faintly at this, but she was still too amazed to take it all in.

"Clara did get quite a few recipes from Doreen, though," Daniel went on. "They swapped recipes all night, while Hiro and Terry were down in your brother's shop talking woodworking."

"And...and Maria? You said that she went, too? Wasn't she afraid to leave the house after what happened on Friday?"

"I think she was," Daniel said. "I think she was terrified, but she knew that we were making this visit for your sake, and so she forced herself to go even though she hated to leave the safety of the house."

"And once she was there..."

"Once she was there, she had a wonderful time watching all the kids playing. She sat all evening cuddling that fat baby on her knee and looked like she was going to melt away with happiness."

Jamie gave him a misty smile. "I wish I could have been there," she said softly. "It sounds just wonderful, all of it."

"I told Maria this morning that I was coming to see you," Daniel went on casually. "She said to tell you that she's fine, and she's going to try again tomorrow to go downtown by herself. She said that seeing your brother's children made her want more than ever to get herself back into the real world."

"Oh..." Jamie said, her face softening with affection. "Oh, Daniel, that's wonderful." All at once her features darkened in concern. "But if she's going tomorrow, I won't even be there...I should be there, Daniel, in case she..."

"Jamie, you can't always be there. You have to let people take some responsibility for their own lives. It's bearing all the weight of everyone's problems on your shoulders that's wearing you out so much. At least," he added with an abashed grin, "that's what Doreen tells me."

Jamie flushed, her blue eyes full of warmth. "Daniel, it really was so nice of you to..."

She paused awkwardly, gazing down at the rough floorboards, and then looked up at him again, trying to smile.

"And what about you, Daniel?" she asked in a more casual tone. "What did *you* do all evening at my brother's barbecue?"

"Mostly, I talked with your father. He's a delightful man, Jamie. I really liked him."

Jamie smiled again, warmed and pleased by his words, and by the picture of Daniel and her father in conversation.

"What did the two of you talk about?"

"Well...let's see. About the Blue Jays' chances for the pennant next year, since the Blue Jays are always a next year's team, and about Irish history, and your father's early days working in the shipyards. Fascinating, that man's life, Jamie. I've never set a book in Ireland, you know. Just after my accident, I tried to start one, even tried to go to Belfast for the research, but then—"

He broke off abruptly and they avoided one another's eyes for a moment, watching as a little gray squirrel, bolder than his fellows, ran along the railing near Daniel's elbow and paused to sit erect, regarding the bright chrome of the wheelchair with a comical astonished look.

"So," Daniel said finally, "Doreen decided that I wasn't a threat to you after all, and that it even might be good for us to get together and have a talk about things. She told me how to find you, and Terry suggested this van rental, and here I am."

"And here you are," Jamie echoed, dreading his next words.

"And now, Jamie, it's time to quit stalling and have a serious talk."

"Daniel," Jamie murmured, her eyes lowered, "I don't think I can . . ."

"Look at me, Jamie," he said gently.

She lifted her head and met his gaze, her face drawn with pain.

"Jamie, I love you."

"Oh, Daniel . . ."

"Please don't look on that as any kind of pressure from me, Jamie. I just want you to know that—" He gave her a small sad smile, and hesitated "—that my intentions are honest, I guess. I know that I've been harsh with you a lot of times, and I've accused you of . . . of having the wrong motivations, and so on, but I've been trying to deny my own feelings to protect myself, and it's been completely wrong of me. The truth is that I love you, really love you, and the last thing I want is to cause you any pain or unhappiness."

Jamie set her mug carefully on the railing and folded her hands together in her lap, staring down at them in tense silence.

"I know," Daniel went on steadily, "that I have nothing to offer you but my name and my money, and I also know how little money matters to someone like you. I'll never be a whole man, Jamie, and it's selfish of me to want you all to myself under those circumstances. What I want to tell you is that I'll be satisfied with as much of you as you feel you can give. Even if you can bring yourself to come back and be my therapist, and just give me your friendship, then I'll try to be content with that. From now on, I won't pressure you to give more than you feel you can."

His words surged through her like a powerful electric shock, filling her with rich, bracing indignation. She looked up, her cheeks flushed, her eyes sparkling with anger.

"Daniel, do you think it matters to me, any of that? You know that I don't care about your money. Do you honestly think I care about your legs, either? Do you really think I'd be unable to love you just because you have a disability?"

"I don't know, Jamie," he said, his dark thoughtful gaze resting intently on her face. "Why don't you tell me? *Would* you ever be able to love me?"

Her blue eyes met his, gazing at him with all the uncompromising honesty of her rich and generous spirit, and his features were suddenly taut with stunned amazement.

"Say it, Jamie," he whispered urgently. "I want to hear you say it."

"I love you, Daniel," she said steadily. "I love you with all my heart and soul, and I always will."

"Oh, God," Daniel said in a choked voice. "Oh, my God..." He gripped the wheels of his chair in his strong brown hands to propel it across the rough floorboards, but was checked abruptly by something in her voice as she spoke again.

"I think I loved you the first minute I saw you, even though you were so infuriating," she went on in that same controlled, toneless voice, "but it took me such a long time to recognize my feelings for what they were. When we made love, that first time..."

She gave him a brief questioning glance, her cheeks flushed at the memory, and he nodded silently.

"Well, then I was really confused," she continued. "You accused me of behaving that way just out of pity, and I thought maybe you were right, even though I could hardly keep my hands off you all the time."

"Jamie," he interrupted with a sudden flash of white teeth in his tanned face, "it's your job to have your hands on me all the time."

"Come on. You know what I mean."

"Lord, yes," he agreed fervently. "I know what you mean."

"And then the other night, when you wanted me to..." She hesitated awkwardly, and then plunged ahead. "Well, I wanted to then, too. Wanted it terribly, but I still didn't know why. It wasn't until I got out here and had a chance to be alone and think things through that I realized there *was* no deep terrible ulterior motive. I just love you, that's all," she concluded simply. "And I want you, all the time."

"Jamie, darling, why is this not a happy story? The woman I adore tells me that she loves me for myself, without reservations, and I still have the feeling that she's a million light-years away from me. Why, Jamie? What's the matter?"

She looked quietly across the width of the veranda at him, searching for words. "Daniel," she began at last, "you told me the other day that you're starting a new book after Christmas. It's going to be an adventure story about a circle of art thieves, I think."

"Yes," he agreed, startled by the sudden change of subject. "Yes, that's true."

"You said it's going to be set mostly in Paris, didn't you? At the Louvre?"

"Yes, I said that."

"Daniel, when you write that book, how are you going to research it?"

He flung his head up, his flashing dark gaze raking briefly over her face before he answered.

"I'll assign my research staff to the project right away," he began slowly, "and then when I'm ready to put the ideas together, I'll send somebody over to Paris, one of the senior people that I really trust, to give me a set of firsthand technical details on gallery security measures, as well as some background and color."

"But you won't go yourself," Jamie said quietly.

"No," he agreed, just as quietly. "I won't go myself."

"Absolutely not? Not ever?"

"Not ever."

Jamie's warm expressive face clouded with pain, and she gazed unhappily out across the glimmering surface of the lake.

"That's what this is all about, Jamie? You can't allow yourself to love me because you don't approve of the way I'm living my life?"

"I can't stop myself from loving you, Daniel," Jamie said in a low voice. "But I can't allow my life to become involved with yours if I don't accept your outlook and actions."

"That seems terribly harsh, Jamie."

Jamie turned to look at him. "I don't think it does. I think it's the right thing to do. I think this is the only mature way to behave. You see, when a woman is young, Daniel, especially a woman like me," Jamie said with a small bitter smile, "she always thinks that she's the person who can make everything better. Unconsciously she even looks for a man who needs her desperately, because then she can be the one to fix things and help and encourage him and build him up. Do you know what I mean?"

Daniel nodded, still looking at her with burning intensity. "But when she grows up . . ." he said.

"When she grows up," Jamie went on, "she realizes that she can't fix anything. Nothing at all. People all have to do their own fixing, and if they get too dependent on someone else for strength and help, then their love can quickly turn to hatred."

"I'd never hate you, Jamie. Never."

She turned to him, her blue eyes blazing with conviction. "You might be surprised, Daniel. You might be surprised how much you could get to hate me, a few years down the road, because I'm free to come and go as I please while you're still trapped by your own fears."

His face turned white, but his steady gaze never wavered. "You're a hard woman, you know, Jamie."

"I love you. Real love isn't soft, Daniel. It has to be hard, or it can't be strong. If you really wanted to overcome this," she went on, "I'd give you every ounce of love and support that I'm capable of. But if you absolutely refuse to help yourself, then I can't afford to get involved. Ultimately, there would just be too much pain. For both of us."

He sat for a moment longer, studying her silent profile. Finally, as if coming to some painful decision, he wheeled his chair abruptly toward the edge of the veranda and rolled slowly down the makeshift ramp. Safely on the ground, he paused and looked over his shoulder.

Jamie turned quickly away and gazed off across the lake, battling a sudden stormy burst of passionate desire. Just the set of his broad shoulders in the warm red jacket, the firm arrogance of his mouth, the line of his tanned cheek and chin against the rich green backdrop of the woods were enough to make her weak and shaky with longing. But she kept her face silent and still, betraying none of her turbulent emotions.

"Are you coming home?" he asked without expression. "If I promise none of this will ever be mentioned, and you'll be free to do your job with no more interference or pressure from me?"

"I don't think so," Jamie said slowly. "I'll come and get my things, but I really don't think...don't think I can bear to come back, Daniel."

"There's more than just me to consider, Jamie," he said, looking at her intently. "Think about Steven, and Maria...all the others who love you."

"Daniel..." she began helplessly.

"At least consider it," he said abruptly. "Stay here and rest, and think about things for a few days. Later in the week, you can come back to see me and we'll talk."

"And if I still don't feel I can live there..."

"Then you're entirely free to go," he said quietly. "I mean it, Jamie. No more pressure."

Jamie nodded miserably, looking down at her hands.

Daniel paused, and then turned without speaking and wheeled himself rapidly across the uneven ground toward the big silver van.

She watched him wrestle with the sliding door and the lever-operated ramp, feeling an almost uncontrollable urge to go and help him. But instinct told Jamie that help from her was the last thing he wanted just now. She sat on the veranda, her hands clenched in her lap, while he finally managed to get himself into the driver's seat and his wheelchair safely installed in its place behind him.

He waved once, a curt polite gesture, wheeled the van around in front of the cabin, and then vanished down the mountain trail in a swirl of dust.

CHAPTER FOURTEEN

"DADDY? Daddy, may I come in?"

Daniel, who was deeply absorbed in a pile of documents scattered across his desk, dragged himself back to reality with some effort and turned toward the door. Steven was there, dressed in his neat school uniform, his hair slick and damp from a fresh combing.

"Pardon, son? Did you want to talk with me?"

"I wanted to ask you something," Steven repeated patiently. "May I come in?"

"Of course."

Daniel looked up at his small son, struck, as he always was, by the boy's fine sensitive features and his shy, vulnerable look.

Steven came into the room and sat carefully on one of the leather chairs, folding his hands politely in his lap. His legs, still brown with their summer tan, looked very thin in his neat gray flannel shorts, and Daniel noted with a brief smile that there was still a healthy scrape from some past adventure healing slowly on one of his knees.

The little boy bit his lip and looked down at his hands for a moment, then faced his father directly.

"Daddy, is Jamie ever coming back?"

Daniel's breath caught, and pain hammered within him like a physical blow. But he kept his face carefully expressionless, moving the mass of papers in front of him into a neat symmetrical pile.

"Of course she's coming back, Steven. Why would you be concerned about that?"

"I just thought . . . I thought maybe she didn't like us, or something," the little boy whispered, his face pale with anguish. "I thought maybe she was like Mommy, and didn't want to live with us anymore, and she'd go away and never come back."

With considerable effort, Daniel summoned enough calm to return his son's gaze steadily.

"Listen to me, Steven," he said slowly. "When Mommy left, it had nothing to do with you. Nothing at all. You're a good boy, and she still loves you, in her own way. And Jamie loves you, too. She cares about you a great deal."

"Then why did she go away?" Steven asked, his voice pleading. "I don't mind so much about Mommy," he went on with the innocent honesty of childhood. "She never really wanted me around much, or anything. But Jamie's always so—"

His voice broke and he dropped his head, searching for words, while Daniel watched him in troubled silence.

"If Jamie doesn't come back, I'll just die," Steven said at last in a muffled voice. "I love Jamie."

"So do I, son," Daniel said sadly, his dark eyes resting on some faraway place that only he could see. "So do I."

Before he could say more, Maria appeared in the open doorway, casting Daniel a quick apologetic glance before she turned her attention to Steven.

"Steven," she said briskly, "you've got to hurry. The bus is going to be—" Suddenly she paused, looking down at him in alarm. "You're crying, Steven. What's the matter?"

The little boy climbed down from the chair, brushing hastily at his eyes and turning toward the door. Maria looked at Daniel with growing concern.

"He's worried about Jamie," Daniel explained over his son's sleek dark head. "He's afraid Jamie might not come back."

Maria nodded in understanding and bent to give the little boy a hug. "Steven, you *know* that Jamie's coming back," she murmured. "Your daddy told us she'd be home in just a few days."

"Sometimes people say that," Steven said stubbornly, "and then they never come back. What if Jamie doesn't come back?"

"Jamie's coming back," Maria said firmly. "She loves us all too much to just go away and leave us. You wait and see. Jamie will be back before the weekend, and then Clara will make rhubarb pie for supper."

Steven looked up at the small gentle woman, his eyes brightening. "Rhubarb pie is Jamie's favorite."

"It certainly is," Maria said with a smile, stroking his hair. "And you have to finish coloring those nice pictures of the flower garden for her, too. You know how she loves flowers."

Comforted, the little boy went over to give his father a brief affectionate kiss and then moved toward the door, followed by Maria.

"Steven," Daniel said suddenly behind them, "you run down and get your schoolbooks from Clara, all right? I want to talk to Maria for a moment."

"Okay. 'Bye, Daddy. 'Bye, Maria. See you after school." Steven paused in the doorway, turning to look back hopefully. "Do you think Jamie might be here tonight when I get home, Daddy?"

Daniel shook his head. "Probably not. I think she'll be home later in the week, son. She's just having a holiday and a little rest."

The boy hesitated, then nodded and vanished down the hallway.

Daniel sat for a moment staring thoughtfully at the empty doorway before he turned to Maria, who waited shyly just inside the room.

Since the arrival of Jamie, and all the momentous things that had happened since, Maria no longer seemed quite so nervous and terrified in his presence, Daniel thought. But her very nature would probably always make her a little shy.

"I hope I'm telling him the truth, Maria," he said with a small unhappy smile.

"About Jamie, sir?"

Daniel nodded, his fine handsome features drawn and silent as he gazed down at the pile of papers beneath his hands.

"I'm sure you are," Maria said loyally. "I can't believe Jamie wouldn't come back to us. She really cares about us. She's like—"

"Like one of the family?" Daniel asked with a quick glance from his dark brilliant eyes.

"Yes," Maria said softly. "Like one of the family."

"Oh, God," Daniel muttered with a rare and revealing flash of emotion. "Oh, my God—"

Abruptly he composed himself and studied his lean brown hands, gripped tightly together on his desk.

"Maria," he began, changing the subject with deliberate calm, "I believe you're doing something important today?"

Maria licked her lips and flushed pink to the roots of her hair. "Yes, sir," she whispered. "At least, it's important to me."

"It's important to anyone, Maria. Having the courage to do something you find absolutely terrifying...that's one of the most important things that any of us can do in our lifetime."

Maria gazed at him, her face reflecting a strange mixture of fear, gratitude, and some other emotion, less easily defined.

"Thank you, sir," she murmured.

"What's your plan, exactly?" he asked casually. "What do you plan to do today? Can I help at all?"

"No, thank you, sir. I think it's better *not* to have help, you know? I have to do it alone."

Daniel nodded. "So how will you approach it?"

"Just...just the same as last time, I think, except that I can't allow myself not to go through with it by giving myself some kind of escape route. I have to make sure that I get all the way there."

"And how do you propose to do that?"

Maria hesitated, her face turning an even deeper pink. "I'm going to...arrange to have somebody meet me there," she murmured, unable to look at her employer. "Somebody that I wouldn't want to disappoint, so I'll be sure to keep the appointment."

"Somebody who works downtown?" Daniel asked with a gentle teasing smile. "Say, for instance, in a grocery store?"

She smiled at him, a shy radiant smile that brought a lump to his throat.

"Have you called him yet, Maria?" he asked.

Maria shook her head. "I'm going to call in...in a few minutes. I wanted to make sure first that I would be able to do it. And," she added with a small proud lift of her chin that Daniel found enormously moving, "I know that I'll do it. I *won't* give in to my fears any longer. I've wasted enough of my life."

"Maria," he asked with sudden intensity, "what's it like? I mean, when you get out there and make the attempt, when you're actually doing what terrifies you and you're right in the middle of it with no escape, how does it really feel?"

She searched for words to answer him, her eyes thoughtful and faraway. "It's terrible," she said at last. "There are no words to describe how terrible it is. It's like you're going to die, just from fear, because it's hard to believe that you can suffer that much and go on living. But then," the little housemaid went on softly, "you think of the people you love, and everything that's at stake, and what you'll lose if you can't be brave, and you go on and do it. And then," she concluded simply, "you feel just wonderful. Nothing feels more wonderful than... than facing what you're afraid of and not giving in."

Daniel listened in silence, his handsome dark features stilled, his powerful muscular body taut with contained emotion.

"I wish you good luck, Maria," he said quietly. "You're a very brave woman, and you deserve all the happiness in the world."

She looked over at him, startled and warmed by his words, and then turned to leave. Daniel watched the door slide noiselessly shut behind her small trim form before he wheeled his chair slowly across the room. He paused by the window, drew back the drapes, and sat for a long time gazing out at the golden autumn morning.

"OH, HIRO," Maria breathed in delight. "Thank you. It's just beautiful." She smiled, her pale face glowing with pleasure as she turned the small, polished wooden box in her hands.

"Yours is teakwood," Clara commented from across the table, "and mine is mahogany. Look how beautifully the corners are fitted."

Clara held up another little box, extending it across the table for Maria to examine. The cook's austere features were softened with uncharacteristic emotion, and she smiled at Hiro who sat shyly in his place at the table, enjoying their pleasure at his gifts.

"I have one for Jamie, too," he said. "I'll give it to her when she gets back."

"She'll love it," Maria assured him. "She'll just love it, Hiro. You do such beautiful work."

Hiro pushed his chair back, drained his coffee mug and moved to leave, pausing in the doorway to look back at the two seated at the table. "For the women in my life," he commented with a rare teasing smile that illuminated his finely drawn, quiet features, "*nothing* is too good."

Clara chuckled and got to her feet, placing her little box carefully on the windowsill and stroking it gently with her hand before she gathered up her keys and shrugged into an old sweater.

"Well, I'm off. Anything you need?" she asked Maria, consulting her shopping list.

"I don't think so, Clara," Maria said, looking up from the sink where she was stacking dishes. "Anyway, I'm going downtown myself," she added with an elaborate attempt at casualness. "Maybe around lunchtime."

Clara looked intently at her friend. "Maria, are you sure that's wise? I mean, you don't want to...rush things, you know, or have another upsetting experience. Don't you think maybe you should wait until Jamie's back, at least?''

Maria shook her head. ''We can't always be dumping all our problems on Jamie. I want to do this myself and show her that I can manage on my own.''

Clara hesitated in the doorway, jingling her keys and thinking. After a few second's silence she nodded with her customary abruptness, closed the door briskly behind her and vanished.

Maria went over to the window, watching as Hiro's little truck and Clara's car disappeared, one behind the other, down the long winding drive.

Then she wiped her hands nervously on her apron, walked haltingly across the room and picked up the telephone.

The number was printed indelibly on her mind even though she had not dialed it for such a long time. Many, many times on lonely afternoons she had opened the phone book and looked at it wistfully, knowing that Tony was at the other end of the line, just seconds away, if only she had the courage to dial this number.

Maria drew a deep, shuddering breath, bit her lip and clutched the receiver tightly in her hand, pushing the dial buttons with a trembling finger.

She heard the harsh jangling ring of the phone in the place where Tony was, heard the brisk tone of the clerk who answered and then her own shaking voice, heard the cheerful voices calling Tony, and his quick footsteps approaching the phone.

''Hello?'' he said.

At the sound of that dear, familiar voice, panic rose up and threatened to engulf her. She couldn't speak, couldn't breathe, couldn't even remember her own name or her reason for calling.

"Hello?" Tony said again. "Is anyone there?"

"It's . . . it's me, Tony," Maria faltered, hating herself for her stupidity, her total ineptitude and miserable cowardice.

"Maria?" he breathed. "Is this *Maria?*"

"Yes . . . yes it is. Tony, I'm sorry to bother you at work, I know I shouldn't have called but I—"

"Maria, this is no bother! If you only knew how many times I—"

Tony's warm masculine voice halted abruptly, and then, in a more casual tone, he continued. "What can I do for you, Maria? Is it something about the reunion?"

"No, not really," she whispered. "I . . . just wanted your help, I guess."

"Maria, if there was ever anything I could do to help you, nothing in the world could stop me."

At his words, a rich thrill of pleasure and excitement flowed through Maria's tense frightened body, warming her and giving her courage.

"Tony, I've had a kind of . . . a kind of problem, I guess. I've had it for a long time, actually, but it's only been really bad for the past couple of years. I don't really know how to tell you. . . ." Maria hesitated, then summoned all her resolve and continued. "I've got . . . something called agoraphobia. Do you know what that is?"

"Yes, I know." He was silent a moment. "Maria, is that why you've been turning me down all the time when I ask you out? You've been afraid to leave the house?"

"Yes, Tony, that's why."

"Why didn't you say so? You should have told me, Maria! I thought you just didn't want to see me anymore, that maybe you'd found somebody else you liked better."

"Oh, Tony," Maria whispered, gripping the phone in trembling fingers and fighting back her tears.

She heard someone calling him in the background, and then a wave of loud teasing voices that swept near him, quelled immediately by his gentle, good-natured response. After that there was quiet on the line, and once again she heard his voice in the receiver.

"Maria, did you say there's some way I can help? Is there something I can do for you? You know I'd do anything you asked me, Maria."

"Well, I've been..." Maria drew a deep breath and plunged ahead. "Tony, I've been trying to get over this. I finally realized... A therapist came here, to work with Mr. Kelleher, and she made me realize that I'm not crazy, Tony, it's just a sickness like anything else, and people can be cured of it. She's been helping me, and I'm a lot better now. I can ride all the way downtown on the bus by myself, even, but I still... I get awfully scared," Maria admitted with an awkward little laugh.

"Oh, Maria," he said softly. "My little Maria..."

The tenderness in his voice was almost more than Maria could bear. She choked and held tight to the edge of the telephone desk, unable to go on.

"Tony," she said finally, "I'm almost thirty years old. I don't want to waste any more of my life. I want... I want to..."

His voice sounded again, strong and warm in her ear. "I know, Maria. I feel the same way. And if I can help somehow..."

"I really want to see you, Tony. That's why I called, actually. I wondered..." Maria paused, gripped by sudden paralyzing terror, and then plunged recklessly ahead. "I wondered what you're doing for lunch."

"Today?" he asked.

"Yes."

"Oh Lord, Maria, I've waited all this time, and now out of the blue... I'm not doing anything for lunch," Tony said with a sudden lift of happiness in his warm, boyish voice. "You name it, kid. I'm all yours."

"I have to warn you," Maria began steadily, "that there's a chance I might not make it, Tony. Last week..." Maria faltered, and then continued. "Last week, I got all the way downtown by myself and then had a panic attack and had to be... brought home in disgrace."

"Oh, Maria...! How about if I come and get you, then? Would that be easier?"

"No!" Maria said abruptly. "I'm not interested in what's easier, Tony. I want to have my life back. I want to do this the hard way, just so I can get back in control."

"All right. You tell me what you want and I'll do it."

"What I want," Maria began steadily, "is to meet you downtown for lunch. What's a good time for you?"

"One o'clock," he said promptly. "If I don't take my lunch break till one o'clock, then I can spend a couple of hours with you."

"That would be lovely," Maria said shyly. "Just lovely, Tony. I'll meet you at one o'clock in front of Eaton's, all right?"

"Maria, are you sure...?"

"I'm sure," she said abruptly. "One o'clock, then?"

"Maria," he began softly, with a rough emotional edge to his voice that thrilled her, "Maria, you just don't know how much I've..."

Voices swelled in the background and drew close to him again, raised in cheerful banter, and he hesitated, then said more formally, "Okay, that's fine, then. One o'clock it is. Goodbye, Maria."

"Goodbye, Tony," Maria said softly.

For a long time after she hung up the phone she sat gazing at it, lips parted, eyes shining, with a dreamy, far-away expression on her face.

THE LUNCH HOUR was not a good time to ride the buses, Maria realized after it was too late. Every coach was jammed with students, commuters and shoppers. People crowded together in the aisles, bumping against one another and jostling rudely for position.

Maria's taut, trembling courage almost failed her when she was shoved over against the window of her bus seat by an enormously fat man in a musty woolen pullover who carried two brown paper bags full of books, and whose breath reeked of salami.

Fortunately, her unsavory seatmate expressed no desire to make conversation, so Maria was free to gaze out the window at the colorful moving landscape beyond the bus, a scene that she had observed often enough in the past months to give a sort of bizarre comforting familiarity.

She sat quietly, hands folded in her lap, strikingly beautiful with her pale delicate features, her black hair drawn back into a simple knot low on her neck, and the vivid red silk suit that she had made for her high school reunion.

I'm glad I decided not to save it for the reunion, she thought, smoothing the lovely soft fabric beneath her work-worn fingers. *After all, this is the most important day of my life.*

The bus stopped, started, lurched forward, opened and closed its doors to absorb and disgorge a steady stream of passengers. Car horns blared, people shouted rudely, and dust swirled down the street in front of a gusty autumn wind. Slowly and relentlessly the world beyond the windows began to change, turning into a sinister landscape full of nameless threats.

Maria bit her lip and stared ahead blindly, feeling the slow hopeless slide into numbing terror that always preceded one of her panic attacks. She tried to think of pleasant things, of Steven and Kevin giggling in the tree house, of Clara's pleasure with her new camera, of Hiro and his woodworking and the sunshine flaming in Jamie's curls. She thought desperately of Tony, with his dark curly hair and his dimpled chin, and the deep and endless kindness in his eyes, waiting for her right now on a windy downtown street.

But all the beloved figures in her life were tiny and faraway, as distant and unreal as objects viewed through the wrong end of a telescope. She had been mistaken to assume that a date with Tony, momentous though it was, would be enough to hold her terrors at bay. She loved Tony, and she longed to see him, but with the tide of panic that was beginning to wash over her and pull her under, Tony might just as well be on the far side of the moon.

Maria whimpered in despair and gripped her hands tightly together, trying to keep herself from leaping out of her seat, stumbling down the aisle of the moving bus and flinging herself out onto the street where she could run, run blindly toward some quiet shelter. Back home, back to her room, back to the place she should never have left....

Something penetrated the dark swirling fog that surged inside her head, a voice, heard dimly, saying something strange.

Maria moaned under her breath and shook her head, trying desperately to clear her clouded thoughts, but the voice continued.

She felt a heavy warm hand gripping the thin silken fabric covering her arm, smelled a hot overpowering gust of salami, very close to her face and heard the voice again, muttering, growling in her ear.

Maria opened her mouth to scream, drowning in terror. The hand tightened on her arm. All at once she caught a few words, and listened in stunned, bewildered amazement. The voice that accompanied the salami-laden breath was talking, it seemed, about dogs. In fact, about one specific dog, apparently named George.

"...and he hates to have his bath," the voice rumbled cheerfully. "Just hates it, poor old boy. But what can I do? He goes out all the time and rolls in the neighbor's compost heap, so I don't have much choice, do I? But then, after he's bathed, he adores it when I brush him with his own little hairbrush, and make him all smooth and silky...."

The voice droned on above her head, soothing and monotonous, discussing George's eating habits, his handsome appearance, his fondness for the postman and his incredible cleverness at doing tricks.

Maria clenched her hands into fists and turned her head slightly, peeping up at the man beside her. He was fat and unkempt, with a round pink face bulging above his soiled turtleneck, giving him the look of a sweet, elderly baby.

Her companion sensed her eyes upon him and turned to smile down at Maria. "Are you feeling a little better now, my dear?" he rumbled.

The fresh gust of salami was almost overwhelming, but Maria was now able to sense the kindness that accompanied it. She looked quickly down at her hands, struggling against the waves of helpless misery.

"A...a little better, I guess," she murmured. "I was having...a sort of panic attack."

"Of course you were," the big man agreed comfortably. "I find that George is a very soothing presence when I'm in distress, so I thought it might help you if I talked about him."

"You're . . . you're very kind," Maria whispered.

"It has been my lifelong observation that taken individually, people are surprisingly kind," her companion said. "Don't ever forget that, my dear. In any extremity, it's usually possible to find someone who will care enough to help. I think that's an enormously comforting thing to be aware of."

Maria's suffocating horror began to ebb, and her emotions, though still shaky and tentative, gradually steadied. She thought of the dreadful attack she had somehow miraculously survived, of the generous kindness that this strange fat man was able to show to a total stranger, of Tony waiting, quiet and loyal, on a street that was now very close to her.

Suddenly she felt a surge of happiness almost as devastating as her earlier terror. It washed over her, flooded her mind with light, radiated from her like a shining aura. She smiled at her seatmate with a glowing incandescence that clearly startled him.

"Thank you," she whispered, gripping his plump brown-spotted hand and squeezing it warmly. "Thank you so much. You'll never know what you did for me today. I'm so grateful. . . ."

The bus jolted to a stop and Maria peered outside. Then she gave a little jump and hastily gathered up her handbag.

"This is my stop," she said, edging out past the man's bulky form. "Thank you again."

She walked down the aisle with a step so light and a smile so joyous that dozens of eyes followed her, and many faces reflected admiration at her slim scarlet figure and her gleaming black hair.

But Maria was not aware of any of them. She saw only one face, a quiet rugged face partly obscured by the swarm of noon hour commuters, looking for her, full of anxious concern.

"Tony!" Maria called. "Tony, here I am!"

He turned and saw her, and his gentle features lighted with joy. He held out his arms and Maria ran to him, caught up in his embrace, laughing and crying.

She forgot who she was, where she was, what a momentous thing she had accomplished. All she felt, singing through her whole being, was a rich, deep, completely satisfying assurance that at last she had come home.

JAMIE TURNED THE KEY in the lock and opened the door quietly, slipping through the silent deserted kitchen and moving across into the spacious luxury of the foyer. After almost a week in her family's rustic cabin, Daniel's home looked unbelievably opulent and beautiful. Jamie thought of her own comfortable room with a kind of wistful sadness, wondering miserably how she could ever bear to leave this house and all the people in it that she loved so much.

Suddenly, she looked around in concern. The house was so quiet.

Just as she framed the thought, Maria appeared, hurrying briskly along the hallway with her arms full of towels. When she saw Jamie, the smaller woman stopped short for a moment, then uttered a cry of delight and flew to hug her friend.

"Jamie! It's so good to see you! We were wondering when you were coming back!"

Maria stood back, looking up with a glowing smile, her dark eyes sparkling.

"Maria," Jamie said slowly, "what's happened to you? You look different. You look so—"

"So happy," Maria concluded. "And I am, Jamie. I'm so happy, and I owe to all to you. Oh, Jamie. I'm just so—"

"Here, hold on," Jamie said, laughing as she interrupted the tumbling flow of words. "Tell me some details, okay? What's happened?"

"On Monday," Maria said softly, her eyes still shining, "I went downtown on the bus all by myself, Jamie. And I met Tony down there, and we had lunch together."

Jamie stared down at her, speechless with amazement.

"And since then," Maria went on with a dreamy rapturous smile, "we've been out somewhere every night... over to visit his mother and out for dinner at the most beautiful restaurant and once to a movie. Jamie, do you know how long it's been since I've seen a movie?"

"I'm just stunned, Maria," Jamie said helplessly. "How did all this come about?"

"I called him," Maria said simply, "and asked him to meet me downtown. I knew that was the only way I'd ever do it."

"But... what about the reunion?"

"I decided that the reunion was just a crutch, something that I didn't really need anymore. The idea of it helped me a lot at the start, but when it comes right down to it, like I said to Tony, you have to live for every day, not special occasions."

"That's right," Jamie said warmly. "That's absolutely right. So," she added with a smile, "How's it going? Pretty well, I take it?"

"Oh, Jamie," Maria began with a blissful sigh. "I can't wait to tell you...."

A telephone rang somewhere in the silent house, quickly stilled by the answering machine.

"Where is everybody, anyhow?" Jamie asked, glancing around her.

"Steven's at school, of course. And Clara and Hiro are out in the garage, making a bigger bed for the puppy. That's where I've been, finding some more soft towels for his—"

"Puppy!" Jamie interrupted. "*What* puppy?"

"Mr. Kelleher decided to buy a puppy for Steven after all. He's a furry little spaniel, Jamie, and he's just so adorable. Wait'll you see him! We're going to call him George," Maria added, with a private little smile. "Steven let me name him, and that's what I wanted to call him."

Jamie shook her head. "What a group!" she muttered in mock despair. "I turn my back for no more than a couple of days, and you're all out buying puppies, going to movies, doing all kinds of amazing things." She paused, and then, with a quick shadow of pain, she asked, "What about...what about Mr. Kelleher, Maria? What's he been doing, besides buying puppies?"

Maria shook her head. "I don't know. He's hardly been downstairs at all, the past few days, except just to give Steven the puppy."

"Oh," Jamie murmured unhappily. "I was afraid of that."

"He called me up to see him, though," Maria went on. "The other day, after I went downtown on the bus alone. He asked me a whole lot of questions about it, how it felt and what happened and how I managed, and everything. He seemed really interested."

At Maria's words, Jamie felt, for some reason, a cold little shiver of alarm. She dropped her suitcase beside her, hesitated and then turned toward the elevator.

"Maria, I think I'll just ... I'll run up to see him right now. Then in a few minutes I'll come out to meet George, okay?"

"No, wait Jamie. He's not there."

"Not there?"

"He left this morning, Jamie. Said he was going out of town for a few days. He didn't even say where he was going or anything, but he left a letter for you."

"A letter?" Jamie repeated.

Maria nodded and pulled a white envelope out of her apron pocket and handed it to Jamie, who just stared at it with a mounting sense of dread.

Maria cast a concerned look at her friend, then hurried off.

With her shaking hands, Jamie at last ripped the envelope open, unfolded a single sheet of Daniel's heavy plain stationery, and read the brief message he had written:

Jamie
I've gone away for few days. Don't worry about me.
I hope that you'll be hearing from me before long.
Please stay until then, and give me one more chance
to change your mind about leaving us. I love you.

The note was signed with his hasty powerful scrawl, and nothing more.

Jamie stood staring at the paper in her hand, white faced and silent. In the stillness of the big empty room she could hear a cold autumn wind that sobbed and howled around the corners of the house as it carried little drifts of withered dried leaves down the curving driveway and out of sight.

CHAPTER FIFTEEN

ON THE SATURDAY NIGHT after Jamie's homecoming, there was a killing frost that blackened the tree branches and shriveled the brilliant autumn chrysanthemums still blooming in the flower beds around the house. Next morning, they woke to a fresh snowfall, big soft flakes that drifted lazily to the ground and slowly whitened the spacious lawns and gardens.

Jamie stood by her bedroom window in her fleecy blue pajamas and socks, gazing out at the world of white. For a moment she felt a surge of pure happiness at the hushed loveliness of the day, and then it all came flooding back— her last conversation with Daniel, his strange disappearance, undoubtedly prompted by all the harsh things she had said to him, and the nagging worries that tormented her, day and night.

She frowned and turned aside, heading in the direction of her shower, but was interrupted by a knock on the door of her suite.

"Come in," she called. "It's open."

The door edged open and Steven appeared, clutching his puppy. The little dog reclined against his master's chest, liquid brown eyes alert with interest, small silky ears raised.

Jamie smiled. "Hi, Steven. Hi, George. What kind of night did you two have?"

"He was really good," Steven said. "He only cried a little bit, and then I . . ." He paused, biting his lip.

"And then you took him into your bed, and he was good," Jamie finished. "Right?"

Steven nodded, avoiding her eyes.

Jamie stood with her hands on her hips, gazing down at him. "Steven," she began helplessly, "you *know* that Daddy said George was supposed to sleep in the garage."

"Daddy doesn't mind if George sleeps in my room!" Steven said. "He just didn't want him to be making a lot of noise and stuff. And now," the little boy added, his face clouding, "Daddy isn't even home, so it doesn't matter anyhow."

Jamie looked down at his thin anxious face, and his arms gripping the warm little puppy with such fierce protectiveness, and her heart melted.

"I guess you're right," she said. "As long as he's trained by the time Daddy gets back, and he'll be just as quiet as a little mouse up there."

"He will!" Steven promised, his eyes lighting. "He will, Jamie!" He turned and hurried off toward the kitchen to prepare George's breakfast, passing Maria who came into Jamie's room just as the little boy disappeared down the hall.

"Good morning, Maria," Jamie said. "Isn't the snow lovely?"

Maria smiled in agreement and then cast a teasing glance at the Donald Duck decal on Jamie's pajamas. "You know, I just love those pajamas," she said innocently. "They're so sexy."

"Maria!" Jamie protested, pretending to be shocked.

But as she spoke, her treacherous emotions almost betrayed her once more. As clearly as if it had happened yesterday, she remembered Daniel's teasing remarks about these same pajamas, the night she went to him in his bedroom. All at once she was assailed by a deep longing for him, a lonely, urgent yearning that was almost unbearable.

Maria saw her expression and her smile faded. "Jamie, what is it?"

Jamie sank into one of her little armchairs, hugging a big pillow, and Maria sat down across from her, leaning forward in concern.

"Oh, Maria, I'm just so worried about him. I'm so terribly, terribly scared...."

"Jamie, you said yourself that he's perfectly capable of looking after himself, and he can't possibly be in any danger. Remember all those things you've been telling Steven?"

"I know, I know. But I keep thinking... I think of all the things that could happen, and how long it's been since he's travelled at all, and he's had so little experience traveling in his wheelchair...."

Jamie raised her head and looked at her friend, her eyes wretched with appeal.

"I wish I was with him, Maria," she whispered. "I wish I could be there, helping him."

Maria shook her head with small sad smile. "I never thought I'd ever, ever have anything in common with Mr. Kelleher, but I know now that I do. We both have the same kind of fears, and they're fears that nobody can really help with, Jamie. When it comes right down to it, you have to find the courage to do it all by yourself, or you'll never succeed at all."

Jamie nodded, but her face remained drawn and unhappy, her lovely blue eyes shadowed with concern as she gazed out at the gentle drifting snow.

"Jamie..." Maria began softly. "Jamie, you love him, don't you?"

Jamie glanced up, startled, and her cheeks grew warm. "Yes, Maria," she whispered finally. "I love him. I never ealized just how much until I went away by myself to hink about things. And even then, I was determined that aothing would ever come of it, because he wasn't willing o face his own fears and get his life back under control. But when I came back and found he'd gone... Oh, Maria, sometimes I can hardly bear it!" Jamie said in a rush of emotion. "Sometimes I feel like I'm going to die if I can't see him soon, and know what he's doing, and be ure that he's safe."

"He'll be just fine," Maria said soothingly. "If there vas anything wrong, we'd have been the first to know."

Jamie nodded, unconvinced.

"He loves you, too, you know," Maria went on, her voice soft. "He's been like a different man, ever since you came to live here. And, Jamie, you should see the look on his face whenever your name is mentioned, or when he ooks at you and he thinks nobody's watching. He just adores you."

Jamie looked over at her friend, almost unbearably moved by her words. Awkwardly, she laughed and tossed her pillow aside, getting lightly to her feet.

"What a household, Maria," she said. "Everybody's n love. Clara adores her new camera, and Hiro loves his ools, and Steven loves George, and you... You're so much in love with your Tony that it's just shocking. And hen there's me..."

Her voice caught. She moved restlessly to the window, pulling the drapes aside and peering out at the silent nuffled world.

Maria came over, slipped her arm around Jamie, and ested her head against the taller woman's shoulder. "You'll hear from him soon," she murmured. "He'll call or something. Probably today, Jamie. Just wait and see."

As IT TURNED OUT, though, Maria was wrong by several days. Word from Daniel didn't arrive until much later in the week, and when it did, it was in a surprising and unexpected form.

Jamie was on the pool deck, wearing her yellow maillot and tights. She had her small stereo set up there, with a pile of tapes beside it, and she was working through the music and moves for a whole series of new aerobic routines, taking advantage of her unexpected free time to prepare programs for a full complement of classes now just beginning the new season.

"And heel and toe and up, two, three," she panted, "and back and side and up, two, three. . . ."

Maria appeared in the foyer entrance, her small body taut with excitement. Jamie glanced over at her and then, feeling suddenly tense and breathless, she switched off the stereo.

"What is it, Maria?"

"There's—Jamie, there's a courier van here. With a personal delivery for you."

"Oh . . . oh, my goodness . . ."

The two women exchanged an eloquent glance. Jamie searched frantically for her wrap skirt, pulling it on and buttoning it around her slender waist with trembling fingers before she ran past Maria and into the kitchen.

The courier driver, neat and expressionless in his blue uniform, handed her a large square envelope covered with packing slips and markings. The only thing that Jamie recognized, obliterating everything else from her mind, was her own name in Daniel's vigorous handwriting. Hastily, barely able to hold the pen, she signed for the envelope and ran through the silent hallways to her own room, closing the door behind her. Then, with pounding heart and pent breath she opened the big envelope and looked in astonishment at its contents.

There were only two things inside the envelope. One was a brief typed note, and the other was a folder containing an airline ticket.

Jamie stared blankly at the ticket, then opened the note and read it with growing bewilderment.

The letter was from Daniel, but it was completely impersonal. In fact, it was really nothing more than a list of instructions, telling her how to use the plane ticket, how she would be met at her destination, what hotel she would be taken to when she arrived, and concluding politely with the statement that he looked forward to seeing her and hoped that she would be able to make the journey.

Jamie opened the folder and studied the ticket. She was booked on a flight out of Calgary leaving early the next morning. Her destination was Dallas, Texas.

She felt dizzy, light-headed, unsure of whether to laugh or cry.

"Oh, Daniel," she whispered. "Daniel, what on earth are you doing?"

She hesitated a moment longer. Then, with a surge of excitement she crossed the room, hauled her Pullman case out of the closet and began to pack.

CLOUDS MASSED and billowed and separated beneath the wing of the plane that was visible from her seat. Jamie gazed down at them impatiently, willing them to dissipate and vanish so she could see the land below. She glanced briefly at her watch, and then peered out the window again.

If they were on schedule, they should be crossing Colorado by now....

As if in response to her thoughts, the clouds grew thinner and began to drift apart, giving her a glimpse of the rugged, towering magnificence of the Rockies. Jamie marveled at this mighty range of mountains, flung across the face of North America all the way to Alaska, and then shivered at the breadth and hugeness of the vast continent that the big jet was crossing.

Soon the mountainous terrain flattened and dulled, the colors fading from snow-splashed green to red and brown, to umber and ocher and tan, as they flew over the deserts and canyons of New Mexico.

Jamie's throat tightened. She could barely contain her excitement, realizing how close she was getting to her destination, to Daniel, and whatever he had planned for her.

In the airport terminal, she was approached by a small polite man in dark livery who had clearly been instructed to watch for a tall woman with bright red hair. The man presented the identification card that Daniel had mentioned in his note, and then led Jamie across the vastness of the crowded terminal.

Impeccably trained though he appeared to be, he was still unable to refrain from casting a furtive, deeply appreciative glance at Jamie's shapely legs and tall curving body, beautifully dressed in a light creamy suit and vivid orange silk shirt. Jamie caught his swift eloquent look and grinned cheerfully, feeling all at once a good deal more confident.

Her escort led her to a luxurious car parked near the exit doors and helped her inside, then vanished briefly to deal with her luggage while Jamie waited, looking around curiously at the sun-drenched parking area.

In Calgary, when she had left early that morning, there had still been patches of slush and dirty snow heaped everywhere, and a cold west wind that howled and whistled through the dark deserted streets. Now, she had the strange disoriented impression that she had traveled in a few hours from winter to summer.

Her escort returned and maneuvered the big car expertly through the downtown area to a huge sprawling hotel complex near the city center. Jamie looked out at the massive structure and then over at the driver.

"Is this it?" she asked nervously. "Is this where Daniel's staying?"

"Mr. Kelleher is here," her companion said expressionlessly.

"Is he waiting for me now? Are you taking me to his room, or what?"

"You'll go to your own private room just now. You'll have twenty minutes to freshen up, and then I'll call for you again."

"And take me to Daniel's room?"

"I'll take you to where Mr. Kelleher is."

Jamie looked over at him again, but he was staring straight ahead, his face silent and unreadable behind his dark glasses. She sighed, nodded and followed him to the door of her room.

He departed politely, after reminding her once more of the twenty-minute time limit. Jamie stepped inside the small suite that had been provided for her, and gasped, stunned by its luxury. Flowers and fruit baskets seemed to be set casually on every available surface. On the gleaming rosewood sideboard a small gift-wrapped package was placed discreetly near a vase of glowing vivid autumn flowers.

Jamie moved haltingly across the room, lifted and opened the little package, and then drew her breath in sharply. The wrappings parted to reveal a tiny, heavy, beautifully sculpted reclining lion of solid gold, with sparkling sapphires for eyes. She gazed down in amazement, holding the lovely object in her hands, stunned by its perfection. A folded note fell out of the tissue. Jamie opened it, and read,

My darling,
Steven always used to say that you reminded him of
a beautiful golden lion, and I have learned to understand why. You are strong, lovely, graceful and fear-
less, and I love you, dearest Jamie, with all my heart
and soul.

A flood of pure love washed through Jamie, leaving her
feeling weak and hollow. She folded the note with a misty
smile and tucked it into her handbag, placed the exquisite sculpture tenderly on the sideboard, and hurried into
the opulent white-and-gold bathroom to repair her hair
and makeup.

Punctual to the very second, her nameless escort
knocked on her door and then stood aside politely to follow her down the hallway in the direction he indicated.
Jamie strode along the broad silent corridor, lithe and
graceful even in her heels, wondering where Daniel's room
was and what they would say to each other when he
opened his door and saw her.

She smiled and quickened her steps, thinking with
amusement about all the trouble he had gone to just to
prove to her that he was able to travel on his own, to deal
with the world beyond his own city and make complex
arrangements for both of them.

Oh, Daniel, she thought tenderly, *you didn't really have
to bring me all the way across the continent to make your
point, you know. But that's just your way, I guess. You're
certainly not a man to do things halfway, are you?*

"Here we are," her escort said calmly, interrupting her
thoughts. "We'll take the elevator now and go down to the
main floor."

"The main floor?" Jamie echoed, bewildered. "But I
thought...I thought you said you were taking me to
Daniel's room."

"I said I would take you to where Mr. Kelleher is," the small dark man replied imperturbably. "And that's where we're going."

A little of Jamie's buoyant optimism faded, to be replaced by growing puzzlement and a quick stirring of alarm. Her escort took her arm, guiding her through the plush elegant lobby and into a network of carpeted corridors beyond the reception desk.

They paused at a massive double door set into a beautifully paneled wall, and he turned to Jamie with brief smile of encouragement.

"I believe they've already started," her companion murmured. "I'll find an usher to take you to your seat, and then leave you. You'll be all right from here on."

"My *seat*? What are you talking about?" Jamie whispered frantically. "What is this place? What's going on inside there?"

"It's a convention of writers and book publishers," her unknown escort replied serenely. "Mr. Kelleher has reserved a seat for you."

Helplessly, Jamie followed him as he opened the huge doors and turned to murmur something to a uniformed usher who hurried up to them on swift silent feet. The usher nodded, offering his arm, and Jamie walked beside him through a vast, dimly lit auditorium packed with people.

Tense and breathless with startled nervous surprise, Jamie gained only a few scattered impressions as they progressed toward the front of the room, of golden sconces and exquisite oil paintings in lighted alcoves, of silks and furs and jewelry, of hundreds and hundreds of pale faces glimmering in the dusky immensity of the huge, carpeted lecture hall.

They walked all the way to the front of the room, to the very first row, where the young usher handed her courteously into a vacant seat. It was the only empty place that she could see, and Jamie held her breath, looking cautiously around for Daniel.

He was nowhere to be seen.

Suddenly, as her eyes adjusted to the dim light, Jamie forgot about Daniel for a moment and gasped in amazement. Seated all around her were people she recognized, faces she had seen and admired on dust jackets for all the years she had loved and devoured books. The names of the people gathered at the front of this hall were household words, famous all over the world. The craggy, rumpled pipe-smoking man on her left, for instance, was one of the foremost contemporary novelists in America, while the plump, sweet-faced lady at her other side wrote big, sweeping historical sagas that sold millions of copies.

As Jamie peeped over at her in awe, the silver-haired woman smiled warmly and then turned her attention back to the stage.

Jamie returned the smile uncertainly, stunned and shaken by this new development. Her head was spinning, and she frowned and bit her lip, trying desperately to gather her confused thoughts into some kind of sense and order.

She knew, of course, had known for months, that Daniel feared and shunned contact with his fellow writers since his accident. He couldn't bear the thought of being seen in his wheelchair, helpless and diminished, and he never accepted invitations to writers' groups and conferences anymore. He even avoided meetings with his own agent and publishers, preferring to conduct all his business by telephone.

One thing was obvious, Jamie realized. When Daniel had finally set out to prove something to her, he'd chosen to do it in a big way. Not only was he determined to show her that he could travel on his own, he also intended to make it clear that he was not afraid to meet and mingle with his old colleagues.

But in that case, where was he?

Jamie glanced furtively around, trembling and chilled with fear.

What if Daniel had set this all up, and then found himself unable at the last moment to go through with it? What if he was, even now, huddled in a room somewhere in the hotel, suffering from a panic attack like the ones that Maria had to struggle against, wretched and bitterly disappointed with himself for failing in courage and letting her down after bringing her all this way?

Oh, Daniel, Jamie thought in agony. *Daniel...*

Her mind was in such a turmoil that she was completely unaware of what the speaker on the stage was saying. She paid no attention to him at all until his remarks were suddenly punctuated by a few scattered bursts of applause. The speaker paused, smiling cheerfully at the interruption, and then stepped close to the podium again and continued.

"And, so, ladies and gentlemen," he said, "I know that you don't want to hear any more from me. Without further ado, I give you our feature speaker of the day!"

With a theatrical flourish, he waved his arm toward the wings. Jamie, along with a thousand others, turned in the direction he indicated, and then clutched the padded arms of her chair, afraid that she was going to faint.

Daniel Kelleher emerged from the darkened area beyond the draperies and rolled his wheelchair slowly to center stage, followed by a spotlight that lingered brilliantly about him, glinting on the bright chrome of the chair and illuminating Daniel's thick dark hair, his handsome tanned features and his finely cut gray tweed jacket.

A roar of surprise and delight rose from the massed ranks of the audience, echoing thunderously to the high vaulted ceiling. The distinguished novelist beside Jamie leaped to his feet, his coat tails flapping, yelling incoherently and beating his hands together in a fury of applause. All over the room, others rose from their chairs in an undulating wave of humanity and a solid wall of noise that went on and on, flooding the whole vast auditorium.

Jamie found herself standing as well, pulled to her feet by the same powerful, irresistible force that drew them all up, clapping and smiling, totally unaware of the tears that streamed down her cheeks.

She could see Daniel looking for her, frowning intently at the dark cavernous depths below him. When at last he found her, he gave her a private, almost imperceptible, thumbs-up sign. All at once he smiled down at her, his rare boyish smile that spoke to her of victory, of joy and courage and an endless, wondrous, triumphant love.

Then he turned away and rolled his chair into the spotlight at center stage, looking calmly out at the shouting mass of people and waiting in silence for their thunderous roar of applause to subside so he could begin his speech.

EPILOGUE

JAMIE WOKE in a square of early morning sunshine that lay warmly across the big four-poster bed, dappled with light and shadow by the heavy lace curtains at the window. She gazed drowsily through the leaded glass panes at the small fountain in the courtyard of the villa, delighting in the sparkle of sunlight on the gentle cascades of water.

Then she turned her head slowly on the pillow and smiled. Even after all these months of marriage, she could never quite get over the joy of seeing Daniel's face in the early morning, of knowing that they were together and always would be.

She studied the fine contours of his profile as he slept, feeling weak with love. The familiar shock of rumpled dark hair fell across his forehand, and his sleeping face looked boyish and tired. He had been working so hard, spending long days at the Louvre and other galleries in Paris, researching his new book on fine art theft.

Now his work was finished, and they had a whole week to themselves before they went back to Canada. They were staying at the home of an old friend of Daniel's, a writer so famous that Jamie still felt awed to share a table with him. But their host was witty, gracious and kind, allowing his young guests all kinds of time together to relax, to love each other, to watch as spring flowed softly and gloriously across the rolling acres of vineyards and orchards.

Daniel's eyes flickered open and he gazed at her, smiling. "Good morning, sweetheart," he whispered.

Jamie smiled back, suddenly overwhelmed by the need to tell him. She had planned to keep her news to herself until they got home, but they were in love, and it was Paris, and it was springtime. It was time to tell him.

"Daniel," she murmured, "remember last Tuesday when you were at the Louvre, talking with the security staff?"

He nodded, his fine dark eyes puzzled.

"Well, I went to see the doctor."

Jamie laughed at the flare of panic on his handsome face and hugged him.

"I'm pregnant, darling," she whispered. "We're going to have a baby. A little brother or sister for Steven," she added with a smile. "He'll be almost as happy as I am."

Daniel's face lighted with incredulous, overwhelming joy. He gathered his wife into his arms, kissing her passionately and murmuring broken, incoherent endearments while the doves whispered on the windowsill and the fountain threw sprays of glittering rainbows toward the morning sun.

A Note from Margot Dalton

The idea for *Daniel and the Lion* was born one day at a
shopping mall when I noticed an extremely handsome
man in a wheelchair ... a man who looked much like
Daniel Kelleher. I started to think about him and what his
life must be like. Soon I completely forgot what I was
shopping for, and a book started growing in my mind.

As I researched the story, I was awed and humbled by the
courage shown by disabled people, who routinely deal with
problems that would devastate most of us. I became
determined that Daniel was going to have the warmest,
sweetest, most fulfilling love story that I could possibly
give him!

Love isn't just for "the beautiful people," the famous
athletes, movie stars and jet-setters. This miracle
is available for anyone with a loving heart and a
generous spirit.

You, the readers of romance novels, are wonderful proof
of this. You are the people who truly believe in love and
who treasure it for yourselves and others. Like Daniel, you
deserve the very best stories a writer can give.

Letters to Margot Dalton can be sent c/o:

> *Harlequin Reader Service*
> *P.O. Box 1397*
> *Buffalo, New York 14240*

If you enjoyed *Daniel and the Lion,* you'll love

COWBOYS AND CABERNET
by Margot Dalton

Tyler McKinney is out to prove a Texas ranch is the perfect place for a vineyard. Vintner Ruth Holden thinks Tyler is too stubborn, too impatient...too Texas. And far too difficult to resist!

COWBOYS AND CABERNET
Book Two of

A town where you'll find hot Texas nights, smooth Texas charm and dangerously sexy cowboys.

A series of twelve books that feature the rugged individuals who live and love in the Lone Star State. And each one ends with the same invitation...

Y'ALL COME BACK...REAL SOON!

In March, don't miss Book One of Crystal Creek: DEEP IN THE HEART by Barbara Kaye. Then in April, look for Book Two: COWBOYS AND CABERNET by Margot Dalton!

MDCC1

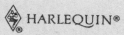

The most romantic day of the year is here! Escape into the exquisite world of love with MY VALENTINE 1993. What better way to celebrate Valentine's Day than with this very romantic, sensuous collection of four original short stories, written by some of Harlequin's most popular authors.

**ANNE STUART
JUDITH ARNOLD
ANNE McALLISTER
LINDA RANDALL WISDOM**

**THIS VALENTINE'S DAY, DISCOVER ROMANCE
WITH MY VALENTINE 1993**

Available in February wherever Harlequin Books are sold. VAL93

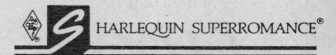

HARLEQUIN SUPERROMANCE®

COMING NEXT MONTH

#534 UNCOMMON STOCK • Terri Lynn
Dashing businessman Duncan McKeon had romance on his
mind. He was determined to woo stockbroker Blythe Summers
with every means available: flowers, candle-lit dinners,
moonlight walks. But Blythe associated romance with
ephemeral affairs. It was up to Duncan to prove to her that the
love they could share would last forever!

#535 DREAM BUILDER • Julie Meyers
Joy Porter had no idea why Charlie Comfort had refused to
design a playground for the children of Sacramento. It wasn't
money—she'd offered him double his usual fee. Some dark
secret haunted him, a secret Joy had to uncover if she was to
honor her father's dying wish.

#536 REFLECTIONS OF BECCA • Lynda Trent
P.I. Tyler Hart had a very good reason for not wanting to find
Becca Chambers's birth mother, but he couldn't refuse the
assignment. What he found was far beyond either of their
expectations. If Becca didn't have a twin sister, there had been a
very strange accident of genetics!

#537 WINGS OF TIME • Carol Duncan Perry
Women Who Dare Book 2
When Libby Carmichael flew her antique airplane into a
thunderstorm, she was thrown back in time to the year 1925.
Swooping out of a suddenly clear sky, she rescued stunt pilot
Shamus Fitzgerald from a carload of gun-toting gangsters. So
began the story of Libby and Shamus, an adventure that defied
time, a romance that dared fate....

AVAILABLE NOW:

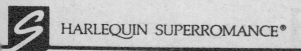

HARLEQUIN SUPERROMANCE®

WOMEN WHO DARE DRIVE RACE CARS?!

During 1993, each Harlequin Superromance WOMEN WHO DARE title will have a single italicized letter on the Women Who Dare back-page ads. Collect the letters, spell D A R E and you can receive a free copy of *RACE FOR TOMORROW*, written by popular author Elaine Barbieri. This is an exciting novel about a female race-car driver, WHO DARES ANYTHING . . . FOR LOVE!

OFFER CERTIFICATE

To receive your free gift, send us the 4 letters that spell DARE from any Harlequin Superromance Women Who Dare title with the offer certificate properly completed, along with a check or money order for $1.00 for postage and handling (do not send cash) payable to Harlequin Superromance Women Who Dare Offer.

Name: _____

Address: _____

_____

City: _____ State/Prov.: _____

Zip/Postal Code: _____

Mail this certificate, designated letters spelling DARE, and check or money order for postage and handling to: In the U.S.—WOMEN WHO DARE, P.O. Box 9069, Buffalo, NY 14269-9069; In Canada—WOMEN WHO DARE, P.O. Box 622, Fort Erie, Ontario L2A 5X3.

Requests must be received by January 31, 1994.
Allow 4-6 weeks after receipt of order for delivery.

WWDDIR

HARLEQUIN SUPERROMANCE®

HARLEQUIN SUPERROMANCE WANTS TO INTRODUCE YOU TO A DARING NEW CONCEPT IN ROMANCE...

WOMEN WHO DARE!
Bright, bold, beautiful...
Brave and caring, strong and passionate...
They're unique women who know their
own minds and will dare anything...
for love!

One title per month in 1993, written by popular Superromance authors, will highlight our special heroines as they face unusual, challenging and sometimes dangerous situations.

Travel through time next month with:
#537 WINGS OF TIME by Carol Duncan Perry
Available in February wherever Harlequin Superromance novels are sold.

If you missed #533 *Daniel and the Lion* and would like to order it, send your name, address, zip or postal code along with a check or money order for $3.39 for each book ordered (do not send cash), plus 75¢ ($1.00 in Canada) for postage and handling, payable to Harlequin Reader Service, to:

In the U.S.
3010 Walden Avenue
P.O. Box 1325
Buffalo, NY 14269-1325

In Canada
P.O. Box 609
Fort Erie, Ontario
L2A 5X3

Please specify book title with your order.
Canadian residents add applicable federal and provincial taxes.

Collect letters and win!
See previous page
for details.

WWD-FL